Borisov to America

By:
Anthony Bykowski

Prologue

For a 93-year-old immigrant from Byelorussia (now Belarus) of the old Soviet Union, our mother Pauline was doing quite well. She was still mobile, fun-loving, even sipped occasionally on some "b-o-o-o-o-z-e." She always stretched out that word and seemed to enjoy pronouncing it, slowly and deliberately, particularly in front of her bible banging, abstaining oldest daughter Tamara. She had laughed so much more, reminisced so much more, in those thirteen years since the death of her hard-to-love husband John. Davenport wasn't glitzy or that exciting. But, here in heartland America, it had been a safe, comfortable home for sixty-plus years…sixty-plus years since her immigration (or maybe more accurately her necessary escape?) from Belarus and her hometown Borisov.

It was a "maybe 93rd birthday" because among so many contradictions and questions about her life, she wasn't sure in what year she was born. It was a lighthearted, continuing joke among our family as to which birthday should be celebrated and how many candles should be blown out. Even she would laugh at this, though in that laugh you could detect some confusion, maybe a little embarrassment as well.

Pauline, the common American name, was also a "maybe." "Maybe" because, as we children eventually learned, it was in fact a conveniently adopted American variation on Polahaya, her Byelorussian birth name. But, Polahaya could also be considered a "maybe" since her stated name on various immigration documents identified her as Apolonia, a very common Polish name. From a Byelorussian Polahaya, to a Polish Apolonia, to an American Pauline. Her names, changing over three decades, provided a brief but useful summary of her thirty year journey from her Byelorussian hometown of Borisov to America

At her birthday celebration, a party highlight was her youngest son serenading his mother with a sweet, original composition, complete with guitar accompaniment. George had a fine voice, and had even booked his share of week-end gigs over the years. And, our mother dearly loved that soft tenor voice from her youngest child. He was a successful business executive who had risen from the entry level ranks of a telephone technician to a very senior position at a major telecommunications company. He epitomized that enviable American success story, combining a strong work ethic, leadership skills, and an engaging personality to climb the corporate ladder and enjoy a comfortable lifestyle. And on weekends, he could, and did, shed the sedate corporate suit and became a fun-loving, hellraising, doo rag-wearing biker. Despite the fondness for her youngest son, our mother never fully understood nor appreciated the significance of that great success story. Instead, in her innocent but unfiltered way, she all too often scolded George, though ever so gently, about his seemingly dangerous biking trips and his wild weekend lifestyle. "Not very professional," she reminded him in her charming and very broken accent.

Five months later at a family Thanksgiving festival our mother shocked us by announcing she had been diagnosed with terminal cancer. And, within the week she passed away.

Over the next five days we three siblings prodded (maybe begged?) our mother to share details of her childhood in the old Soviet Republic of Byelorussia, her five years as a post- war refugee in Germany, and her eventual immigration - complete with husband and two infants – to the US. Our collective prodding became more intense during that all too brief final week after that terminal cancer bombshell. Our mother's health was rapidly failing and there still were so many mysteries, so many unanswered questions. I, the middle son, the corporate lawyer, took the lead as investigator. And, that collective prodding, or "nagging" as our mother preferred to call my efforts, led to one more confirmation and two eye-opening revelations.

Responding to me, her inquisitive, nagging lawyer son, and punctuated with our mother's classic "oy, oy, oy", our mother confirmed that she and John, her husband of over 50 years, had in fact been properly married. We children had witnessed decades of a turbulent, love/hate relationship and few helpful documents, memorabilia or photos. There was no wedding certificate, no wedding portrait, nothing. So it wasn't that far-fetched a question for us to ask.

With less calm, and a little irritation, mother also debunked the long-standing myth that her husband, our father, had come from some Moscow aristocracy, a noble aristocracy which had fallen on hard times. The decades long story had been that the Bolshevik Revolution in now Soviet Byelorussia had no tolerance for any aristocratic lifestyle or capitalist wealth. That part of the story was historically accurate. Consequently, John's family was forced to relocate to a more modest home in rural Borisov. On the contrary, our mother informed us that John was just another country boy, hardly any "nobility" or "aristocrat", relocating from a nearby village.

The most startling revelation came next. When she married John in 1943 he was currently married to another woman. And, he was also the father of a young child. The label of "bigamist" was never used. And quite possibly our mother didn't even know such a descriptive label. But, labels weren't necessary. The now corrected, deathbed portrait of her husband John was very clear. The father of her three children was not from some noble family. And, that father also was not some innocent, and honorable, country lad, falling in love and marrying for the first time. After I shared this revelation with my siblings there was wild speculation. Was there some former "spouse" of John's still alive somewhere? And, there was the intriguing possibility that somewhere – maybe Belarus, maybe Germany, maybe the United States - a spry, entertaining step-brother was waiting to reunite with his stateside siblings.

For our mother these revelations, made with such relative ease, would have been impossible 13 years ago. It had been 13 years since her husband's death. And, it was 13 years since the start of what we children affectionately labeled her "emancipation." With that emancipation a more self-confident Pauline visited more, talked more, revealed more, debunked various other family myths. She also became, on occasion, too blunt, too unfiltered in her opinions about people. This also included the advice - too often unsolicited - she offered to people. But, she was never intentionally cruel or calculating. She was simply an unsophisticated, innocent, poorly educated girl from Belarus. Despite 50 some years after her immigration from post-war Germany, she never fully assimilated into 20th century America. And, in her own clumsy way, she was thoroughly enjoying that emancipation.

It was an emancipation, not from any literal imprisonment, but from 50+ years of hardship, modest comforts at best, and recurring physical and mental abuse. During those 50 years, our family did have food on the table, though basic and hardly in generous quantities. We children were clothed, though in modest, hardly fashion forward styles. And there was some occasional fun and laughter, particularly when a "refugee" party was scheduled at some family's home on a Saturday night. Seven or eight families would gather, and on that festive occasion there would be an overabundance of food, lots of kids to play with one another, and an overabundance of drinks. The typical format was to have "Schakov" bring his accordion to play. That was his last name. He was never called by any other name and it was somewhat of a mystery which country he called home. He was a short, slightly built "refugee" who said very little but had a perpetual smile. And he loved to play an old, very weathered accordion. The kids who watched the refugee party from the shadows of the party basement would giggle and on occasion shout out "Schakov" just like the drunken adults did. It was "Schakov play more", "Schakov, play this…play that." Every house also had a record player. And when Schakov ran out of songs or energy, out came oldie records that entertained everyone, young and old, with spirited Russian ballads or more subdued tango tunes. And, almost on cue, our father, Big John to his fellow refugees, would take center stage, belting out two, or three, or four romantic ballads. No one ever complained because he had a fine, powerful baritone voice. The tango tunes also produced one other ritual. Big John would go over to our mother, usually sitting in a corner, largely ignored and remaining low profile thus far. He would take her two hands, often a bit too tightly, and insist they dance. Each time, almost on cue, our mother would resist, Big John would persist, and eventually his reluctant dance partner would rise off her chair. Continuing the ritual, she would first offer a theatrical grimace and then offer a feeble smile to her fellow refugees. And then they would dance. First, slowly tango style, then more energetically, even with some hint of passion and affection. They were good, really good. And, they actually appeared to like, maybe love, one another and enjoy one another's company.

Sadly, those affectionate moments were too few and too far between the recurring marital chaos. Big John was a vain, dictatorial and cruel husband. He was a stereotypical tough guy tolerating no sass or defiance, even regularly dressing in a tawdry wife beater tee shirt. There were noisy, drunken returns to the home in the middle of the night, often accompanied with fists and slaps, followed by heart wrenching screams and sobs from our mother. We children would awaken, sobbing and sometimes bravely attempting to come to her defense. There was the frequent verbal abuse, accusing our mother of anything and everything and tossing out an entire dictionary of obscenities and demeaning words for extra cruel effect. And, there were the occasional female visitors. Whether brazen, or just simple, the women would come to our front door, usually at night. And, those female visitors were uniformly trashy lowlifes, tough and ill-mannered. They would ask if "Big John" was home. As for our mother, it was difficult to assess her reaction to these unexpected visits. Infuriated or embarrassed, or maybe just reconciled to this too frequent pattern? Probably a sad mix of all of those emotions.

Over the years we children, as well as close friends, urged her to leave her husband. She was tempted, but never did so during their 50+ year marriage. Some of the refusal to leave him must have been due to her own indecision, plus understandable fear, as to what she would do, and how she would survive on her own. Maybe the refusal was due in part to an old-world, old-fashioned duty to stay with her husband for better or worse as the wedding vow is recited. And maybe, just maybe, it was some love between the two of them, despite those turbulent 50+ years.

As for the "love" factor, we children frequently talked about and speculated whether there was any of that between husband and wife. During one of those recurring conversations, someone playfully mentioned a lovely and insightful song from the Broadway musical "Fiddler on the Roof." Throughout the musical Tevye and his wife Golda are constantly quarreling, never agreeing on anything. And during one of those insignificant quarrels, they pause for a few minutes, and Golda changes the subject and asks her combative husband, "Do you love me?" Tevya is caught off guard by the query but gains his composure and responds by cataloging all the good things he's done for his wife. But he doesn't answer the question. Golda responds in kind with a lengthy catalog of her own good deeds. But she also doesn't answer the question. They counterpunch back and forth with their good deeds until Tevya restates, in his tough, gruff but musical voice, Golda's first question, "Do you love me?" There's a very long pause and silence from both of them. Then Golda responds in a soft near whisper, "I guess I do." There's an equally long pause and then Tevya, appearing somewhat surprised by his own impending confession of sorts, responds "I guess I do too." Love, slowly, awkwardly and grudgingly acknowledged, but love nonetheless. After that sibling conversation we all agreed that this musical exchange could very possibly describe the essence of Pauline and John's marriage and their decades-long emotional attachment to one another, for better or worse.

At John's funeral there wasn't too much ceremony or sadness. Our father had softened in his last six months, but he was still a difficult man, or father, or husband to love. The family, plus a few friends, proceeded down the short path toward the gravesite. Our mother was tenderly escorted between her two sons, arm in arm. She had a steady gait and a semblance of a smile. But, suddenly her knees buckled, she stopped, and for the first time that day she let herself go with sobs and tears. With us at her side we heard her say softly and painfully "John, oh John, I miss you." Possibly she said "I love you." But, if so, no one heard her. And, no one could confidently recall if she ever said "I love you" to John. During that pause, amidst the sobs and tears, she also said, "John, I'm sorry, so sorry." She buried her husband that day. But, also she left us children puzzled and frustrated with that cryptic farewell "I'm sorry." It was just one more addition to over eighty years of myths and mysteries, sometimes lies, about our parents.

Summer Research, Summer Memories

During that hectic, fun-filled summer birthday gathering we three siblings found a few quiet moments to share memories. We also confessed our common concern. Though spry and healthy looking, our mother was 93. How many more years could we enjoy her, enjoy her fractured English accent? Though we had coaxed and prodded her, and occasionally nagged her, to share her pre-American years, collectively we knew oh so little. And with our father's passing she was literally our one and only family historian. We knew of no aunts or uncles, no elderly cousins, no known living grandparents.

There was very little documentation. There were a few puzzling photos. But to our collective surprise, we discovered there was a fair volume of oral history each of us had respectively accumulated over the decades. During the parents' Colorado visits to their youngest son there were stories told, some myths debunked. In particular, a one-time visit to a quaint Denver Russian restaurant, aided by nostalgic balalaika music and generous pours of vodka, had produced a treasure trove of family facts. The occasional Ohio luncheon date, with just mother and daughter, had generated its share of complaints and confessions about our parents' turbulent romance. Illinois visits, aided by summer sunsets and sips of wine, which wines were off limits in Ohio, also provided historical bits and pieces of the parents' five plus years as post war displaced persons in Germany. Or the parents described themselves during that time period, they were just struggling "DP's."

We had far more extensive historical data than we realized. But it was scattered among the three of us. It certainly was unintentional, but we had failed to share those conversations, those historical vignettes, among ourselves. Though it was unspoken, we collectively sensed a greater urgency to explore deeper, share better, recollect more of those vignettes. There was still a deep historical hole we wanted to and needed to fill. And though again it was unintentional, we had to acknowledge that we had been too lazy in working to fill that hole. In hindsight our instincts, that sense of urgency that summer, proved to be very sound because our sole surviving historian was gone from us just five months later. However, as a partial defense, our collective, even if inconsistent, efforts to fill that historic hole were fiercely and repeatedly stymied by our father. While he was alive, he rarely shared any history about any of the places they had lived prior to their immigration to America. In his brusque manner, he replied that any of that history was too painful to discuss. Or with added anger in his voice, he simply declared he would not answer any questions. The dutiful, subservient wife was also ordered, with his equally angry voice, not to talk about their past.

After that summertime birthday party, we said our good-byes on a Sunday afternoon. We also pledged to free ourselves of our decades long inertia. It was an all too frequent inertia that had us announcing "I'll start more researching/work harder on my recollections, first thing next week," Or maybe next month. Or next year. Over those intervening five months we were in fact far more tenacious and successful. We accelerated our efforts to collect old documents, to recollect old conversations and revelations about our parents' childhood during their Borisov years, their Hannover encampment, the immigration challenge. Quite possibly our mother also sensed some added urgency as she more readily shared their European odyssey. Intuitively we all realized time was not our ally.

This summer research produced both sadness and surprise for us. Part of our collective sadness arose out of our concern about our mother's health. She was relatively spry and energetic for her years, but her pace was much slower, as was her speech. Her hair, long and lush in her youth, was now little more than a head full of tight curls struggling to provide some cover. Her eyes, bright and hazel in a rare recently discovered youthful portrait, weren't as bright. And, in those eyes the sadness was all too evident, and the sadness appeared all too often. Maybe she was recalling some ancient painful chapter of her thirty year journey. Sometimes when we prodded her too much during our research summer she would frustrate us with her abrupt and long silence. We could also see some fear in her eyes. Did she imagine, maybe see, the ghost of her domineering husband, glaring at her, warning her to remain the decades long submissive wife who damn well better not tell stories, or reveal secrets, from their European past? But, there was the occasional surprise for us as well when those eyes lit up and she boldly and enthusiastically, almost defiantly, shared some European adventure. Or two or three adventures. She would reimagine and recount her early youthful, rebellious years. And, we would just watch and listen and smile, surprised and delighted as we were to see her and hear her share those decades long secrets. Those eyes could even sparkle as she reminisced about that one very special, and very wild, back road four wheeler ride with her handsome young grandson-in-law. It was during the first summer road trip for her after the springtime death of her husband. It was also her first tentative effort to explore her newly found emancipation. Careening through gullies and small streams, she held on with a death grip around his waist. And, she laughed and laughed like a little girl as she retold that memorable ride. And we laughed as well. We hoped for more surprises, not knowing how long we would enjoy our historian.

As we worked on that historic excavation, we also unearthed some of our own personal favorite memories. There was a recurring Christmas spectacle of everyone talking, mumbling, or grumbling, and usually all at the same time. And in the middle of that playful chaos the family patriarch insisted we all take turns saying something, anything, into our father's tiny handheld microphone.

Also during those messy Christmas gatherings, we were herded together around a large sofa with a sickly Christmas tree as a backdrop, and commanded, (semi-politely) to sit still and smile (or try to) as the patriarch failed (once again) to remove the lens cap or load film into his ancient Kodak. That Christmas photo spectacle was comical and embarrassing. But in retrospect, it was a spectacle that provided an endearing mental picture of our patriarch trying to capture a fleeting moment of family unity. It also might have been his desire to memorialize evidence of the American dream he and his wife had painfully pursued and proudly realized.

In addition to old memories now revisited, our five-month project created an expanding list of questions that begged for answers. Why two tattered pairs of boxing gloves? Why a Tennessee address on that rickety wooden chest in the basement? Who was this mysterious German officer? Why Hannover? What happened to grandparents, or cousins, or aunts or uncles? What was the story behind the scars on our father and those cryptic tattoos on his knuckles? The list went on and on. But where to begin? Maybe we should begin seventy plus years ago in Borisov.

Chapter 1 - Polahaya, the Early Years

"Birth and death, we all move between these two unknowns."

Anonymous

It was the early 20th century, three years into the newly formed, expanding Soviet Union. Russia, the mother Republic and birthplace of the Bolshevik Revolution, had absorbed its close cultural and historic neighbor, Byelorussia. That's the original name of the country on Russia's western border. Literally translated it means "White Russia." And when pronounced slowly in Russian, "Byelorussia" is pleasant sounding, even a bit melodic. But, the cold, efficient Soviets, abetted by the international community, changed that melodic Byelorussia to a more boring, sterile Belarus.

Soviet communism was coming to Belarus, and it was coming to the midsize town of Borisov where Pauline, our Byelorussian Polahaya, was born. There was still some lingering old wealth and aristocracy. There were servants, maids, farm hands, factory workers and merchants. Collective farms, purges, and pogroms would arrive soon enough. Pauline's mother, Nashtya, enjoyed a simple life in early twentieth century Borisov.

"Enjoyed?" Maybe not quite, but seventeen-year-old Nashtya was resourceful, very pretty, and had a decent job as a maid for a successful merchant and landowner. The merchant had a pleasant, soft-spoken nearly invisible wife, and a loud, very visible, very wild young son, Alexi. Alexi was very handsome, athletic, reasonably bright, but very lazy. The family business could definitely use the son's help. But, moving boxes, making deliveries, or performing any manual labor were tasks far beneath playboy Alexi. He was much more adept at hustling his young friends at cards or hustling the young ladies at the local taverns. And, when Nashtya was hired, Alexi turned his attention, almost full time, to this lovely maid.

He was crude at times, very suave and charming at other times. And he was the son of Nashtya's employer, a fact which he never hesitated to point out. Charming yet offensive, Alexi overwhelmed Nashtya with a variety of gifts, both trivial and occasionally quite extravagant. One day it was a cute little bracelet, another day it was an elegant necklace or a finely embroidered shawl. For a poor, illiterate maid, these were gifts she could hardly refuse, nor did she want to. And, though he never took her out for what could be considered a date, he did spend hours chatting with and escorting her about the merchant's sizable garden. He was handsome and irresistible to this naive young servant girl. And, he was very, very persistent. Inevitably, one night she said "yes" to that predictable question. And, eight weeks later she started to show an unmistakable baby bump.

For the first few months after Alexi's conquest he continued to be charming. But, his charm and attention faded as Nashtya turned more visibly pregnant. Alexi had to confess to being the likely father-to-be and the merchant grudgingly kept Nashtya in his employ as long as she was able to perform her daily chores. To his credit, the merchant also provided food and a modest extra payment to Nashtya as she approached her delivery date. But as the due date approached, Alexi, the playboy but soon to be a parent, gave her even less time and attention. He didn't even make an appearance on the delivery date. He was probably too busy hustling another young woman, putting together another seduction. And in June 1920 Nashtya delivered a healthy, very cute, little Polahaya. Later in her youth she would be called "Polya", then "Apolonia" in Germany, then "Pauline" in America.

The first half dozen years of motherhood were not kind to Nashtya or to Polahaya. To no one's surprise the rich merchant distanced himself from his former maid. He offered only a meager and infrequent "gift" of some cash and food. The charity dwindled even more as the Bolsheviks advanced and seized more property and wealth. And the playboy son refused to take on any responsibilities or provide support. In fact, a few months after Nashtya gave birth, Alexi abruptly left Borisov for some unknown location and some ambiguous and supposedly important "job." Nashtya's parents were hard-working, very religious, and not very wealthy. And they were also very outraged by their daughter's carelessness. They grudgingly allowed Nashtya and Polahaya to live with them. But, the parents, just like the merchant and his prodigal son, gave very little time, care and affection to the unwed mother and child.

Nashtya didn't help her cause either. Publicly she showed no shame or remorse. She wasn't a churchgoer in deeply Orthodox Byelorussia. (But communism would make church going far less relevant very soon anyway.) She was still young, pretty and quite the flirt. In the eyes of many, Nashtya was the town tramp. She struggled to pick up any steady work because of little Polahaya. And little Polahaya, likewise, was branded and shunned as the poor bastard child of the town tramp. This wasn't the childhood on which fond, lifelong memories were built. Then along came Temofay.

Temofay Ilyonich Bekovsky was the pride and joy, and the only child, of Ilya and Katerina Bekovsky. As a healthy, not too mischievous young lad, Temofay helped at his father's modest carpentry shop. As his carpentry skills improved in his late teens, Temofay handled an increasingly large share of the family's business. Ilya became just a polite part-time contributor to that business, with Temofay providing the daily hard labor and maintaining the family's comfortable standard of living. They weren't rich but they lived well. Temofay hired three other workers along with his part-time father. And, to everyone's surprise and relief, the local communist leaders (more like troublemakers than leaders) left the business alone.

With the expanded workforce at the carpentry shop, Temofay was able to leave the business periodically and pursue his other occupational passion. Just like the dreams of countless young boys and men, Temofay wanted to be a fireman. Though Borisov was growing, there was no official fire department. Consequently, it was an all volunteer force, and Temofay was ready and very willing to help.

He was an imposing figure, lean and muscular and six feet tall. And with his perpetual smile, any damsel would gladly be rescued by Temofay. He knew everyone in town and was a friend to all. When the fire alarm bell rang, he would dash out of the carpentry shop, knocking over a project or two, and routinely be the first to show up at the fire. He was courageous, a bit reckless, but he truly loved the thrill and the danger of the fire emergency. This second, but for him his first serious occupation, earned him the respect of the townspeople. It made him the envy of many other young men and also made him the most eligible bachelor in Borisov. Handsome, dashing and daring, and reasonably wealthy. What a catch for any young lady. There were even a number of not so young ladies who competed for his time and attention. Temofay did date some, but not much. Nor was he in any hurry for marriage. But, among the countless eligible females to choose from, he turned his attention to Nashtya.

Yes, she was a beautiful young lady. But, she was only 19, six years younger than Temofay. Nashtya also carried so much baggage. She was the town "tramp." And a poor tramp at that, barely working, barely tolerated by her own parents, and deserted by that despicable rich boy. And she carried with her one more very visible bundle of "baggage," her cute two-year-old Polahaya.

Maybe, it was that collective baggage that drew Temofay to Nashtya. He had a reputation as a charming, sensitive gentleman. Consequently, here was a classic portrait of a damsel in distress (flawed as this damsel was) needing some charity, support, maybe even a little affection. And Temofay provided all of that and more. Their first meeting was accidental… maybe. One afternoon Nashtya changed her route from her daily stroll and walked past Temofay's carpentry workshop. On the second day on that new route there was the shop owner, covered in copious amounts of sawdust, standing in the shop's doorway. Apparently, he was taking a short break, also maybe accidently, at that very moment. The two looked at one another, a brief hello and a friendly wave of the hand were exchanged, and Nashtya continued on her motherly stroll. Whether it was initially accidental or intentional, Nashtya continued on that new route, strolling by Temofay's workshop, cute "baggage" in her arms, two or three times a week. There were polite, shy hellos exchanged. And little Polahaya, almost on cue, would squirm and giggle as Temofay routinely paused his work, ambled over to mother and child, and delighted them both with his huge grin and a small soft cookie. Temofay had perfected his routine of always having that little cookie in his overalls. He also hurriedly brushed off some of the workshop sawdust beforehand to look slightly more presentable. The sidewalk stops became more lengthy and lighthearted, the infant's giggles continued. Temofay also introduced an extra weekly ritual of inviting Nashtya to pause from her walk to join him for his afternoon cup of tea, and maybe a small cookie, or two. The shop was constantly busy and there was an extensive backlog of projects that needed attention. But the projects simply had to wait for an extra half hour as Temofay played the weekly teatime host. The weekly rendezvous, the halting conversations, grew less awkward.

This was as old fashioned a courtship as anyone could script: slow and very innocent. But it was clearly blossoming into a far more serious romance. And after those sought-after teatime pauses, Temofay increasingly wondered about and worried about the future. "Where is this silly little romance going?" And more importantly, "Where should it go?" He was a highly visible town gentleman. Everyone knew and admired his kindness, his missionary mindset, his constant offering of a helping hand. Consequently, offering a smile, conversation and tea to a struggling young mother certainly could be viewed as entirely proper and charitable. But Temofay was also very sensitive to public opinion, maybe gossip, about his intentions. After all, this single mother was the scandalized town tramp (a very beautiful tramp, but a tramp nonetheless.) Temofay admitted to himself that he could and probably should do far better in finding some other woman to court. A gossiping public might readily, though wrongly, suspect his supposedly noble missionary interest was not quite so noble.

Nashtya, in her reflective moments, likewise wondered why the town's most eligible bachelor was lavishing so much time and attention on her. She knew Temofay could do far far better. He was so polished. She was so quiet, so uneducated, so tarnished. She questioned his motives and contemplated putting an end to the courtship. Nashtya's mother didn't offer any helpful advice for her daughter's dilemma, aggressively prodding her daughter to do anything, be anything, to land the town's most eligible male trophy. Nashtya continued the courtship.

Despite their respective qualms and questions, plus the random town gossip, the romance did blossom. The town's consummate gentleman loved not only the town's tarnished mother but also that mother's innocent, always giggly, daughter. And that tarnished mother wanted desperately to provide her daughter with a better life and a good man, a very good man, that Polahaya could call a father. And little Polahaya became the common denominator to further strengthen that romance.

Over the next two years, and despite the predictable and often cruel gossip, Temofay altered and expanded their meetings. He visited Nashtya's home often, provided extra food, some money, and the occasional gifts to both Nashtya and Polahaya. He took Polahaya on little adventures to the park and was very much the caring, loving father figure.

Over those two years Temofay discarded his "bachelor forever" mindset and eventually married Nashtya, adopting the cute little "baggage" as well. The resourceful, energetic carpenter also built a new home for the family. With that marriage and a home, the gossip faded away. And for Nashtya, as well as for her young daughter, the stigma of illegitimacy started to fade away.

The family also grew. Halya was born two years later and Pyotr followed the following year. Life was simple, uneventful, and still fairly unaffected by the Bolshevik Revolution. The one recurring challenge in the growing household was Pyotr. He was a scrawny boy but a boy with a rebellious streak, a quick tongue and a quick temper. It was a troublesome personality that would cause his early childhood death and bring heartbreak for the family, especially for big protective sister Polahaya.

Around the home, and around the entire town, he was known as Pyotr the Pest, or just "the Pest." Not only was he a scrawny kid, he was also short for his years. That stature, or lack of it, produced the stereotypic Napoleonic complex in the Pest. He was entirely too bossy for his own good or his health. He didn't hesitate to push and shove anyone he found who was more of a runt than he was. The only asset he did possess, which saved him time and again, was fast feet. Actually, he had one more asset and that was his older sister Polahaya.

 It was very close to an exhausting, full time job dragging him away from a beating he was only moments away from. Or she would pull some young tough kid off the Pest, saving poor Pyotr from more of the beating he was currently receiving, and which he probably deserved. After a rescue Polahaya would smack the troublemaker brother on the back of the head, yank once or twice on his ear as she hustled him back home. Then she would deliver her stern lecture about his bad behavior and his very bad mouth. Next came one last smack on the head, as was the ritual, followed by a big hug and a kiss. He was a pest, a persistent pest, but he was her little brother. And, she was the loving, protective big sister. Until that fateful, tragic day.

Temofay's family owned a small pasture for grazing cattle. Pyotr was assigned a semi-regular task of bringing a small milking herd from the pasture and then across a bridge on the creek separating Temofay's house from the pasture. The creek wasn't that wide, but it was always deep and swift. Polahaya didn't go with Pyotr that afternoon though it was her regular ritual with her little Pest. And, as darkness was approaching Pyotr had not returned. Father and big sister went searching but with no success. Sadly, a neighbor some distance from Temofay's house, and some distance downstream, came to the house later that day and dropped the devastating news that Pyotr had drowned. Shock. Confusion. Feelings of guilt by big sister who should have been with Pyotr. Compounding the tragedy, the rumor started circulating that Pyotr had not accidentally fallen into the creek. Three older boys, tough boys, had been sighted around the bridge that late afternoon. And, according to the boys, Poytr, the clumsy foul mouthed punk that he was, had shouted some insults, then ran, then tripped and caused his own drowning death. Or maybe it was more pushing and less accidental tripping.

Either way, it was doubly tragic but also maybe convenient for those boys that Pyotr had not learned to swim. The rumors about the actual cause of the drowning remained just that, and nothing further was done about the suspect "accident." All that was left was a grieving family needing to arrange a proper burial.

Late that afternoon Temofay drove the barnyard wagon with Pyotr lying in the wagon and in the middle of a thick pile of straw. He was wrapped in a wool blanket, his head uncovered and resting on another folded blanket. The boy looked as if he was just resting or sleeping. That was how Temofay wanted the family to see their boy, peaceful and warm, not cold and damp. As Polahaya ran out of the house and stared into the wagon she whispered to her little brother, "Wake up, please wake up." She had heard the terrible news, knew Pyotr was dead, but couldn't bring herself to accept that painful fact. Not yet. Her troublemaking little brother was always involved in some prank, some stupid little joke. Maybe, just maybe, he was lying very still, pretending to be asleep or even pretending to be dead. How dumb! But even at her young innocent age, Polahaya knew she was the one pretending. And after another few minutes of staring at her brother she broke down into uncontrollable sobs and tears. Her mother and father collectively embraced her, saying nothing, just hugging and crying as well. As they nudged her back into the house Polahaya turned back to the wagon and whispered, "Please forgive me. I should never have let you go out alone. I should have forced you to learn how to swim. But you were too darn stubborn, and I was too darn lazy." Her parents tenderly insisted Polahaya was not to blame for her brother's death. And they repeated that heartfelt message time and again over the next several days. But Polahaya would struggle all her life with the misguided belief she was responsible for the death of little Pyotr.

She also had to be a participant and spectator throughout the time honored but macabre spectacle of a Russian Orthodox funeral and its preparatory three-day period of repose. There in the small family room of the Bekovsky home Nashtya placed her little Pyotr. A small side table was cleared of its portraits and decorative pottery and converted into a ceremonial stand for the diminutive body. Nashtya draped the table with her finest tablecloth and adorned it with flowers, religious icons and memorabilia. And there Pyotr lay. And lay. Initially Polahaya was more curious than terrified about the ceremonial table and its occupant. The first day of repose she even brought over a small stool and placed it next to the table to provide her more of an up close and personal viewing. There she was in her simple, very proper black dress staring at her little brother clothed in his finest party clothes. But those party clothes and all those fragile decorative items placed around Pyotr struck Polahaya as entirely wrong. Pyotr always had dirt on his face, dirt on his clothes, and he never stopped running around or running into something, anything. This Pyotr was lifeless, literally, and stiff and cold. After that first peek atop the footstool Polahaya avoided looking at the body, even avoided going anywhere near the table. In a quiet trembling voice, she repeatedly begged her parents, "Can you take him away now?" But traditions and rituals needed to be observed, and there Pyotr lay in the family's front room. What a sight, what a memory for this grief stricken eight-year-old.

Mercifully for Polahaya, maybe for all of the family, the repose period finally ended. A small graveside service followed. Kind words were offered, tears were shed, and there was a small but supportive gathering of friends at the gravesite. Everyone was still dressed in respectful and not very cheery funeral attire. But once the last rites were offered and Pyotr was lowered into the grave Temofay declared in a loud and cheerful voice, "Let us celebrate." And there at the gravesite he and Nashtya brought out food from his cart. Others generously contributed as well and everyone settled into a hearty luncheon feast. Since this was Polahaya's first encounter with death and its attendant Orthodox rituals she was at first confused and surprised. But those thoughts were quickly replaced by smiles and some excitement as she saw the food festival being set out at the gravesite. Those feelings of guilt and responsibility would resurface over the years for Polahaya. But for now she ate heartily, laughed heartily with her mother and father, reliving some of Pyotr's wild, stupid misadventures and the countless times Polahaya rescued him from yet another beating. Life goes on.

Chapter 2 -   Growing and Rebelling

"Adolescent stories are almost all beginnings. There are never any endings."

Alan Chambers

Polahaya still had a younger sister to care for, chores to help with and a fairly comfortable day-to-day existence. Her mother had landed a job in the local furniture factory and took Polahaya with her frequently. That was fun and she was informally picking up some sound apprentice skills. Over the next half dozen years Polahaya graduated from mother's little helper and curious bystander to a part-time employee. Child labor laws didn't exist, working conditions were dirty and dangerous. But, the factory manager observed some real talent developing, and the factory could use the extra, and very cheap, labor. Polahaya was paid a part-time wage though she was increasingly putting in a full 12-to-14-hour day alongside her mother. The income was helpful, however small the amount, though sadly for Polahaya all that money went to her mother.

 The payment scale changed when Polahaya turned sixteen at the factory and was officially designated "full-time." She had been just that, full-time, for almost two full years. But, now she received a modest bump in pay as she switched to piecework. And, her mother agreed, even if reluctantly, to allow Polahaya to keep her earnings.

 Polahaya's factory workstation was fairly straightforward and simple, at least in theory. She was assigned the task of shaping wooden legs for the chairs and tables which were the factory's specialty. There was a lathe, precision chisels, and tons and tons of hard oak boards. The chisels were fine but very sharp and dangerous. The lathe, or what passed for a lathe, must have been a hundred years old and with no electrical connection. Power to turn the spindle with its chunk of wood waiting to be shaped was simple, old fashioned foot power applied to a large, heavy pedal. For a petite and slender young teen it was a grueling non-stop effort to keep that spindled block of wood rotating fast enough to chisel out the expected design.

There were the early mishaps, but no injuries. Polahaya contributed her share to the factory floor's scrap pile. But, she became very proficient and very fast with that piecework assignment. She even boldly approached the factory manager with a design change to the legs. The proposed change wasn't that radical or that different. But, it was a bit more stylish, even a little more artistic. Though the manager had a very strong and hardly subtle anti-female bias, he gave his hearty endorsement. Nashtya was very surprised by Polahaya's boldness, but she was also very proud of her daughter.

In those first years at the factory Polahaya was a quiet, shy, soft spoken child laborer. She listened, observed, and learned. Predictably, the harsh work environment shaped her into a more mature, self-confident Polahaya, street smart beyond her years, and at times more defiant and outspoken than she prudently should be. She became more adept at rough and crude trash talk though she could turn on impish, innocent girlish charm when necessary. She also developed a growing intolerance for factory politics or managerial pecking orders.

One year after Polahaya became a full-time employee her friend Ludmilla joined her at the factory. Ludmilla was two years older, petite like her friend but equally ambitious and unafraid of hard labor. They had been dear friends and mutual troublemakers since early childhood. They also came from troubled households in their early years. Ludmilla had been working at a smaller competitor's factory but saw an opportunity for a better position, maybe better pay. And, she hoped she might be lucky enough to be placed at a work station alongside her old friend. Polahaya was equally delighted to have her dear friend join her as a workmate. But, Polahaya also felt the need to paint a blunt picture of the challenges awaiting Ludmilla in her new workplace.

The two friends gathered at Polahaya's home on Sunday night before Ludmilla's first day at the factory. Polahaya sat down with her friend and offered her insights about the factory's cultural environment. "We have lots of old women on the floor, old but also very skilled. But they and their skills don't count. It's a good old boys' workplace. Actually, they're not old boys. They're young boys, arrogant, very fond of themselves and barely tolerant of any of us "girls," young or old. And those boys are loved and tolerated by their not so young but also equally arrogant boss. He's a nasty old pig, and he'll grab and grope you any chance he gets." (The "male chauvinist pig" label wouldn't become fashionable until decades later.) Polahaya offered this description with quiet calm. Her friend listened attentively and wasn't too surprised by what she heard. Disappointed, yes, but not surprised.

Polahaya became more animated as she continued. "Forget about all that communist propaganda: No classes! No aristocracy! Equal pay and equal opportunity! Don't expect or believe any of that garbage in this factory. The factory boys think and act like aristocrats, and think they are the "special" talented, most skilled workers. They are not!" Polahaya rose from her chair, took a deep breath. Her angry expression changed, replaced with a smile and a wink to her friend and new workmate. "We're going to change that workplace and those damnable attitudes. And, we're going to do it quickly, just you and me." Ludmilla's first day on the job confirmed everything Polahaya had described.

These arrogant, chauvinist pigs proved to be no match for Polahaya and Ludmilla. After only two days together on the floor, and after enduring an endless barrage of abusive language and crude behavior, the women put together their own factory offensive. Over vodkas at Polahaya's apartment, Polahaya laid out their grand strategy. "We'll go to the manager and politely, but confidently, tell him we can work on those supposedly most complicated spindles. Give us a chance! He's a dirty old man who can't say no to us if we ask and act so sweetly and politely." Polahaya paused for another sip, Ludmilla practiced her best sexy pose, and Polahaya continued. "Let's even present this as a challenge. Watch how good, or rotten, we are compared to his boys. If we don't deliver, he can demote us to the lowest level of piecework and we'll quietly do our job, no complaints. Assuming we persuade the manager to accept our proposition, you and I will then make it our daily mission to distract and annoy those same arrogant bastards as often as we can. We won't sabotage the factory production. We'll just make it a bit harder for the boys to focus on their work and meet their production numbers. You and I will make our quotas, and so much more, easily. I know we can, and we will. Quite frankly, I look forward to annoying and humiliating those self-proclaimed "superior" workers." Polahaya looked over at her friend and co-conspirator expecting a comment, maybe a question. Ludmilla only smiled, nodded her head in agreement, and they enjoyed one more vodka toast.

Once every week, at the end of the workday, the factory boss came out of his office and yelled at the women to march up to his office. "Get up here, now," he growled. The two dutifully presented their sweetest, most innocent smiles and sheepishly gazed at their boss. Only those two could make that short fifteen step walk seductive, and anything but sweet and innocent, for their ancient bachelor boss. With his sternest look and a forced harshness in his voice he said, "You two have to stop taking so damn many breaks during the day. You can't possibly be that thirsty or that constantly in need of a toilet break. And you absolutely have to stop bothering my boys, chatting with them, bumping into them as they're working, messing up their hair. I see you do this every day. And it has to stop!" The manager's lecture was almost the same every week. But he never came across as too serious, definitely not that angry. The women alternated weekly in responding to the complaints. It was Ludmilla's turn this week. In her sultry, soft voice, with her head bowed, she delivered her apologetic reply. "We're sorry, truly sorry, if we've caused any trouble. Have our piecework numbers gone down? Are we no longer your two highest performing workers? Have any of your boys complained to you about us?" And then after a pause to allow some kind of rebuttal, though none was expected, she continued. "As for those toilet breaks, you know we girls just have to go more often. Can't change that. Honest." This weekly ritual was always the same. The manager's regular and very weak complaint wasn't that compelling either since all three knew the women remained the factory's best and brightest. And, they were this dirty old man's most attractive workers. On cue both women promised to try to do better the next week, just as they promised every week. Then Polahaya, followed by Ludmilla, walked up to their boss and gave the old bachelor a polite kiss on the cheek. While the boss watched they repeated their seductive walk back down the stairs. Half-way down the stairs to the plant floor they always stopped, turned back up the stairs to their plant manager, waved oh so playfully and innocently, and then returned to their stations. And every afternoon, after that half-hearted scolding from the manager, the two star employees, and clever actresses, casually walked to their local tavern and toasted their ongoing success.

They became quite the dynamic duo on the floor. Collectively they were the source of dramatically increased productivity. They remained the source of continuing headaches for their manager. But, no one, absolutely no one, could compete against the duo in speed and quality. Those skills in turn generated both envy and at times hostility, though neither girl seemed to care.

Polahaya had so much, enjoyed so much as a confident, carefree teenager. But, despite all this success there was something she did not have, something she sorely missed. The missing something was also an ever present source of frustration and embarrassment. Polahaya did not have a basic education. She was so street smart but not at all school smart. She was not dumb nor suffered from any diagnosed mental disability. She had good people skills. But, from her very first year in a classroom she struggled with school and struggled to stay focused on her studies. She passed her first five years of school, though she had to retake her fifth-grade finals. Fortunately, Polahaya was blessed to have the support of a young, dedicated grade school teacher, Stefan Mirovich. He tutored her as much as he could, helped her master that fifth grade retake. However, in sixth grade Polahaya struggled even more, failing to pass her sixth-grade finals, not just once, but twice. Stefan came to the rescue, or tried once again, offering to tutor Polahaya for a third try. But, with equal parts humiliation and defiance Polahaya said no, there would be no more tests. There would be no more school. Her mother didn't help any, since she herself was illiterate. And instead of school Polahaya joined her mother as a child laborer at the factory. That ended Polahaya's formal education. And throughout her life Polahaya would look back on the decision to drop out of school with embarrassment and tearful regret. One small consolation was that Stefan, the young, caring school teacher, continued to provide informal classroom sessions. He promised Polahaya that he would continue to guide and support her, as a teacher and as a friend. And Stefan Mirovich would keep that promise over another twenty plus years.

Through kindness and love from Temofay, Nashtya regained some respectability and lost that "town tramp" label. Polahaya likewise profited from that kindness and love. She grew into a beautiful teenager and a skilled maker of furniture components. Later in life, Polahaya would struggle to recount any glowing achievements or proud moments throughout her 30+ years in Belarus or Germany. But, when pressed by her children she would brag that she was a real "expert" at shaping beautiful furniture legs. That was it, that's all she could declare to her children and the world at large as her lifetime achievement. What a shame.

There was some emotional and social growth during those teenage years. Polahaya joined a local communist youth club and attended the frequent rallies and marches. She attempted a reconnection with her mother's parents. But, that was a brief and hardly warm reception from her grandparents. She also had one brief and painful encounter with her birth father.

It was a late summer afternoon, still providing a warm breeze and wispy clouds for Polahaya as she walked home from the factory. It had been a good day, a highly productive day, and Polahaya took her time. Her usual walking companion and work partner, Ludmilla, had other plans this afternoon and wasn't with Polahaya. The street she took home was safe and friendly with few fellow travelers. Therefore, it was a little unsettling for Polahaya to see a stranger leaning against a streetside tree. He appeared to be waiting for someone. As she continued down the street, he turned his head and stared intently at her. Her smile vanished, and her pace slowed, as she approached the stranger. As her smile vanished an awkward looking smile appeared on the stranger's face.

He turned directly to her, stretched his arms out in a welcoming gesture and said in almost a whisper, "Hello, my dear little Polya." Still in a whispered voice as well as some stuttering, the stranger said, "It, it, it's me, your father. Don't you recognize me?" Of, course, how could she know it was her long-lost father, if it truly was who he claimed to be? He had deserted the family when Polahaya was barely a year old, with little if any memories at that age. Stupid as the question was, Polahayak instinctively sensed this was in fact her father. "So, you did your homework," she said, "and you learned where I work, probably where I live. Good for you. Now why are you here?" He took two steps forward, attempting a clumsy hug which Polahaya avoided. Then with a stronger though still trembling voice he said," I'm so very, very sorry I left you and your mother. No, that's wrong. I didn't leave you. I deserted both of you. And I'm truly sorry for that cowardly decision." Tears welled up in his eyes. In contrast, Polahaya stood in front of him and showed no emotion. The stranger continued. "I'm here to ask for your forgiveness. I'm also here to take you back into my life as my dear daughter. Come with me and I promise I can and will provide you a far, far better life than you can ever hope to enjoy here in Borisov." Before she could offer any answer, the stranger continued with his apology. "I know I owe you an explanation of what I did, where I've been all these years." And, before Polahaya could reply, "No, no I'm not interested," he blurted out a lengthy, at times rambling, account of his travels and troubles. Polahaya was polite enough not to interrupt as he continued with his combination confession/explanation as to where he had been the past fifteen years of her life.

It began as a tearful apology, once again, for his actions and his absence. And there were pathetic, almost laughable, explanations he offered. Yes, he had not been very attentive, nor even present, during the last few weeks before Polahaya was born. And, yes, he had given very little time and attention to the new mother and his new daughter. The reasons? Some general panic. Some immature confusion as to how he should act. Even some lingering question as to whether he was in fact the father. But, the real reason, he had to confess finally, was his overwhelming panic about becoming a responsible parent, a responsible spouse. That simply and very bluntly was not him, nor could it be him. He was just a young, irresponsible, privileged playboy.

His parents were embarrassed by the scandal, angry with their stupid, irresponsible son, annoyed about their unexpected and certainly unwanted new role as grandparents. They made the impulsive decision to send him away to some distant relative, somewhere far across the Urals. They undertook the responsibility of caring for Nashtya and the newborn. But they did so half-heartedly.

This mystery man, this self-proclaimed long lost father, blurted out all that history, with what sounded like genuine regret and shame. Then after all that history and explanations, and another awkward apology behind him, he asked her, one more time, to go away with him, father with daughter.

Throughout that lengthy, pathetic story, Polahaya paid little if any attention to what she dismissed as ancient and irrelevant history. And for several minutes she just stood in silence. There was silence from him as well (he never even introduced himself by a proper name) while he waited for her answer. Then with an air of confidence, as well as defiance, well beyond her years, Polahaya shouted out, "No! Never! You didn't want me or need me all those years. You weren't a father. And you will never be my father." Then with a calm, quiet voice, and the hint of a smile, she said, "Good bye." Then she continued on her walk home.

She had gone only a few steps toward home when, in a trembling voice, and barely above a whisper, she heard this man, supposedly her father, speak. "Please, please, give me a chance to be a father, your father." Polahaya stopped and partly turned around. She saw a pathetic figure staring at her, even on his knees, arms outstretched and with a few tears flowing down his cheeks. For a moment, just a brief moment, she felt some pity and sadness for that person. No love for him, just some understandable emotions toward a person in distress. But after that brief emotional pause she felt only indifference as she stared at this stranger. She turned once again toward home, with a firm, confident stride and even more of a smile. Over her shoulder she shouted out "good-bye" once again. With that second goodbye Polahaya would never see nor hear from her father again.

Young, beautiful Polahaya grew more independent, a little less sweet, and more rebellious. But, this evolving personality made her the town trophy for every young man to pursue. In a few years, when the Germans invaded, she would also be pursued by more than one handsome German officer. Polahaya loved the attention, dated and dismissed young suitors with ease. And then along came Ivan.

Summer Research, Summer Memories

Our deceased father and his very sparse and often very vague European history presented a daunting summertime challenge. We needed to separate facts from myths, collect and connect random comments and contradictory statements. We had our share of unpleasant American memories, some memories better forgotten than relived. But there were good memories as well, the better parts of an otherwise complicated man. Those better memories, principally reconstructed by us two brothers who worked with him, and played with him, offered some insight into his past.

He was the consummate, never tiring opportunist. We boys were constantly recruited (maybe more accurately forced?) to help with endless weekend "opportunities." There were regular weekend roofing jobs, often beginning at 6:00 a.m. on a steamy Saturday. The grunt work, at $1 an hour, required us to haul 85-pound bundles of shingles up a ladder. And sometimes it was a far more strenuous haul up to a second story roof. Weighing little more than those huge bundles, we boys would start at a third of a bundle with each climb, eventually toughen up enough to tackle a half bundle. And finally, and proudly, we'd manage a full bundle. With that triumphant benchmark behind us, but still at $1 an hour, we'd apprentice at laying and nailing shingles. There were similar Saturday "invitations" for a new concrete floor or driveway job. This again required us kids, still short on muscles, to move unstable and very heavy wheelbarrows of so-called "mud" and to do so again on a sweltering Saturday afternoon. We also remembered one unusual late afternoon trip to an elementary school gymnasium. Our opportunity this time was to literally tear out that gymnasium's old oak flooring and haul it away to our recently purchased very first home. This was a real home, a nice home, and not just another rundown rental. The gym floor tear away/removal project was entirely proper, our father having offered some sweat equity carpentry repairs at the school in exchange for the flooring which otherwise would have been pulled up and then thrown away. After that gym floor removal project, we were again "invited" the next weekend to spend that entire weekend installing the reclaimed flooring into our new home. No even $1 an hour this time, just our contribution to our new home. Despite the hard labor and the denial of our youthful free time, we witnessed and grew to admire our father's tenacity and his opportunistic mind. Those repeatedly found new projects, his shrewdly bartered labor trade-offs, also provided modest but satisfying wages for us. And we boys began to develop a few more muscles for that next weekend "invitation."

We relived Sunday group picnics at a local lake. Our father would parade around the picnic grounds, barrel chested and deeply tanned from shirtless summer workdays. He was the biggest, toughest male and he had no qualms about belittling the other pale skinned welterweight male picnickers. Despite the enviable tan, our father offered some self-inflicted comic relief. He had that strong, barrel-chested, bronzed upper body, but his legs, protruding from his baggy swim trunks, were pale white. A glaring pale white. He could have worn work shorts on those hot summer days like so many of his fellow building tradesmen. But he stubbornly refused to do so. Therefore, it was a comical Sunday spectacle: bronze top with albino legs down below. Comical, yes, but no one dared to laugh.

In that bright summer sun, on that deep tan, the long scar on our father's chest, as well as the long scar on his right cheek, stood out so conspicuously. His fellow picnic goers never dared to ask. We children, out of innocent curiosity, occasionally made the mistake of asking. But all we ever received in response, in addition to an occasional slap on the head, was a fierce scowl and a steely eyed stare. The scars weren't ugly or scary to us. We were simply curious. But it never went beyond curiosity.

We also recalled our enjoyment with, but also our curiosity about, the Saturday night immigrant social gatherings and the Sunday afternoon chess gatherings. In particular we never understood our father's fondness for one very irascible immigrant, plus his diminutive, very talkative wife. This immigrant was a constant invitee on Saturdays and Sundays. To everyone he was simply the "Cossack." And it was an open question if anyone actually knew his real name besides "Cossack." Later in life, after he passed away, our mother informed us he was an actual real life transplanted Cossack, having immigrated, somehow, prior to the war. We were saddened by the news of his death, followed just one week later by his wife's passing. We had always been curious as to what a "Cossack" was but had been afraid to ask. Now we felt slightly less uneasy asking about those strange weekend visitors. Our mother and our father belatedly tried to offer an explanation. Cossacks were not part of some distinct ethnic group. They weren't Russian or Ukrainian or Turkish or anything, just simply "Cossacks." Historically they were a self-ruled community of horsemen, or "freemen" and "adventurers," first documented in the fourteenth century out of the plains, or "steppes'" of central Asia. They had the reputation of being formidable fighters, fighting for anyone or no one. They were described as wild, fierce, proud and independent. And, that is what our family's self-proclaimed "Cossack" was: wild, fierce, proud and independent. "Unpredictable" could also be added to that description.

He was short, maybe only 5 feet 8 or 9, but muscular and barrel chested, just like our father. From the conversations we overheard it was very evident he had a sharp mind. But he also had a very sharp tongue. He delighted in bragging about his Cossack roots, even hinted at some ancestral aristocracy. But they were only vague hints. If a fellow immigrant dared to probe for more details about those roots the Cossack would simply roar, "I'm a Cossack! That's all you need to know!" We children would sneak down the stairs on those Saturday nights to watch and listen as the Cossack used his distinct booming voice to frequently argue with someone over something, anything. All in all there wasn't much to endear him to anyone. We suspected he was invited and tolerated because he was an immigrant, just like all the other attendees. Fortunately for him, as well as his fellow immigrants, the Cossack was also married to a much more cheerful, though slightly eccentric, wife. She routinely entertained the crowd with her silly jokes and butchered songs. Whatever his reasons were for doing so, our father clearly enjoyed the Cossack's company, apparently also enjoyed that all too combative personality. We certainly didn't understand why. But our opinions didn't count.

Chapter 3 - Ivan the Terrible

"A father is a man who expects his son to be as good as he was meant to be."

Carol Oates

In his first 10 years, Ivan Kupraschonik lived a simple and uneventful life. Later in his teen years, Ivan would acquire the sometimes flattering, sometimes derisive, nickname of Ivan the Terrible. At times the label was well deserved. And with his westward escape to Germany, and eventually to America, he would change his name, once again, into a far more common sounding and far less notorious Jan Bykowski. Maybe there was, and is, some semi-secret catalog of adoptable European immigrant names. Census records of post-war arrivals to America recorded countless thousands of "Jan Bykowski's." Ivan became one of those countless thousands.

Ivan's father Andreyev, wife Galena, and Ivan's two younger siblings eked out a modest but comfortable existence on a small farm outside Borisov. There was some livestock, a decent acreage of wheat, and a small but sturdy home. Communism and its "great peoples' revolution" was rapidly eliminating any symbols of bourgeois society: aristocracy, rank, personal wealth, personal land ownership. Land in particular was being confiscated from its owners, whether peasants or aristocrats, and absorbed into large "peoples" collective farms. The Kupraschoniks' modest farmstead would suffer that same fate in a few years. But, for the moment their farm belonged to them.

Ivan's father was a big, rough, heavily muscled man. He was tough in appearance and attitude, and quarrelsome by nature. These less than flattering traits were evident at home. They likewise were very evident in his contacts with others. As the man of the house, he made frequent trips to town for provisions at the general store. A stop at his favorite drinking hall was for him a regular, and indispensable, part of that weekly routine. Along with weekly provisions Andreeyev all too frequently brought back bruises, bloodied knuckles, the occasional black eye. A torn shirt or a scuffed knee were all too common as well. He was entirely too quick to take offense at some stupid but harmless comment or an inadvertent bump. Andreeyev was collecting a growing lineup of enemies, and few friends. But he didn't mind. It was just tough guy talk, the occasional fight, but no serious injuries or serious threats.

In contrast to the tough guy exterior, Andreyev also had a softer, gentler side. Unfortunately, very few other townsfolk saw that side. Despite a very basic elementary education, Andreyev learned to read quite well. And, he was a voracious reader of any books he could get, borrow, or maybe steal. There must have been some unique genetic marker at work because Ivan developed that same reading skill and passion. And, that lifelong love of literature might have helped to soften the tough every day exterior of Ivan the Terrible.

Sadly, at age ten, Ivan's simple, uneventful life changed drastically. Ivan, out of necessity, evolved into a tougher, more assertive, at times reckless young man. That evolution began with a seemingly senseless murder of his father, witnessed firsthand by Ivan in the family's front yard.

Ivan was out by the small shed stacking wood. His father was at the house examining a very old, covered porch that was badly in need of repairs. Ivan enjoyed helping his father, occasionally driving a few nails or sawing a board. But that fateful day he was relegated to the routine task of stacking wood. And fortunately for Ivan, he was not at his father's side.

Down the dirt road, heading to the front of the house, Ivan spotted a small horse drawn cart moving at a very quick pace. As the horse and driver moved past Ivan who was working at the shed, Ivan vaguely recognized the man. Maybe he had seen him in town during a visit with his father. Though Ivan had only some vague recollection of who the stranger might be, Ivan definitely recognized the expression on the man's face. It was an expression of intense anger, and the stranger directed the same angry, hateful stare at Ivan as he raced past Ivan to the house. And toward Ivan's father. Sadly, Ivan, even though so young, knew that look, knew that stare. He had seen that look all too often from his own quick-tempered father. Instinctively Ivan started walking, half running to the house. But his father, seeing Ivan approach, shouted out, "Ivan, stay where you are! Go back to the woodpile." From the woodpile Ivan saw the tragedy unfold.

With dust and dirt floating and flying everywhere, the stranger reined his horse, and, through the dust, bolted out of his cart and toward Andreyev Kupraschonik. The stranger was short, slightly built and quite the physical contrast to much taller, stockier Andreyev. The size difference clearly didn't matter to the stranger as he walked up, now almost belly to belly, and glared at Ivan's father. Then he broke the brief silence and exploded with a violent outburst of words and curses. Ivan, even from his safe distance, could hear everything though he couldn't understand much. He did know some of the vile curses, curses he probably shouldn't know nor repeat. But Ivan clearly heard and understood a repeated combination of "liar, cheater, thief" directed at his father. In addition to the assault of curses and the repeated "liar, cheater, thief" accusations the diminutive, but very enraged, stranger started shoving Andreyev. With that first shove Ivan's father, who thus far had stood at the porch front and said nothing, shoved back.

Ivan, frightened and confused by what he was seeing, thought to himself, 'That little man is crazy! My dad will beat him to a bloody mess, maybe kill him, if that idiot keeps this up." But just as he thought that, and just as big, stronger Andreyev shoved the stranger and almost knocked him down, Ivan saw the stranger reach into his coat pocket. Again, out of some primitive instinct Ivan tried to run to his father. But the boy couldn't. He just stood there frozen in place, unable to move. All he could do was to scream out, "Father! Watch…" Before Ivan could shout out anything else and warn his father the stranger pulled out a pistol and fired one shot.

Still unable to move, Ivan could only stare at the stranger. The stranger stared back at Ivan but only for a moment. Then he put the pistol back in his pocket, casually walked back to his cart, climbed aboard and then slowly trotted his horse down that dusty road. Ivan was never able to provide a helpful description of his father's murderer. Nor did Ivan see that vaguely familiar stranger again.

The murderer seemingly vanished. No villagers volunteered any clues as to who the shooter was or why Ivan's father was killed. Ivan's mother may have known what triggered that violent exchange that afternoon. But if she did, she never shared it with Ivan. Sadly, Andreyev's reputation and frequent fights might have produced a lengthy list of suspects. Whatever the motive, and whoever the murderer was, the death of Andreyev quickly became and remained just an unsolved crime. And, life in revolutionary Byelorussia would go on as usual. As usual except for Ivan's life.

Back at the porch front Ivan was finally able to free himself from his paralysis and fear and run to his father who lay still and lifeless in the dirt. By the time he raced over, his mother was outside as well.

Sadly all she could do was to stand on that dilapidated porch and stare at her dead husband. Andreyev Kupraschonik had done everything, made every decision, and ran the house in a stern, efficient manner. She was the good and dutiful wife, the good mother. Sadly, she was totally dependent on her domineering Andreyev. She remained standing on the porch, sobbing and saying nothing, and just staring at Ivan, her young but oldest child. Ivan, despite the years, had to take charge, helping his mother, helping his siblings get through this tragic afternoon. Neighbors were called to help. Funeral arrangements were made. Ivan also had to endure that awkward, macabre Russian Orthodox ritual for the dead, where the body lay in repose for 3 days in the house. In an ironic twist of fate, Ivan's future wife, at an equally young age, would likewise be a participant in that Orthodox ritual.

Ivan at that very young age became the de facto head of the family. His mother, the typical quiet subservient housewife, struggled to run the home except for making meals. She was always on the verge of being healthy, but not healthy enough or energetic enough to contribute much. And, there were two younger children to care for.

Ivan had to and did capably take charge. He grew up tougher, mentally and physically, and adopted some of the same brash, combative traits of his deceased father. He increasingly spent more time in Borišov, switching from farm boy to a street savvy urban opportunist. He became more of that "Ivan the Terrible" instead of just Ivan. He quickly developed an interchangeable trio of everyday street skills: hustle, intimidation and charm. And Ivan easily and skillfully applied those three skills in whatever current "business" opportunities he pursued. A normal day job wouldn't do for Ivan. Nor would the dull, daily existence of a farmer.

Ivan did make a brief attempt at carpentry, having learned some skills from his handyman father. Ivan quickly became proficient at measuring, sawing, and nailing at the small carpentry shop that hired him. But, at this shop that was pretty much it day in and day out: measure, saw, nail, toss in a little sanding every so often. Ivan was making boxes, big boxes and little boxes and medium sized boxes. There were no challenges. There was just the day-to-day monotony and boredom of being a box builder. After just four weeks Ivan said goodbye. Ironically, twenty years later Ivan returned to that first career opportunity he rejected in Borisov. Ivan, later Big John to his fellow carpentry tradesmen, refined those rudimentary box making skills to become a proud, very well-respected finish carpenter. Instead of boxes, he made intricate hand-crafted cabinets, complex crown moldings, ornate doors and frames.

After that first brief and unsatisfying attempt at carpentry Ivan returned to the streets and its shopkeepers, once again searching for a job, any job. He saw a sign posted at the storefront of Gregor Trotkov, the town's sole watchmaker and repairman. The watchmaker needed an apprentice. Big, tough ham-fisted Ivan would not have been on a shortlist of candidates. However, Gregor had been an old friend of Ivan's murdered father. Those old friends had gulped down countless vodka shots, smoked countless cigars, and had participated in their share of barroom brawls. Actually, it was somewhat of a miracle the watchmaker still had hands skilled enough for delicate watchmaking and repair. Gregor saw much of his old friend Andreyev in Ivan. And, largely out of charity instead of good sense, Gregor invited Ivan in for a visit and an interview.

Ivan entered the small shop and was instantly taken aback by the vast assortment of small and large table clocks, several very expensive looking cuckoo clocks and countless watches. These items were spread over two large workbenches, all items apparently in need of repair. With that shop inventory scattered everywhere there was barely room to move around. And here was big burly Ivan clumsily bumping into just about everything, though luckily with no breakage, as he followed Gregor to his main workbench. Ivan's well recognized tough guy walk, arms and shoulders freely swaying and big feet thundering with every step, was a very bad fit in Gregor's shop. Ivan was very much that classic bull in a china shop, in this case in a watchmaker's shop. Ivan's big powerful handshake, with his hand totally engulfing Gregor's hand, was also totally wrong for the job. Nonetheless Gregor continued with the interview. Old friendships and old fond memories run deep. "Hello, my dear little Ivan," he said. "Though you obviously aren't that little. I knew your father very well. I'm aware of the challenges in helping your mother and providing for the family. You've been a good son. I'm also aware of the nickname you've picked up around town. Ivan the Terrible!! Well, I don't need an Ivan the Terrible in my shop. I do need and expect soft careful steps around my shop. I need patience, not impatience or a quick temper. And I certainly don't need to hear about any barroom brawls that mess up my apprentice's delicate hands. Do we understand each other?" Ivan sheepishly replied, "I understand." And Ivan started his apprenticeship the very next day.

That charitable experiment was doomed to fail after just the first few weeks. Ivan was very grateful for the opportunity, and he was an eager and hardworking new hire. But, big muscular Ivan, complete with big hands and boundless energy, struggled with the slowness, patience and fine touch required of a watchmaker's apprentice. And, there was a growing pile of delicate gears and levers that were tossed into the "ruined" basket and rarely deposited in the "repaired" basket. Ivan wanted to succeed, wanted to please his father's old friend, actually wanted a real, respectable job. But, this was definitely not his career path.

After three weeks Gregor gave Ivan the bad, but not surprising, news. As Gregor was closing up for the day, he asked Ivan to stay for a few minutes. Ivan rose up from his workbench, sweaty as always, but not because the shop was hot and stifling. Poor Ivan sweated profusely as he struggled every day to avoid another failed repair, or some irreparable break in a timepiece, or maybe another dropped wall clock. Gregor walked over to his sweaty apprentice, gave him a big hug, and with a tender smile he said, "You're fired." Ivan was disappointed but not that surprised. "I simply can't afford you, my dear big Ivan," Gregor continued. "There are entirely too many pieces that need to be repaired, new parts that need to be ordered, too many timepieces I have to give away to unhappy customers to replace a timepiece that's beyond repair. I'm losing money, not making money, with your help. I know your heart's in the right place and you've tried very hard to become a good apprentice. But you and your big hands just don't fit here." Ivan smiled, offered no protest or rebuttal and simply replied with a very sincere "Thank you." They exchanged hearty hugs and handshakes. Gregor even gave Ivan a few extra rubles as severance pay. And, Ivan was off again in search of a job.

With nothing but a firm handshake, small change in his pocket, and an increasingly unappealing employment resume, Ivan decided on a brief pause back at his family farm. Maybe a simple pastoral farm life wouldn't be that intolerable. He knew his mother could use his help and might enjoy his daily presence. He certainly wasn't averse to hard work. But it needed to be simple hard work that better utilized his nervous energy and youthful strength. And farm work would be far more tolerant of his occasional clumsiness. A bull in the barn was far better than a bull in a china shop, or a watchmaker's shop.

A farming life offered comfortable stability. Get up early, work hard and long, enjoy a home cooked meal, enjoy a vodka or two, and call it a day. But it also could, and would, turn Ivan into one of countless other young, energetic and very anonymous males in Borisov. And Ivan couldn't allow himself to be anonymous. He had experienced that anonymity in his early youth, just helping out and struggling to get by after the death of his father. Ivan had no intention of revisiting that past.

He could continue as an occasional street hustler, a handsome hustler, but otherwise still anonymous and unimportant. But he was confident enough, arrogant enough, certainly clever enough to keep pursuing that elusive "important," and as yet undefined, "opportunity." It would be that opportunity that would move him out of the borderline poverty with which he struggled every day. The elusive opportunity which would deliver to him the respect and recognition Ivan also craved. If a little intimidation was required to gain the sought-after respect and recognition, so be it. For Ivan, fear was an acceptable substitute for respect. An "opportunity," one that fueled his youthful vanity and his need to be important, sent Ivan back to the city streets after a three-day respite.

Over the next three decades that opportunistic drive would present Ivan with four critical decisions. The first one of Ivan's youthful decisions, to find a steady and honest job, saw him struggle as a clumsy box builder and then as an equally clumsy watchmaker. Those two honest work "opportunities" had provided Ivan with little more than a shabby resume. That collective experience then sent him to a far more rewarding and exciting, but very questionable, business opportunity with a black marketeer Cossack. The opportunity also earned him the unflattering and lingering label of a gangster. Later, during the German occupation of his town, Ivan seized a third business opportunity, this time working with his German occupiers in a seemingly harmless, non-violent guard position. The Cossack "opportunity" and the German "opportunity" provided Ivan with short term, superficial benefits. But, Ivan's pursuit of those opportunities also produced unintended and very adverse consequences, those very undesirable fruits of his opportunistic labors. The fourth opportunity, an escape from his past, he seized as a refugee amidst the chaos of post-war Germany. This opportunity would prove to be the most challenging for Ivan. It would also be the most rewarding.

Searching for that next great opportunity, Ivan learned there was one very successful town merchant who just might need the kind of hustle and energy that Ivan could easily provide. And, the job description was vague enough, and suggested it would pay well enough, to be a potential perfect fit for Ivan. Little did Ivan know, nor did he at the time care, this impending opportunity would brand him an intimidating, thuggish gangster. Would he be Important? Yes. Respected? Maybe. Admired? Not so much.

Nikolai Lenkov ran a combination grocery and mercantile store. Much of the daily business was devoted to selling, or rationing, basic commodities under the increasing control of the local communist "comrade." There were also a few odds and ends available which might be called "luxuries:" a pretty scarf, a new shirt, some fragrant soaps, maybe some jewelry. Nikolai, the one and only salesman on the floor, was quite good at closing a sale. When asked, he was vague about his background, but he did love to boast about his Cossack roots. He played up **the** Cossack mystique by strutting around the store in a gaudy Cossack outfit, complete with the traditional hat and high-stepping boots. And, if prodded just a little he could offer a brief dancing display. To the general public he was a jovial, smooth-talking merchant, and a successful one at that.

Beneath this jovial Cossack exterior was a shrewd and at times ruthless black marketeer. The store had its inventory of nondescript, drab basics that were shipped in weekly. This business and its regular shipments were common enough and dull enough that they didn't invite any questions or complaints from the communist watch dogs. However, there were other vaguely marked boxes, small crates, large bags, and barrels which showed up regularly, and discreetly, at the store's alley entrance at night. Some deliveries remained at the store for **an** equally discreet sale, typically after regular store hours. There also were numerous deliveries to be made to other small merchants around Borisov, even a few to Minsk, the Byelorussian capital. The deliveries outside the store weren't strictly C.O.D. but close to it. There still was some semblance of good will and trust, though not much, within the black-market community. An item was delivered, and payment was expected one week after the prearranged delivery.

Ivan's employment record was not too stellar. He had walked out of one opportunity, if that lumbering/nailing job could be called an "opportunity." And he had been fired from the watchmaking opportunity, though the firing had been semi-polite and understandable. With such a tarnished resume, but with limitless self-confidence, Ivan entered the Cossack's store for what was now Ivan's third job interview. Though it was relatively short, it was nonetheless a very entertaining interview to watch.

In walked Ivan, straight and tall and lean and muscular. The walk was slow and confident, that well known Ivan walk. Along with the confident walk, Ivan offered a slight but confident smile. The overall impression was of a brash young man with a very large ego and self-image. Lack of employment, at worst just temporary unemployment, was not an obstacle. Nor was it a check on that outsized ego.

On the other side of the store's check-out counter stood Ivan's prospective employer with his own equally large, unrestrained ego. In contrast to Ivan, the Cossack was three inches shorter and with a physique that could hardly be labeled lean. No, not lean, since he was a good thirty pounds heavier than Ivan, thick in the chest, thick in the legs, and exceptionally thick and muscular in the arms. Ivan struggled hard to suppress a large smile as he imagined how this short, stout man could perform his trademark Cossack dance kicks.

The applicant charged right in. He said, with an air of confidence, maybe a little arrogance, "The word on the street is you're looking for a man, a young and tough man, for a variety of odd jobs in the store and out on the street. I don't care what the jobs are, what the hours are. I'm your man."

The Cossack looked up at his smug applicant then stared at him, not saying a word, for what felt like an eternity for Ivan. Ivan waited and waited, expecting to explain, or defend, that unimpressive employment record. After **a seemingly** interminable silence the Cossack finally asked Ivan, "Ok, my tough, smug job applicant. Can you count?" Long pause, then, "Can you read?" Another long pause and then, "Can you dance? And sing?" Caught off guard with this surprising litany of baffling questions, Ivan's first very impulsive reaction was to stomp out of the shop. "This isn't a serious interview," Ivan thought. "This is a joke. That arrogant, self-proclaimed "Cossack" is just playing some stupid game with me, asking stupid questions, expecting me to grovel and give him equally stupid answers. Not going to happen!" Ivan flashed a brief scowl and was a moment away from ending his third job interview. But practicality triumphed over stubborn pride and Ivan's scowl turned into a slight smile. "So, what if the questions are irrelevant and very stupid," Ivan asked himself. "I need a job, hopefully this job." Ivan also had to admit to himself, "He's strange, no question about that. But I think I could end up liking this strange Cossack, even with his boots and weird hat and Cossack high stepping."

With his well-practiced charming smile now firmly back on display, Ivan finally shouted out a rapid fire "Yes, Yes, Yes and Yes." The Cossack flashed a small smile and then asked, actually ordered, Ivan, "Show me your best, inviting smile. Then give me a fearsome scowl. And then an intimidating stare. Sometimes a look is all you will need, and no words." After that facial audition the Cossack produced his own intimidating scowl, quickly followed by a smile, and then told Ivan, "Show me your big hands and then turn them into big fists. You'll probably need them on occasion, just like you'll need your smiles and scowls." Ivan regained his composure after completing the unexpected combination interview/audition. Maybe now the Cossack would quiz Ivan about his prior jobs. Ivan was ready with some quick-witted explanations. But instead of prior employment questions, the Cossack produced a much larger and engaging smile, extended an equally large and imposing hand and said to Ivan, "You're hired and you can start this afternoon at 5:00." Shocked but delighted, Ivan blurted out loud, "Yes, Yes, I can start right now if you want me." The Cossack pumped Ivan's hand, then gave Ivan's chest a friendly but firm punch and replied, "No, five o'clock is just fine. And, yes, you're hired. Now do you want a description of the job you so eagerly, but naively, committed to?" Feeling less self-confident and also feeling embarrassed by his impulsive and immature "Yes, I'll do anything" response, Ivan now meekly asked for the job description. The Cossack's reply offered few details and a great amount of ambiguity. "You'll have no regular hours. I'll expect you at the store every day, except Sunday, to do some cleaning, some stocking, a little selling using that big smile of yours. When I said there will be no regular hours that means I'll expect you to be around and available for after-hours delivery and pick-up. Much of that will be not just after hours but after dark. As a matter of fact there will be a considerable amount of night work, if you demonstrate to me you have that talent you supposedly have. I'll expect you to make late night deliveries and pick-ups. And if you're as smart and talented as you claim to be with your reading and arithmetic, I might put you on my collection team."

Ivan understood pick-ups and deliveries and didn't care if the work was daytime or nighttime. And he could always produce an engaging smile or belt out a short but lively song. The only concern he had, though he didn't dare to point it out to the Cossack, was that the nighttime work could interfere with his ongoing romance with Polahaya, the town's loveliest eligible female. Comfortable with the interesting, even if vague, job description so far, Ivan nonetheless had to ask, "OK, so far, but what about my dancing? And what about my fists that you seem to be so excited about? You going to turn me into some nighttime street boxer? From what I hear so far, I might not be much more than a glorified delivery boy." The Cossack smiled, briefly, and then turned very serious as he answered Ivan. "Dancing feet suggest to me you have quick feet. If you're delivering or picking up I'll expect you to make those rounds briskly. No lazy, slow shuffling from place to place, making time with some dumb girls. And if I put you on collection detail - and that will be nighttime collection work - you will definitely need to be quick on your feet. Chasing someone one night. Maybe being chased by some unhappy, maybe violent, customer the next night." Giving Ivan a few minutes to reflect, the Cossack then asked, "Want to rethink that quick, impulsive "yes" answer? Oh, and as to those big time, intimidating fists of yours, you will very likely need them if and when you start collection work. There will be uncooperative customers who might need some extra, let's call it 'persuasion', to pay their bills in full. After another brief pause the Cossack asked, "Still a yes?" And Ivan replied immediately, "Damn right, it's a yes!" The added job description with its emphasis on risky, maybe dangerous night collection work was a perfect fit for Ivan Kupraschonik, the tough, reckless bad boy of Borisov.

There was only one more detail of this job offer to address. Regaining his composure and his macho attitude, Ivan flashed that big time smile and declared, "I'm definitely your man. Now, tell me what you plan to pay me for my feet and fists." That response drew an equally large smile and hearty laugh from the Cossack. This was the Ivan the Cossack wanted and would hire: brash, cocky, a bit too irreverent and short on proper deference to his new employer. But, Ivan was in fact the man for the job, especially the collection work. Answering the salary question the Cossack said, "I'll pay you ten rubles each week. When I put you on full-time collection work, I'll pay you an additional ten percent of the payments you collect each week from my "special" customers. Collect on time, collect the right amount, and you'll have more rubles than you can possibly spend on that beauty you've been chasing around town."

For the first week Ivan tackled the miscellaneous, and very boring, chores around the store. The next week the Cossack sent Ivan out on deliveries, a few during store hours but far more after hours. At the end of that second week there was considerably more after hour delivery work. And along with the increasing after hour delivery volume, the Cossack gave Ivan written instructions on where and from whom Ivan would begin collection work. With those first written collection instructions the Cossack also gave Ivan a small leather bag. The Cossack's message was short and simple. "Use this only if you absolutely need to. Don't hesitate, but don't be a fool. And don't be some stupid kid strutting around town bragging about your fancy new toy. Understood?" Ivan understood.

Nikolai's job interview with Ivan ended with another hearty handshake and a bone crushing bear hug. The Cossack could definitely use the hustle and energy that were quite apparent in this big, muscular job applicant. Small, delicate watchmaker hands were not necessary. And for the time being, Ivan did not need to know, and probably didn't even care about what might be in those secretive deliveries coming in and going out of the Cossack's store.

Ivan had a job, and a decent paying job at that, and that's all that mattered. Ivan started out making some routine deliveries. Unfortunately, there were also buyers of merchandise – whether legal or illegal merchandise – who did not pay or didn't pay in a timely manner. Therefore, Ivan, the energetic and ambitious store clerk/delivery man/handyman quickly became the merchant's chief bill collector and enforcer. Ivan took on that additional responsibility gladly, and very enthusiastically. If he couldn't charm the delinquent bill payer to settle up, Ivan easily became the intimidator.

Communism was firmly entrenched throughout the expanding Soviet empire. There were fewer and fewer small businesses, fewer and fewer goods and services available to the common folk. There was the ever present communist "comrade," acting so self-important and sanctimonious, ordering the closure of this, the confiscation of that. All this fervent anti-capitalism, the pursuit of some ill-defined, simple proletarian paradise, produced the inevitable black market. And, Nikolai, the jovial, high-stepping Cossack merchant easily filled the black-market void.

The initial after-hours deliveries and collections by Ivan were fairly benign and occasionally pleasant. One of Ivan's frequent customers was an elderly but very spry seamstress, Tatiana Gorodin. Skilled and very respected, Tatiana had her adequate stockpile of fabrics and mending supplies. But, her real specialty was in fashioning elegant scarves, shawls, and dresses. Her merchandise was far more capitalist than proletarian. And, it was created from far better quality linen, cotton or silk than a pedestrian would see in her display window. The finished products were of such quality that Tatiana even had a sizable clientele in Minsk.

The Cossack was glad to supply the raw materials. Ivan was glad to deliver. He was equally glad to collect the required payment the following week. Grandmotherly Tatiana always paid, did so with a smile and a thank you. Actually, it was Tatiana's charming granddaughter who offered the payment, along with her own cute smile, every week. Tatiana's nine-year-old cherub accompanied her grandmother on Ivan's second week of collections. Ana was petite, polite, well-spoken and not at all intimidated by the imposing collector who entered the grandmother's back room. Ana extended her tiny hand to the collector and said, "My grandmother told me your name is Ivan the Terrible. But I should only call you Mr. Ivan. Hello, Mr. Ivan. Are you terrible?" The grandmother was startled and horrified by the question and very worried about Ivan's reaction. Ivan released the little hand, offered a big smile and replied, "No, I'm not really terrible. That's just a silly name someone gave to me as a joke. Just a silly joke and a silly name. But even if I was terrible - and I am not - I would never be terrible in front of a beautiful little lady or her grandmother. That's my promise to you and we can shake on that if you wish." Ana extended her hand which Ivan gently placed in his hand. The two shook, Tatiana paid her collector, and Ivan left for his next collection site.

The subsequent week Ana was present with her grandmother, and a heartwarming little ritual began. Ana approached the big, bad collector, extended her hand and said in a loud, confident voice, "Hello, Mr Ivan." Then with a very serious expression and with a tiny, accusatory finger pointed up at Ivan she asked, "Have you been terrible this week?" With his own very serious expression, but working hard to suppress a smile, Ivan bent down to look little Ana directly in her eyes and replied, "No, I have not been terrible." Ana replied with a simple "Good." Then she, not the grandmother, presented the week's payment to Ivan. And, as was their little ritual, Ivan would tussle the little girl's hair, bow ever so low and slowly, and accept payment from her petite hands into Ivan's huge hands. Not too bad a collection job.

A second client of the Cossack's was, ironically, Ivan's former short-term employer, Gregor, the watchmaker. Despite the nondescript boxes, it wasn't hard for Ivan to identify the blackmarket goods he delivered: cigars and cigarettes. These weren't the cheap varieties readily available at the local communist commissary. There were elegant, firmly rolled and fragrant cigars, cigarettes, even slim women's cigarillos from faraway places. The old boss was always glad to see Ivan though these deliveries were irregular. And on C.O.D. day, actually C.O.D. night, the old boss routinely invited Ivan to pause for a smoke on a good cigar. Ivan received the necessary payment along with a hearty pat on the back plus two free packs of Gregor's black market addictive treasures. The collection business was good for Ivan, and he was enjoying some unexpected fringe benefits of the job.

However, there were no fringes or freebies offered by another Cossack customer, Leonid, the town's only blacksmith. After hour deliveries consisted of 10 to 12 long rectangular crates painted in what might pass for military olive drab. With rare exceptions, Leonid paid on the delivery day. For Leonid, there was no need, definitely no desire, for more contact or maybe meddlesome chatter with his delivery man. Ivan's educated guess was these were crates packed with rifles, probably ammunition as well. Maybe they were destined for some anarchist group, maybe some partisan zealots yearning for the return of a Czar. Ivan speculated, but he didn't dare ask. He made the delivery, received payment, and received a grunt and a nod of the head that was probably intended as a thank you and good-bye.

In contrast to silent Leonid, Ivan received more than his share of conversation, as well as abuse, from Ilya, the local apothecary. Ilya was healthy though he looked decades older than his mid-50's. He was irascible, short-tempered, and displayed the people skills of a troll. But, he was very good at his profession, barking out a medication regime, formulating a pill or potion with speed and accuracy. Despite that offensive personality, Ilya the apothecary transformed into quite the smooth salesman when a patron quietly inquired about Ilya's "lekarstva." That was the Russian word for a medicine, any generic medicine. But, when a patron asked about Ilya's "lekarstva" the patron was asking about Ilya's behind the counter liquor store.

The Cossack, through Ivan, kept Ilya's liquor store well stocked. There were cognacs, French wines, fine sipping Polish vodka, some of that hard-to-get Polish buffalo grass infused vodka. There was even some fine distilled vodka from Moscow, which was certainly far more palatable than any of the 110-proof swill from the Borisov distillery. Ilya's sizable inventory became all the more desirable as self-important party officials continued to confiscate and then ration whatever vodka was produced.

There were several boxes and small crates Ivan dropped off after closing every week. Though there were no labels, Ivan easily determined the varied contents. Ilya was there at every single delivery yelling at Ivan to be ever so careful about Ilya's lifesaving "lecarstva." Ivan was an oaf, and a very clumsy one at that according to Ilya's ranting and raving. But, there was not a single crate dropped, not a single drop of "lecarstva" spilled.

The following week, on C.O.D. night, Ivan would endure another round of abuse. The previous week's delivery inventory was always double-checked, and Ilya would sign off. But, on collection night the surly apothecary always insisted he had not received his full shipment. Ivan must have miscounted. Ivan must have stolen a box, probably three. A crate with its precious contents must have been dropped or knocked over by the clumsy oaf. No lifesaving "lecarstva" was salvaged. And, Ilya could not, and would not, pay the exorbitant amount demanded by Ivan. Payment not demanded by the Cossack big boss, but demanded by this crude, unpolished errand boy Ivan!

Ivan always listened to the excuses, the abuse, in silence. He knew, as did the surly apothecary, this was at most half-serious gamesmanship which Ilya enjoyed, and Ivan was Ilya's captive audience. Nikolai, the savvy black marketeer, gave Ivan full discretion to negotiate a compromise if Ivan chose to do so. The compromise might be nothing one week. It might be up to 20 rubles another week. With each week's haggling behind them, and with payment made, Ilya always forced a smile, delivered the traditional bone-crushing bear hug, and offered a few generous shots of his own special and healthy "lecarstva" to Ivan.

There were other less interesting clients for the Cossack's black-market goods. There were also more mysterious packages and equally mysterious delivery sites. Ivan also had to contend with far more difficult clients than a harmless haggler like Ilya the apothecary. There was the occasional slow pay, or an attempt to stall for a payment until the next delivery. But, on Ivan's collection route that delay would happen once, and only once.

Ivan quickly learned that his employer, that seemingly successful, though at times ruthless, merchant was the employer of several other young toughs. Collectively the merchant (Ivan never even knew his name except the "Cossack") ruled over a sizable gang. And, Ivan earned the dual title of a capable employee as well as gang member. He even earned the right, more likely an obligation, to have the gang symbol - four elaborately designed cryptic numbers - tattooed crudely on his right hand knuckles. Few in town knew the precise intent or symbolism of the knuckle numbers. But, if the townspeople didn't know the details, they knew or suspected enough to be both fearful and respectful of the wearer of that body "art."

Armed with a pistol, pocketknife, and graphic knuckles, Ivan went about his delivery and collection work. The collection work wasn't without its challenges and dangers, however. One late night he was heading down a dimly lit street in a rundown part of Borisov to visit a tough, grizzled and very delinquent customer. As Ivan approached the customer's door someone jumped out of the dark from a nearby alley and stabbed Ivan in his right chest. Fortunately, it was on the right side, not the left. Ivan was a strong barrel chested 18-year-old. The knife stuck, but not too deeply, and the shadowy assailant simply stabbed and fled. Ivan gamely walked back to his merchant's headquarters and explained, with some fear and embarrassment, that the collection was unsuccessful.

To Ivan's surprise and great relief, the merchant was very calm and sympathetic. He provided Ivan the medical attention needed though without any stitches. This would leave a large chest scar which became for Ivan an extra decoration to complement his rugged good looks. Ivan also gained some added respect and stature within the gang.

Building on his expanding tough guy persona, Ivan volunteered, just one week after the attack, to go back and collect from the delinquent customer. However, the merchant told Ivan the collection effort was not necessary. All had been "settled," whatever that meant. And, as Ivan learned, that customer had disappeared, quite suddenly, a day after that night time attack.

Ivan continued to work hard, though his reputation and good looks also allowed him to play hard. It wasn't the most flattering of reputations, based more so on fear than some admiration or respect. Lots of drinking, the occasional bar brawl, countless young women vying for his attention. Countless young ladies, except for one exceptionally lovely young woman.

Summer Research, Summer Memories

One of our greatest summertime challenges, and one of our biggest frustrations, was trying to extract more details of our parents' courtship and marriage. We knew and saw too much of their turbulent American marital life. There must have been more of an innocent storybook romance, or so we hoped. We uncovered an old but still glossy photo of each of them, which photo had been stored and then forgotten in that beaten up old wooden chest. Mother was a stunning young beauty, and he was a very handsome young man, both fashionably dressed and both displaying confident smiles. They were probably in their late teens, still in Borisov we suspected. The two could have been the present-day prom queen and her football hero. But the fashionable attire for two teenagers in gritty Borisov seemed too out of place. Another mystery.

We prodded our mother for details. But as she revealed more, we realized our hoped for, and very naive, portrayal of two teenagers in love wasn't anywhere close to accurate. She didn't share any warm memories of a Borisov courtship, if there were any memories to share. The courtship picture she grudgingly did share was simple and unromantic. The handsome town hustler was aggressive and unrelenting in his pursuit of the Borisov beauty. No more details of any courtship were offered. Nor was there any spoken admission that she loved her husband to be. He was simply persistent. No. He was persistent and annoying. And eventually the town beauty did say yes to a marriage. But why?

Despite that unromantic portrait of a so-called courtship, without any two-way old fashioned "love", we three fondly remembered those Saturday night immigrant gatherings. Among the playful chaos of twenty-some DP's gathered in our basement or backyard we did remember some interaction that might pass for affection, maybe even love. Our parents had somehow collected a sizable record library. Whether it came over from Europe or was collected stateside we didn't know. But there were certain romantic tango tunes our parents delighted in playing and replaying. John, or Jan to his fellow DP's, would serenade his wife in his fine tenor voice. And if he wasn't serenading her, he was coaxing her, very playfully, to join him center stage and show off their sultry tango moves. They clearly, unquestionably, enjoyed the dancing, enjoyed each other. Maybe they loved one another? Once upon a time.

That summer there was one other romantic angle we attempted to pursue, but with minimal success. We wanted more details, actually any details, about a mysterious German officer. We assumed the first contact was in Borisov during the lengthy German occupation. There was very little information our mother shared. She worked for the officer, he was very kind, she liked him very much, and she reconnected with him in Hannover. She added that our father was very hostile toward this mysterious German. Periodically our father would launch an ugly verbal assault at our mother and that German even though it was many years after we all were settled in America. We suspected our mother might have fallen in love with that German officer in his fancy uniform, maybe loved him far more than she ever loved her husband. And maybe, just maybe, she had been unfaithful to her husband with that hated officer, somewhere, sometime. Yes, we children were curious, trying to extract more details, sort out the accusations and maybe some lies.

There was one pointed revelation our sister did draw out that final summer. Again, over a mother/daughter luncheon our mother admitted she was very fond of that kind German officer. Maybe that fondness turned into love, but our mother wasn't sure. She also admitted she did secretly meet with the officer a few times after the wedding and before their exit from Borisov. He was so pleasant to talk with, confide in. But, with a firm almost defiant tone in her voice she stated she was never, never unfaithful. Never! Despite the recurring accusations and the cruel insults from her husband over the years, she consistently declared her innocence. She had always been a faithful wife!

Chapter 4 - The Pursuer and the Pursued

"It is hard to learn about your parents' courtship."

Michael Reagan

Just as Ivan was now the "trophy" for Borisov's young women, Polahaya continued to evolve from sweet and innocent into a seductive trophy for the town's young men. She was rebellious, carefree, largely independent, and self-sufficient. Polahaya was drawn to Ivan, not just because of his handsome looks but also because of his rebellious nature. There was an air about him that both frightened her but also drew her to him. Unfortunately, there was also an aggressiveness, a bluntness in his pursuit of Polahaya, his sought after town trophy, that caused her to be more cautious and slow in building on the budding romance.

Ivan was undeterred and persistent. They did date though the dating was largely confined to meeting at the local drinking hall. They also became quite the celebrated dance couple, high stepping through local folk songs. Ivan also had a fine tenor voice to add to the dancing. But, most impressively, the two of them offered the bar patrons quite the show with their precise, energetic, and seductive tango moves. Oh, how they moved, how they embraced, how they appeared to be in love. But, appearances can be deceiving.

Despite Ivan's persistence he couldn't persuade Polahaya to marry him. She still clung to that independence she had worked for and earned through her early years. She also enjoyed playing the seductive flirt who could turn on the charm for that drink or two, maybe for that pretty little scarf, or some fragrance soap.

Regrettably, that flirtatious side of Polahaya could, and did, produce some ugly reactions from Ivan. There was the all too frequent tough guy barroom bluster, a shouting match between Ivan and some young man, the occasional pushing and chest thumping. And, one night knives were drawn. No one could confidently recall what was said, who was the aggressor, who was the reacting defendant, if there was some hapless "defendant." It was very evident, however, that night's fight was about Polahaya. After a brief, violent scuffle there at the bar, and in full view of Polahaya, Ivan stood with a long but not deep knife cut on his right cheek. Ivan's attacker, barely looking old enough to be in the bar, stood just a few feet away, a knife on the floor and a very long, deep knife wound on the massive forearm of the knife wielding assailant. The barkeeper shouted out some orders, and a few patrons hustled the young man away for medical help. Polahaya likewise hustled Ivan away to tend to his bloody face.

Throughout the years we children wondered about the distinctive marks on our father. Periodic probes into the history behind the tattooed knuckles, the crudely healed chest wound, the better healed facial scar produced nothing but a curt "I don't want to talk about it." It's sad and unfortunate that the history behind all those distinctive marks was not shared. It's not necessarily a great history, nor a history to brag about. But it is family history. And, this historic chapter, if shared with us, would have provided us children a better appreciation and understanding of the complex life Ivan and Polahaya lived and shared together.

The knife wound was clean enough and it healed well enough that the resulting scar became another cosmetic addition to ruggedly handsome Ivan. Ivan told Polahaya he reacted as he did in the bar because of some cruel and crude comments from the young attacker. Polahaya believed Ivan, and maybe that was what happened. Whatever the real reason, Ivan was, in Polahaya's mind, the wild but loving defender of her honor. And, he had suffered a scar, though an appealing scar, on her behalf. The romance continued. And, then the Germans came to town.

Summer Research, Summer Memories

As young adults we developed a growing interest and curiosity about our parents' Borisov years and their relocation to Hannover, Germany. We were fed a Cliff's Notes account of that two-decade time period. The Germans invaded, and they occupied Borisov for three plus years. The occupying army began a westward retreat in 1944. As part of that retreat, the Germans forced able-bodied Borisov men plus family members into a brutal march back to Germany to supplement a shrinking labor force. It was a forced month-long trek that ended in a German labor camp. The camp was liberated by allied forces, and we eventually immigrated to America. According to our parents, more details were simply too painful to recount or relive. End of story.

That short history was entirely too bland, too short and too suspect. And it did little to satisfy our growing curiosity about our parents' European past. But that remained the only official version until our father's death. With a tag team effort that summer we discovered documents and extracted so much more history, a more honest history, from our mother. Yes, there was a lengthy German occupation but a relatively benign one. From our parents' point of view, their German occupiers were far more benign than the Bolshevik zealots who ruled over Borisov prior to the German invasion. With some defensiveness in her tone, our mother also revealed for the first time that our father was employed by the Germans as an "honor guard." She stressed that the makeshift prison he was hired to guard was not a military combatant prison. Nor was it a so-called "concentration camp" or a hard labor camp. He wasn't even issued a weapon except for a nightstick or baton. But she added that the seemingly innocent guard duty created significant problems both in Borisov and Germany. Because of that honor guard decision, the family's exit from Borisov was not a forced march but a planned and necessary escape from both

Soviets and Borisov natives. And the escape was made possible by a German officer.

That summer our mother produced German documents, with English translations, that listed our official post-war residence as Camp Fallingbostel just outside of Hannover. She produced what appeared to be a birth certificate for me, showing that I was born in another obscure town and hospital north of Hannover. She kept the surprises coming with another document titled "Statement on Oath." It was prepared in the camp in 1949 and we learned it was the family's critical gateway document for our eventual passage to America. She even shared what appeared to be professionally staged family portraits.

The photos must have been taken in Camp Fallingbostel based on the very young appearance of our sister. We were also surprised to view three family members (no infant me in the photos) very elegantly dressed, very healthy looking. This is hardly the picture we expected of refugees who had scrambled around Europe or sought shelter in heavily bombed Hannover. The picture was a mystery, generating more confusion and questions instead of our sought-after clarity. The "Statement on Oath" likewise generated more questions instead of answers. There were repeated references to Polish people and places, and family names we had never heard of before. And our parents, based on that "Statement" were Poles, not Byelorussians.

We stared at those documents and photos. We attempted to make sense of this revised account of what we now had to label the Borisov escape. And each of us had to admit we almost wished we had known only the Cliff's Notes fairy tale. So many questions, so many contradictions.

Chapter - 5 - The Germans are Coming

"Cry havoc.......and let slip the dogs of war."

Shakespeare's "Julius Caesar"

Beginning with the Polish invasion on September 1, 1939 the German Wehrmacht continued to steamroll through eastern Europe. At the start of the invasion there was a disputed eastern border of Poland that had historically included portions of western Byelorussia. In the early months of 1941, despite the invasion of Poland, there still was no German incursion into this part of Byelorussia. Additionally, Byelorussia, including its disputed western border, was currently recognized as a "Republic" of the Soviet Union. The reason behind this convenient acceptance of the respective territorial claims of Germany and the Soviet Union was the so-called Non-Aggression Pact of 1939. In that pact between Hitler, signed in Moscow by Hitler's foreign minister, von Ribbentrop, and Josef Stalin, the two powers agreed not to invade one another for ten years. Hitler had even initially offered to extend that non-aggression pact for 100 years. Stalin decided ten years was more than adequate. Through this marriage of convenience, the dictators would carve up Poland as well as all of eastern Europe without any resistance from the other side. Hitler also generously ceded Lithuania, Estonia and Latvia to the Soviet Union's growing collection of "Republics."

However, that pact became an inconvenience for Hitler. He needed more of eastern Europe for additional German settlement. It was part of his megalomaniacal vision to populate all of Europe with his superior Aryan race. And despite the 1939 marriage of convenience with his Soviet dictator, Hitler harbored a longstanding hatred of communism. Therefore, an invasion of the communist motherland wasn't that surprising. And after all, promises and pacts are all too often broken.

Without offering any warning to his Soviet counterpart, Hitler followed up on his expansionist vision. On June 22, 1941 two million German troops crossed that disputed border that represented western Byelorussia and invaded the Soviet Union. Byelorussia was the strategic centerpiece of that 1941 German campaign. And it would remain an occupied German annexation until August of 1944 when the Soviet Army launched its own Byelorussian invasion under the military code name Operation Bagration. From a propaganda viewpoint, this was a noble and necessary counter invasion to liberate Byelorussia of its German invaders. But for the native Byelorussian population, this was hardly a liberation. It was just an unwelcome switch in occupying armies.

The 1941 German invasion began under the code name Operation Barbarossa. It was so named in honor of a respected 12th century Holy Roman Emperor, Frederick Barbarossa. However, there was such irony in Hitler's choice of that name. Emperor Barbarossa ruled successfully from 1151 until his death in 1190. He was instrumental in unifying a contentious patchwork of individual German states. He was crowned King of Germany in 1152, Holy Roman Emperor in 1155 and also King of Italy that same year. He was considered an exceptional Emperor and a brilliant military strategist. But this Holy Roman Emperor, this renowned military strategist, died in a less than glorious manner during the Third Holy Crusade. It wasn't during the gruesome hand to hand combat of some epic battle to regain the Holy Land. Instead of mortal wounds, Emperor Barbarossa drowned in the Saleph River. There are conflicting accounts of the drowning. By one account, the Emperor drowned due to an ill-advised decision by him to actually swim across the river. The alternate account described Frederick being thrown from his horse while crossing the river, then drowning because he was weighed down by his armor. Whichever was the actual account, this was a less than a heroic end to this Germanic hero's military exploits. There's an added irony in Hitler's choice of Frederick Barbarossa, a Holy Roman Emperor, as the namesake for the ensuing invasion into the Soviet Union's western perimeter. That German invasion was swift, savage and far more unholy than "holy." The invasion was also devoid of any morality or humanity. The entire war, the Byelorussian invasion, Hitler's global pursuit of an Aryan "empire" and a Jewish "final solution" were collectively the antithesis of anything "holy."

On July 2, 1941 the German invasion advanced further into the eastern half of Byelorussia, easily occupying Borišov. The massive multi-front invasion into the Soviet republics had been relatively quick and unencumbered. On that same July 2 date, the German army also successfully concluded its Bialystok-Minsk offensive, demolishing both cities with an intense bombing campaign and then literally encircling a defensive force of 290,000 Soviet troops The end result was a humiliating mass surrender. Borisov's capture was easier and actually more benign.

That capture was not preceded by any intense artillery or aircraft softening of this midsized target. The entire population was only around 50,000. A sizable number of Borisov's young men had already abandoned the city in anticipation of the rumored invasion. Those young men and some women disappeared into the countryside, becoming an annoying, and quite formidable, partisan army that harassed the German invaders during their three-year occupation of Borisov. There was a modest, almost comical, attempt by Borisov's remaining population to defend itself against the German advance. Undertaken by a largely volunteer army, trucks, wagons, and farm equipment were all positioned around the town's western perimeter. It was a noble, but woefully inadequate, attempt to create some semblance of a defensive Maginot Line. But that line had no effect whatsoever against the massive armor that was rumbling into town. A small complement of tanks from the Moscow Motorized Division was also hastily repositioned to provide some deterrent. But, those tanks likewise presented very little resistance against the advance.

Borisov was a mid-sized industrial town with its primary commercial focus on grain and timber. But, its factories could be, and soon would be, converted to light manufacturing of various military parts to support the German eastward advance deeper into the Soviet Union. The town itself had a long, though not that noteworthy, history. It was founded in 1102 by the Prince of Polosk, Rogvolod Vseslavich. Fortunately, he had a less tongue twisting baptismal name of Boris, and his newly acquired territory was aptly named Borisov. The original non-Cyryllic Byelorussian spelling was Barysaw. But its Russian variant spelling, Borisov, became the common spelling version.

When the Germans entered the town, it was largely undamaged. Its main thoroughfare, Garagina Street, was still semi-decent to travel upon, and included its share of bustling storefronts. Some of these were the same shops Ivan frequented on his collection route. More accurately, there were connecting alleys, back doors, and side streets around Garagina on which Ivan conducted his business. The imposing Cathedral of the Resurrection of Christ, colorfully adorned with its beautiful, iconic onion tops, still stood proudly at the northern edge of the town's modest but still inviting Central Square.

Garagina Street, its connecting streets and commercial sites drastically changed in the ensuing occupation years. The German occupation force turned less benign and more oppressive, bombing this commercial trouble spot, bulldozing another annoying facade with a tank. Streets and walkways were torn up to make them impassable. Partisans contributed their share of structural mayhem as well. With some frequency, those partisans likewise felt compelled to bomb this or sabotage that, whether it was to hinder or harass their despised invaders or to punish some suspected German collaborator.

By the spring of 1944, on the eve of the Soviet Army's own massive Operation Bagration, Borisov wasn't much more than a crumbling pile of bricks and broken timbers. It wasn't as severely damaged as Minsk, its capital city just eighty miles away. However, not too much of Borisov's commercial center survived the three year occupation. Remarkably, its venerable Cathedral of the Resurrection suffered only minor small weapons fire and the occasional grenade. Sadly, by the time Operation Bagration's liberation campaign commenced, over 200 hundred Byelorussian towns had been destroyed. Over 9200 villages were completely razed to the ground. And, by war's end in 1945 an estimated 2.5 to 3 million Byelorussian citizens perished. Both the Soviets and the Germans contributed to those appalling statistics.

In addition to that initial June 22, 1941 German invasion, and the related July 2 occupation of Borisov, one other 1941 summer date is worth noting. In an infamous July 31 directive from Hitler to his top aide, Hermann Goring, Goring ordered General Reinhard Heidrich to "submit as soon as possible a general plan of...measures necessary for carrying out the desired final solution to the Jewish question." Leave it to German efficiency and ingenuity to adopt such an innocuous sounding campaign title: the "final solution." All of Europe, including Byelorussia, would witness Heidrich's brutal, inhumane campaign to carry out Hitler's July 31 directive. And millions of Jews, plus countless other non-Aryan undesirables, would die in Heidrich's concentration camps before Nazi Germany finally surrendered in 1945.

Major Heinrich Kohl, a relatively young but respected German army officer, was given the assignment of commanding and controlling a sizable garrison in Borisov, including a number of large makeshift prisons. Despite the relative ease of the initial German invasion and occupation of Borisov, the ongoing occupation proved to be less of a blessing and more of a curse for its commander, Major Kohl. The blessing was that the major's first assignment was at a noteworthy military supply center. The downside curse for the major was that this would probably be only a non-combat assignment. No combat, no danger, no opportunity for some daring military decisions. Despite the absence of actual combat, the administrative burdens of this seemingly comfortable posting became all too evident and overwhelming very quickly.

Before he undertook those overwhelming administrative duties Major Kohl indulged himself by choosing a comfortable headquarters. The northern corner of Central Square, close to the town's historic Cathedral, was an ideal location to explore. If Kohl was being relegated to a non-combat backwater in Byelorussia he decided he could at least conduct his administrative duties in comfort and in a nice neighborhood. He succeeded in finding a nice home, large and stately but not too pretentious. The local communist official, now unemployed but also very cooperative, had recommended this property. The property also was currently unoccupied, for some unexplained reason, and a vacant residence was a prerequisite Major Kohl had insisted upon. He was adamant that he would not evict any resident from his or her home. His house hunting was over and Major Kohl promptly set up headquarters in this house that was so elegant and imposing. He briefly reconsidered the decision, viewing the house as maybe a little too elegant for his personal tastes. But Command Headquarters had urged, actually ordered, Kohl to set up his command post in a property and a neighborhood befitting an officer of the mighty German Army. And, Major Kohl did so, as ordered.

The new home headquarters included an inviting wraparound porch suitable for staff meetings, maybe even a brief relaxing pause, if there was an opportunity to pause. In the coming months the porch would also provide a pleasant setting for conversations with a certain young housemaid. Fortunately for the major his chosen mansion had a large office with a beautiful antique, highly polished office desk as its centerpiece. However, the table would, all too soon, be barely visible as it accumulated a growing mountain of papers. Wehrmacht directives, work orders, requisitions, maps, the infrequent personal and probably unread correspondence. The German war machine loved paperwork, demanded paperwork. Behind the ornate desk and along the entire back wall a extensive library of novels was neatly displayed on bookshelves. This could offer the major an endless collection to peruse and read in his spare time. Sadly, there hardly was any spare time. A large expensive looking oriental rug added a nice touch to the major's new office. But, the expensive rug would suffer from endless daily traffic with junior officers, town officials and visiting senior officers. And with the endless traffic the rug would become far less ornate and oriental and just plain and simple, and very threadbare. The elegant mansion would become a cluttered, unappealing military outpost. Major Heinrich Kohl would dutifully serve at his Borisov outpost for the next three years.

Heinrich Kohl was born in Hannover, Germany, the youngest of three boys. Their father was the owner and manager of a mid-sized factory, and it was the father's hope one or more of his boys would continue in that family business. That father's business, along with the father's hopes, couldn't compete with the incessant Nazi propaganda and the increasing likelihood of war. It came as no surprise that all three boys joined the military, one as a sailor and two as commissioned army officers. Sadly, Heinrich's two siblings were killed in the first year of Germany's European invasion.

Heinrich had rapidly advanced through the ranks of the Wehrmacht. He was bright and showed a real aptitude for logistics and administration. He also demonstrated excellent leadership skills. He had a firm, no nonsense leadership style. But it was a firm, yet polite, style that produced consistent results and consistently good morale from his troops. Though he had no formal education beyond high school Heinrich was a knowledgeable student of Germany's conflicted history after the so-called Great War. And, he was more than willing to help re-establish Germany as a strong economic and military power on the world stage. But an invasion of Poland, as well as the ensuing campaign to conquer all of Europe (maybe the world?), wasn't what Heinrich had in mind. Neither was he obsessed with the propaganda and, for him at least, the myth of Aryan superiority. Nonetheless, here he was firmly entrenched as a rising star in the Wehrmacht. And, if it was to be war, Heinrich Kohl, now Major Kohl, would support the war effort to the best of his ability.

Committing to a military career at such a young age didn't leave Heinrich much time for socializing or building a romantic relationship with a pretty lady. There could have been many such possibilities since the handsome major possessed all of those stereotypic Aryan trademarks: tall, muscular, blond-haired, blue-eyed, and very handsome. Yet, here he was with no leisure time, no romance, no front-line combat assignment and not much more than a desk job in some obscure town in the middle of Byelorussia.

The Germans soon discovered how complicated the occupation could and would be. The native population had little fondness for their former Soviet masters. To the natives' surprise and relief, the German occupation, at least for the first year, was fairly benign. However, that benign relationship was short-lived.

The shift from benign to brutal was almost inevitable in large measure because of the diverse demographic mix in Byelorussia and Borišov. There were those true Byelorussians who despised both of their invading "foreigners," the German Nazis and the Russian Soviets. There was also a sizable expatriate population of Poles, including those who challenged the territorial legitimacy of the Byelorussian western border. And, there was a sizable Jewish population. Some of the current Jewish residents were true natives, some had fled from various homes and villages from the east and/or west, some had been forcibly transplanted out of mother Russia to the Byelorussian backwater. There was even a notable cluster of gypsy encampments throughout Byelorussia including a few on the outskirts of Borisov. This Soviet republic was quite the melting pot, but it was also a very hot, volatile pot.

The German occupation, unwelcome and increasingly harsh as it was, also provided a number of opportunities. Ivan, with his "Terrible" reputation and his persistent search for "opportunities," did enjoy some success. Polahaya did find a job opportunity as well, and she did continue building that budding romance with Ivan. Stefan, the shrewd and sophisticated teacher (now a full professor) found new roles, most critically as a liaison/mediator between the German military command and the local citizens. He also served as job placement guru for both Ivan and Polahaya. For Heinrich Kohl, in command of the infantry regiment occupying Borisov, the three-year assignment presented an exhausting, never-ending challenge to control - or try to control - the violence and hostility between the occupiers and the occupied. His small respite from the turmoil was the periodic light conversation with, plus the frequent polite smile from, his newly hired housekeeper Polahaya. His other small respite was provided by frequent conversations with and advice from Stefan Mirovich, or the "Professor" as Stefan was affectionately called.

Chapter 6 - The Matchmaker/Deal Maker/Professor

"The Dealmaker's Manifesto: Reality is Negotiable."

Tim Ferris

Stefan Mirovich was raised in an aristocratic, old empire household. He very much enjoyed that early childhood, enjoyed the comfortable home, the privileges of czarist nobility. His father had served as a colonel in the old imperial army, but he had stayed apolitical and retired just two years prior to the 1917 Revolution. He kept the family comfortable on what passed for a pension plus inherited land holdings. With that military background the family patriarch commanded his household like a military barracks. Everything was clean, orderly, and very structured. Sadly, it was very short on affection or laughter. Stefan's mother was a schoolteacher and was very loved by all her students. Unfortunately, she, just like Stefan, was somewhat of a prisoner of that cold military house.

For whatever reasons, the parents just had one child, Stefan. And, though Stefan's father was cold and unapproachable, Stefan's mother was very much the attentive caregiver. She spoiled him, or attempted to, though he kept himself very grounded. As a teacher she also supplemented his school lessons and instilled a real passion for literature, any literature. In his teens he also witnessed first-hand the rise of communism and the eventual Bolshevik Revolution. But, to their collective surprise and relief, the family was spared any reprisals or setbacks in their daily lives from the revolution.

Stefan excelled academically at all levels, graduating at the top of his class from the local small, but well respected, university. He studied hard, but he played hard as well. There were other more handsome, maybe more eligible, bachelors around town and around campus. But, Stefan had no problems with the ladies. He was witty and polished, but not too polished. There were a few semi-serious relationships, but they were short-lived, and that was perfectly fine with Stefan. He enjoyed his bachelor status, the freedom from any romantic entanglements.

Bright and personable as he was, the young graduate could have gone far, whether in academia or business, even communist politics. As for politics, Stefan publicly appeared to remain neutral in his hometown. He wasn't an avid supporter of this new revolution. But, he was also prudent enough to mouth the right slogans at the right time and carry that all important party card. As for a career, Stefan's mother remained his loving mentor and role model. Consequently, it was no surprise that Stefan followed in her footsteps and became a teacher as well. He taught at the local public school, tutored on occasion. He even landed an enviable, and well paying, assignment as a history professor, in addition to his full-time public school duties, at the university.

Though the Professor was very popular with his public and university students, as well as administrative staff, he politely, but emphatically, refused to offer any summer classes. Those summer months, he declared, "They are my summer adventure time. Some travel, some education, some relaxation, some new acquaintances." Though the administrative staff offered to assist with travel, maybe book a conference or two, Stefan was again polite and emphatic in declining any assistance.

Off the professor would venture the first week after spring term ended. He did return periodically, not on any discernible schedule and with no explanation, He stayed for a few days or maybe a week. Then he was off again on another so-called "adventure" to parts unknown to anyone, nor disclosed to anyone.

Stefan was always cheerful, or almost always cheerful, on his returns. But when pressed for details of where he had traveled or what he had done our traveler provided a fairly consistent reply. Curiously, it was a slow, deliberate, hardly spontaneous or enthusiastic reply. Stefan appeared to think, maybe think too much, about how to respond to what was an innocent and understandable question. Maybe he was revisiting old answers to similar questions? Maybe he was trying to recollect what he may have previously shared, or not shared, with some casual acquaintance or administrator? With his trademark whimsical smile and a brief wink Stefan's all too common reply was a vague, "Oh, I traveled somewhere you wouldn't know or be interested in, studied some obscure subjects that would bore you, just as they bored me. And, here I am back in good old Borisov. Sorry, gotta run."

However, on some of those summer returns to Borisov Stefan returned slightly less cheerful. His so-called boring "adventures" must have been anything but boring. One late afternoon in June the mild-mannered professor was seen hopping off the westbound train displaying his signature smile. But he was also displaying a collection of black and blue bruises on his face and neck, plus bruises and cuts on his hands and forearms. Stefan's explanation? A clumsy fall. No more explanation offered. Another time our adventurous Professor was seen exiting off a southbound train ever so gingerly and with a severe limp and a severely swollen right knee. Again, it was some foolish clumsiness on his part. And once he returned with his left arm in a sling and evidence of what appeared to be a bandaged wound on his shoulder, possibly from a gunshot. Stefan sheepishly explained he had been off hunting with friends, somewhere, hunting for something. There had been a careless discharge and our professor found himself on the receiving end of that carelessness. But the injury wasn't that serious, Stefan was doing quite well, and a sincere apology had been offered by the clumsy hunter. End of story. To many locals the gunshot story was not very convincing. Summertime hunting by their professor who had shown no passing interest in such activity? And with pistols instead of rifles or shotguns? But this was their admired local Professor. And no one would be so impolite, or so bold, to question or challenge that professorial explanation.

There were other inconsistencies and questions about Professor Stefan's periodic adventures. He was a trim, athletic thirty-something at six feet and 180 pounds. His recurring supposedly casual "adventures" followed by the all too frequent "silly accidents," as Stefan dismissed them, just did not fit together. How could such casual adventures turn into such unfortunate misadventures? If the summertime travel was for rest and relaxation why didn't our athletic, handsome professor fail to bring back an enviable bronze tan, maybe some collectible souvenir? There were even the occasional two- or three-day emergency absences during the academic year, purportedly to visit or advise some mystery friend or relative.

Despite the overall respect and admiration the Professor enjoyed, suspicions and conspiracy theories grew. Maybe the Professor was part time-professor and part-time spy. But for whom? He returned from eastbound trains, westbound trains, southbound trains, and with no regularity or pattern. Maybe he was collaborating with a rebel alliance, trying to undermine the pervasive expansion of the Bolshevik Revolution. Maybe, despite the facade of the prim and proper university professor, Stefan Mirovish was an assassin. Maybe he was a Byelorussian Paladin, the legendary gun for hire, riding off to rescue some poor damsel or to rid a town of its marauding thugs. Despite a decent dual salary, this small-town professor added to his mystique as he dressed a little too well, enjoyed an all too nice home, and escaped all too frequently on what must have been expensive junkets. And despite all of his very public bourgeois ostentation (shoes, clothes, hats, expensive watch) this Professor appeared to be entirely immune from any harassment by the local communist party purists. Stefan Mirovich was quite the Borisov enigma. Adding to his celebrity status as well as the mounting gossip about who this local hero really was, he was conversant in at least five languages: his native Byelorussian (and its Russian variant), Polish, German, English, and survival Italian. The questions persisted, the cryptic "adventures" continued, and life went on in Borisov under its Nazi occupiers.

Stefan's decision to become a schoolteacher led him to his first contact with young Polahaya. She was an average student though she was shy and rarely raised her hand or volunteered an answer. Young children at this age, any age, could be very cruel. And, raggedy Polahaya was all too often the victim of nasty whispered insults in the classroom and equally nasty exclusion from groups and games on the playground. Polahaya could hardly be the only illegitimate child growing up in Borisov. But, she was an easy target for all that adolescent cruelty. Stefan couldn't totally insulate his poor student from that behavior. However, he could, and he did, come to her defense time and again. Yes, at times it was very open favoritism on his part. But, she definitely could use some favoritism. Stefan became her champion, somewhat of a father figure, and certainly a friend. That friendship grew ever stronger, and it would last for the next three decades.

Stefan was well liked and respected by all. And, by many in Borisov he was affectionately referred to as their admired "Professor." That respect, coupled with Stefan's education and political instincts, would serve him well as the Germans made Borisov their far eastern home for the next three plus years.

Within days of the German occupation the young commanding officer "invited" Stefan to visit. Certainly unable to decline that so-called invitation, the two met for several hours at Major Kohl's commandeered home. To say the two became dear friends would be overstating the relationship. A solid level of trust and respect did develop between the two. Stefan emerged as both a confidante to the major as well as the informal spokesman and advocate for Borisov's citizens. Despite that mutual friendship and collaboration, even Major Kohl became increasingly curious, and increasingly troubled, by the Professor's cryptic adventures. Kohl probed, ever so politely. But he did not push too hard, never demanded his Professor partner disclose details of his frequent disappearing acts. Stefan Mirovich was simply too indispensable as the diplomatic liaison between the occupying German army and Borisov's restive citizens.

An immediate though not serious problem for Major Kohl was to find a reliable housekeeper and occasional cook for his headquarters home. Happily Stefan volunteered to take on that assignment, knowing immediately who the ideal candidate could, and definitely should, be. Polahaya, Stefan's young struggling schoolgirl, was working, comfortably making ends meet at the factory. She fiercely guarded her independence. Stefan also continued to tutor her on occasion and continued to be the informal father she had never known.

Despite Polahaya's current comfort and complacency, the Professor's sales pitch to her for the housekeeping job was an easy one. This would be a significant departure from her previous role as the brash, hard working queen of the factory floor. There would be an elegant house to maintain, even if it was German occupied. The German occupant was also a relatively young officer (only 32 years old) and a handsome officer as well. Polahaya would have her own private room, free meals, even a small but helpful salary for her housekeeping duties.

What passed for a job interview was very brief. Major Kohl offered a polite hello and a handshake and began to describe the housekeeping duties. Polahaya declined the invitation to sit down and barely allowed Kohl to get beyond a "Let me tell you about…" before she interrupted him. "My dear Professor told me all about this job. You'll have a clean house. You'll get decent meals every morning, every night, no lunches, and the meals won't be fancy. I don't do fancy. I'll wash your uniforms when you need them to be washed, and I'll press them properly. I like to see an officer, even a German officer, in a clean, well pressed uniform. I do not work on Sunday. Pay me what you think I'm worth. Am I hired?" Kohl smiled, stammered out a brief "Uh, ok, start this Monday." And Polahaya was gone. Her personal "dear Professor" just shrugged his shoulders, smiled at Kohl, and followed Polahaya out of her new office.

There was no hesitation on the part of Major Kohl. Polahaya was the woman for the job. Maybe the woman for him. She started the next Monday and continued in the job for almost two years. That job, however, turned into both a blessing and a curse. For Polahaya there was comfort. There was also the increasing attention the major directed at Polahaya, not Polahaya the housekeeper, but Polahaya the beautiful young woman sharing the major's home. For Polahaya, and for Major Kohl, there was also Ivan.

Major Kohl had far more pressing problems than just finding a housekeeper. Most critically there was a large, very diverse local population. Within that population were distinct rebellious factions to be controlled, to be accommodated, some to be imprisoned. The sizable Jewish and gypsy populations who did not escape as the Germans advanced were immediately imprisoned. Poles likewise were rounded up and added to the prison camps being erected around Borisov. There was also a prison camp erected primarily for local rebels, young and old, who were either courageous enough, or stupid enough, to speak out against the occupation. Some of those rebels stayed silent and invisible during the day but vandalized and sabotaged at night.

Ivan, or Ivan the Terrible to some, was one of those young rebels. Though not liked by many, he was grudgingly admired by many. Ivan was also known to Major Kohl, and in more ways than just the ruggedly handsome local tough guy. Ivan was also a suspected high ranking gang member, a suspected nighttime saboteur, and the man seen frequently arm-in-arm with Polahaya.

Regrettably for Major Kohl the violence and threats to public safety were increasing. In turn the prison population was exploding as more gypsies, Poles and Borisov townspeople were rounded up. Cumulatively, all this was creating an added strain on the German garrison. More temporary prison compounds to be built, more soldiers needed for guard duty, more marauding saboteurs to track down.

Kohl turned once again to his informal counselor, Stefan. Six months after enduring increasing demands for prison guards Stefan suggested a controversial but maybe partial solution to the major's guard shortage. For the sizable non-Borisov prison population why not recruit Borisov men. Those young, maybe rebellious, maybe unemployed, maybe thuggish young men roaming the streets could be recruited, with some modest pay, to work as guards. To lessen the risk as well as the controversy of being a complicit "German guard" the Borisov contingent would be diplomatically labeled an "honor guard." Yes, there would be a uniform, non-German looking, of course. But, there would be a uniform, with its implicit appeal. And, though there would be no weapons issued, each "honor guard" would be issued a large wooden club, to be used only as necessary. The guard assignments would be confined solely to troublesome young hooligans, gypsies, and Poles. No Borisov prisoners would be guarded. At least that was the initial plan, and hopefully this would make Kohl's prison staffing decision more palatable to town folk. Or so Stefan thought. And, so Major Kohl thought.

Strategically for both men, they decided to recruit Ivan the Terrible for this new, seemingly glamorous "honor guard" position. Stefan extended the invitation, Ivan agreed and did so promptly and enthusiastically. For Ivan there was no question at all about accepting the recruitment. And, here he was, once again, the opportunist impulsively hurtling down the path toward another seemingly irresistible opportunity. Was he being mature or thoughtful or deliberate in his decision? Quite the contrary, his decision was based on a short term, myopic vision of the immediate benefits this new employment would provide him.

Ivan could have, and definitely should have, been more deliberate and thoughtful before he blurted out a "yes, I'll take the job" answer. Working for the Germans was the equivalent of "collaboration." And, collaboration could and did take many forms, both benign and damnable.

With the German invasion many Borisov men, young and middle aged, disappeared into the countryside, becoming partisans defending their homeland. But, there also were many others who stayed and willingly collaborated with the occupying Germans as paramilitary or auxiliary soldiers, either in active combat or guard positions. For these able bodied citizens who didn't disappear, the Soviets soldiers and communist officials who ruled over their homeland, were far worse than the Germans. These Soviets, or "Bolsheviks" as they were derisively called by the locals, had taken their lands, fired hard working people from their honest day-to-day jobs, and closed countless local businesses. For these military volunteers it was also safer to side with the Germans as many believed the Germans would be the ultimate winners in this ugly, protracted war. So they willingly signed up with the Germans. They didn't see themselves as collaborators but as German partners.

For those who couldn't or wouldn't take up arms there were numerous non-military positions to consider. There were civil service positions that still needed day to day management whether or not there was an occupying army in town. Those who had been fired by the Bolsheviks were actively recruited to return to old desk jobs. There were local taxes to be collected, mail that had to be delivered, food and fuel to be distributed, roads which still required repairs. Government departments needed to be restaffed and managed: Water Supply and Sewage, Building Inspection, Hospital Administration. For the willing and able this was again hardly any damnable "collaboration with the enemy." Or so one could assume, or maybe hope. It was just a job. Regrettably, not everyone would agree. Certainly not those obstinate patriotic locals who bravely refused to work in any capacity, civilian or military, for their Nazi oppressors.

But the harsh reality was that there was really no option but to accept a German offer, or more bluntly a demand, to work for them. If one refused the offer/demand one of two unpleasant consequences awaited that uncooperative citizen. He or she could be hauled away to a forced labor camp, maybe even a concentration camp. Alternatively, a spouse or child could be threatened with a jail sentence, maybe even beaten or tortured, if a family member refused to accept the work assignment.

Sadly, there was a corresponding threat from the hated Bosheviks, should they return to power, for anyone who collaborated with the Germans. Any collaboration, no matter how benign the work assignment was, would be condemned by those Bolshevilks as disloyal, criminal, traitorous, treasonous. Whatever the label, that collaboration was tantamount to a death sentence.

On balance, there were only bad choices, maybe with some short-term benefits, but inevitable bad consequences for the beleaguered citizens of German occupied Borisov. For Ivan, even if he had deliberated more, analyzed the options more, he still might have replied with the fateful "yes." And, at the moment thoughtful analysis and deliberation, and the consequences of his decision, didn't clutter his mind. What was on his mind was the promise of a uniform.

Yes, the promise of that all important uniform. Not a uniform exactly like that certain Major. But, a uniform that would be clean and crisp, heavily starched and neatly pressed. There also would be shiny buttons, lots of buttons. There would be an equally shiny pair of high-top black boots. Ivan, a very young and very vain man, could easily picture himself in front of the full length mirror, proudly standing tall and erect, night stick in hand, with a serious, impassive face, but maybe with just the hint of a smug, self-satisfied smile. He could also picture himself sauntering down the city street with some lovely lady at his elbow. No, not some lovely lady, but that one lovely lady. How could she resist?

Ivan briefly, but only briefly, considered what his fellow townspeople might think of him. Certainly, they wouldn't question or object, would they? After all, he would be providing a valuable, much needed public service. But then, the arrogant less introspective personality took control, as it often did. And, he quickly convinced himself he really didn't care what others might think or say. He liked what he was, liked what he was going to be. Other opinions be damned. Except, maybe, Polahaya's opinion.

Borisov's newest, very euphoric honor guard recruit exited Major Kohl's headquarters, proudly cradling his new opportunistic trophies in his arms: a uniform (with shiny brass buttons someday soon), military boots, an imposing baton. He confessed to himself he had only the vaguest ideas what "honor guard duties" might be, no idea even where his job site was. But, those were just insignificant details. Ivan would figure it all out. He was ready, right now, to change clothes and start guarding.

Despite being ready to work, Ivan was told his first day on the job wasn't scheduled until next Monday, three days and an eternity from now. Ivan also had been provided with very few details about the new job. Work a 12-hour shift, happily a day shift, six days straight and then a day off on Sunday, then repeat the next week. Ivan had to admit, though grudgingly, that Major Kohl had provided his newest recruit a very comfortable work schedule. The actual details of "guarding" as the major briefly and casually described the job were simple. "Walk the prison yard perimeter. Do it briskly. Look and act like a soldier. Check for breaches in the fence. Break up any brawls but use the baton sparingly. I need you to be firm, to be respected, maybe feared, just a little, by the inmates. But not hated by them." Simple in theory, not so simple in reality, since Ivan would be on the outside of that prison fence while hostile faces glared at him on the inside.

Having committed to this assignment, Ivan also had to admit to himself that he did not know where the prison compound was. He certainly had no intention of going back to his employer and asking for directions. That would only highlight how impulsive and naive Ivan had been in saying "yes" first and not asking any questions. Fortunately, Ivan had no problem getting directions. But he also received some less than friendly stares and questions as to why he, or anyone, would want or need directions to the prison compound.

The compound was located in a large, paved lot adjacent to a partially bombed factory, now abandoned. The compound was roughly the size of three football fields if placed side by side. An eight-foot-tall chain link fence encircled the entire compound and was topped with just one layer of barbed wire. It was quite the less intimidating fencing than what was common at the military prison camps scattered elsewhere throughout Borisov. There was only one entry gate, just large enough for a truck to enter and exit.

Inside the compound Ivan estimated there might be four to five hundred prisoners. All were in street clothes, not some generic prison issue uniform. Scattered throughout the compound German soldiers had set up about forty standard issue military tents. Every prisoner apparently had been issued a blanket, thin but not holey. There were also a few cots scattered here and there. They didn't appear to be used by anyone and they certainly would not fit in the tents. Forty tents for four hundred plus inmates to huddle in, pushing and shoving and jockeying for just a little extra comfort and legroom. Primitive conditions? Yes, but it was better than no shelter at all, no blankets at all.

This was now Ivan's compound, his prison perimeter to guard. This was his constantly grumbling prison population to watch over and listen to. Everyone complained or pleaded or shouted as Ivan walked the perimeter. There were also the occasional obscenities hurled at him, the graphic and gruesome details shouted out as to what an inmate would do to Ivan if he or she got the chance. To his credit, Ivan kept his emotions in check and dutifully marched day after day. After day. The euphoria of this new opportunity was quickly fading away. And on those periodic dreary days as Ivan paraded around his perimeter, he couldn't help but wonder who the prisoner really was.

j

Later in life, both in Germany and America, Ivan would be more thoughtful, more analytic, far more mature in his search for, and decisions about, those ever-tempting opportunities. Yes, he would remain ever the opportunist, but a more careful and cautious one. For now, regrettably, impulsiveness, arrogance and superficial rewards would control him. And, with this "honor guard" decision there would be regrettable consequences.

Chapter 7 - Competing Interests/ Competition/ Conflict

"There is no story if there is no conflict."

Wes Anderson

For Major Heinrich Kohl the command and control of a sizable garrison, complete with makeshift prisons, continued to be less a blessing and much more of a burden. The newly created civilian honor guard group provided a measure of relief. Ivan had been recruited. And as a recognized, if informal, young leader, Ivan built a small but useful bridge between the townspeople - at least the restive young townspeople - and the German command. There were some occasional polite exchanges, maybe even a joke or two, between Kohl and Ivan. Not friendship certainly, but a mutual respect and civility between the two of them.

Vandalism and sabotage were inevitable. That produced a corresponding increase in the brutality of the German response. Makeshift prisons kept growing as the prison population exploded. More and more townspeople also changed their perception of, and tolerance for, the honor guards. Increasingly, the honor guards were seen by the local population as German collaborators. They lost the more charitable image of relatively harmless young men, making a few rubles and keeping the unwanted troublemakers, gypsies and Poles within their prison fences.

Amidst the growing tension and violence, Polahaya continued to enjoy the sanctuary of the major's headquarters. She enjoyed his charming personality, his wit and sophistication, and his occasional chats. But, Polahaya was also quite drawn to her less polished but persistent suitor, Ivan Kupraschonik. Ivan, the wild, ambitious but lovable "gangster," now a former gangster (maybe?) And, now even more attractive in his fancy, form fitting uniform. And, it would be a gross understatement to say Ivan was a persistent suitor.

Ivan definitely was persistent. He was also charming though in a crude and clumsy manner. And, during that courtship he was very vague and evasive about his past. The senseless death of his father was common knowledge even though that tragedy took place in the small village of Zodzina outside Borisov. But, there were rumors that Ivan was not quite the eligible bachelor that he portrayed himself to be. There were also the mysterious overnight trips to visit "an old friend" in Homyelska on the far southeastern border with Russia. If Polahaya was to move forward with a more serious relationship, possibly marriage, she demanded to know more about Ivan's past.

The initial, and not very convincing, admission from Ivan was that there had been an earlier silly, short romance with a young woman in Zodzina. That had all ended and the young woman had moved away. End of story, at least for a while. Polahaya was skeptical and suspicious about Ivan's former love life, but she wasn't that concerned. She was having too much fun playing hard to get while also enjoying the time and attention from Ivan. It became quite the game between the two, she resisting, he persisting. Eventually that persistence by the Borisov bad boy paid off. And the two married in a modest Orthodox wedding in March of 1943. But as Polahaya discovered three months later it wasn't the "end of the story."

One afternoon a letter arrived at their modest little apartment. Addressed to Ivan, it came from a woman Polahaya remembered as Ivan's long forgotten, supposedly brief, romantic partner, the village girl from Zodzina. Understandably curious, Polahaya read the letter and learned the woman was doing well, their young son was doing well, she was moving, once again, with her parents, to Moscow.

She didn't expect any more child support or any more contacts. Essentially it said "good-bye, forever."

Polahaya sat at the kitchen table, stunned, outraged, somewhat embarrassed by this history she should have pursued more aggressively. In addition to those various emotions, Polahaya wasn't that surprised by what she had just learned. She sat at that table all afternoon, the letter there in plain sight, and waited for her "honor guard" to come home. She confronted him with a surprising measure of self-control even though she was furious with her newlywed husband. They sat at that table, Ivan sipping, probably guzzling, vodka, Polahaya drinking more than her typical quota. The letter was still there in plain sight and couldn't be ignored. Ivan, with uncharacteristic humility and awkwardness, finally picked up the letter, quickly read it and then looked up at his newlywed. Polahaya, now with far less poise and self-control, rose from her chair, knocking it over, and shouted out, "Well? How about an honest explanation? Something other than some phony lie about a 'silly short romance'?"

Trying to recover some composure, Ivan stared up at the ceiling, took a deep breath, and gulped two large shots of vodka. He turned back toward Polahaya and flashed one of his signature big smiles. But the smile came across as half-hearted. The smile also did not draw out a glowing affectionate response from Polahaya. All he received was that ongoing glare. Then with an uncharacteristic nervous voice he proceeded. "I was just a young dumb kid. She was just a young dumb girl named Alexana Smirkov from the village of Zodzina. Yeah, she left Zodzina a few years ago with her parents." He paused and gulped nervously. "And when she left she took her infant son…….my son, with her. And for what it's worth we did get married in a small civil ceremony in Zodzina a few months after our son's birthday. There was a long pause from Ivan. And then, unable to look at Polalhaya, Ivan just stared at the floor and muttered "I'm sorry, so sorry."

As Polahaya sat in stunned silence, Ivan slowly tried to explain. It all started as that innocent teenage romance, driven more by lust than love, and not so surprisingly, the romance resulted in a pregnancy. The immature teenage girl wanted that baby. Conversely, Ivan was nowhere close to becoming a parent. Getting married should have been the right and honorable decision, even though both Ivan and Alexana were only sixteen years old. Alexana pushed and prodded Ivan toward domesticity and maybe even more children. However, Ivan enjoyed that wild and reckless lifestyle which his newly found employment with the Borisov Cossack provided him. There was no hostility or hatred between the newlyweds. But, there really was no love either, just mutual regret over their current dilemma. For Ivan there was also no easy escape from this dilemma. Alexana's father was a factory manager in Minsk and a powerful communist party official. He presented an "offer" which Ivan simply could not refuse. Ivan should, and would, marry Alexana even if it was accomplished through a small and discreet civil ceremony. She would leave with her parents and relocate to that new factory assignment in Homyelska. Ivan would provide some financial support. And that would in fact be the "end of the story" for Ivan the parent, Ivan the spouse. For almost two years Ivan dutifully went on secretive overnighters to deliver some support money, bringing a small gift or two as well. They were pleasant enough visits, but the visits looked and felt more like visits from a friend, maybe an uncle, than a parent. The visits became less frequent, payments likewise dwindled. Alexana and Ivan, without any discussion or debate, had arrived at an amicable, though unofficial, divorce. It was just that, however: an "unofficial" divorce.

As Ivan struggled through this confession about his messy marital history Polahaya sat silent and stoic. When he finished, she exploded. "You lied!" Tears flowed. There was hatred in her voice, hatred in her eyes. But all she could repeat was "You lied! You lied!" Then she collapsed back onto her chair and sobbed quietly. No more hatred in her voice, just those sobs. And as she sat there and just stared at the floor she quietly spoke to herself, " And I stupidly married you with those lies! My God! What a fool I was! What a goddamn fool!" She couldn't speak anymore. But her mind was filled with so many thoughts. It wasn't some silly, small and inconsequential lie about his past. There were huge, very consequential lies about that past. And he had perpetuated those lies throughout their two plus years of dating and through their wedding day. Were there other lies, other dark secrets? Would she have said yes to their marriage had she known those "oh, by the way" details of a wife, a child, a very real prior marriage? Ivan offered no defense, no further feeble explanation. But he did read Polahaya's mind and offered a soft spoken, humble promise. "There are no other secrets." Polahaya marched off to the bedroom and closed the door.

For the next week Ivan received nothing but silence, angry stares and a blanket to cover up with anywhere he chose to sleep, anywhere except their bed. The following week Polahaya prepared their first warm meal and invited Ivan back to their bed. To Ivan's surprise Polahaya also said nothing about that annoying technicality of Ivan still being married. Maybe Polahaya decided Ivan's troubled history was not only history but now was ancient history. This married couple was also just trying to survive amidst the current chaos of a European war, a Second World War. Documents, including marriage certificates, were now either irrelevant or nonexistent.

That ancient history was resurrected periodically over their decades-long marriage. Ivan would question Pauline's faithfulness during her employment with the German officer. Pauline would counter with Ivan's marital lie. Except for those periodic ugly, angry jabs at one another Ivan's past did remain just ancient history. The only people who remained interested in that ancient history were we three siblings who fantasized about locating and reuniting with our phantom stepbrother somewhere, someday.

Over the years after our father's death we continued to press our mother about their courtship and marriage. She offered very few additional details as to who, where, how though she did stress there was in fact a proper, if simple, Orthodox marriage ceremony. She did offer a telling comment as to our recurring question about that marriage. Why did she say "yes"? The long awaited reply to us persistent inquisitors was simple and blunt. No, it wasn't a marriage out of necessity because of a pregnancy. For years we had suspected that was the reason for a marriage. And, no, she was not madly, blindly in love with Ivan. With a hint of a smile, coupled with a bit of sadness in her eyes, our mother Polahaya confessed she finally said "yes" to the persistent marriage proposals so her husband-to-be would "stop bugging me." Those were her innocent unfiltered words. Polahaya wanted, probably needed, Ivan to "stop bugging me." We're sure there was some truth in her glib explanation of "why." But despite that bluntness and glibness we believed there also must have been some deeper emotional connection with that brash, opportunistic young Ivan, a connection that would keep them bonded for the next fifty plus years.

After the marriage the two newlyweds moved into a small apartment. It would be far less comfortable and elegant than the major's quarters. But Polahaya continued to work daily at those quarters, enjoyed free meals there, and enjoyed the occasional light hearted conversations with Major Kohl. Ten months after the marriage, Polahaya gave birth to their first child Tamara. But, just months after that birth Polahaya's and Ivan's life was drastically altered. By the spring of 1944 Borisov became a very dangerous place. And, it would force this new family to escape westward to the uncertain and potentially dangerous haven of Germany.

Chapter 8 - Exit Strategy

"The moment one definitely commits oneself then providence moves too. Whatever you think you can do, or believe you can do, begin it."

Wolfgang von Goethe

Nazi Germany's campaign to conquer Europe changed dramatically since its initial lightning fast offensive in to Poland in 1939. For Germany the war had turned far more defensive than offensive on both the eastern and western fronts. The Borisov prison camps kept growing. The German responses to prison revolts, as well as civic unrest, turned increasingly violent. There was also now growing and very open hostility to the Borisov honor guards. Even Polahaya, just a simple housekeeper for the German commander, received a growing number of threats and experienced increasing isolation from the local population. She was labeled and frequently harassed as "that woman," not the wife but just "that woman" who belonged to the German collaborator, Ivan the Terrible. She also became the object of more and more rumors and innuendo about all the time she was spending with the charming "Nazi" officer.

In the spring of 1944 Major Kohl received blunt orders to close the prison camps, as quickly as possible and by whatever means necessary. Kohl was also ordered to undertake a retreat, ideally an orderly retreat, from Borisov. For Ivan, the valued honor guard, he was now out of a job. And, with the imminent retreat of the German occupation force Ivan could no longer enjoy the protective umbrella of Major Kohl. There was only one viable option for Ivan and his family. He, like the Germans, would likewise need to retreat from

Borisov, and quickly. More critically for Ivan, he would need to put together not just a retreat for him from Borisov. He would need to find an escape for his wife and infant Tamara. But, how to escape? And an escape to where?

Ivan, ever the opportunist, was finding few opportunities or options for that escape. The key ingredient, which he lacked, was some form of transportation for not just his family but a larger caravan of escapees. Polahaya had struggled through her pregnancy and was still struggling to recover post-delivery. Polahaya's good friend, Ludmilla, had been and continued to be an invaluable practical nurse, caring for Polahaya and tiny Tamara. Ludmilla needed to be included in any escape plan. Volodya, a friend of Ivan since their earlier teens, remained a good friend. However, Volodya had also been recruited by Major Kohl to serve as the garrison photographer. That photography was lighthearted and innocuous enough and produced a fun-filled gallery of family portraits. However, Volodya also produced an extensive gallery of propaganda shots for the German command. And, in the eyes of many in Borisov, Volodya was as much a collaborator as Ivan, the now despised "honor guard." Volodya needed to be included in the escape caravan.

Surprisingly, the answer to the transportation dilemma came by way of some subtle suggestions from Major Kohl. The imminent German retreat generated its predictable share of confusion, chaos, misplaced and forgotten equipment. The control and protection of equipment was also lax, and that included the motor pool with its assortment of jeeps and trucks. Major Kohl shared this information with Ivan, noting that some small trucks had already been "misplaced." And, at least for the moment, traffic, whatever that traffic might be, didn't encounter that much resistance or risks.

Kohl had struggled with what he could, and should, do with his two "employees." He knew the risks of simply leaving them adrift in

Borisov. He had even considered including them in the retreating garrison, and fully under Kohl's protection. But, Kohl decided Ivan would not accept that invitation. Ivan's pride and vanity would get in the way. Ivan, the opportunist husband and father, would figure out an escape. And, in Ivan's view Major Kohl continued to devote too much time and attention to Polahaya, even after the marriage. An exit in full lockstep with the Germans would also seal their fate as German collaborators. A separate stealthy escape plan out of Borisov, then westward to somewhere, was the best suggestion Major Kohl could offer his former employees. A few days after a strategy meeting between Ivan and Kohl to work out the details, on a moonless night, a small caravan began its escape out of Borisov. It would be a quick and quiet and uneventful escape. Or so they hoped.

The plan was fairly simple, at least in concept. Ivan, plus his expanded company, could slip into the now empty motor pool and commandeer the military truck that Major Kohl had ordered be left behind because it was not salvageable. Then they would quietly slip out of Borisov. But instead of a single "slip in, slip out" escape there were a number of comedic fumbles and stumbles and an initial botched rendezvous. Murphy's Law was very alive and present.

Part one of the plan called for Polahaya to return early in the evening to Major Kohl's residence. Though the motor pool and an escape truck would still be several blocks away, this would shorten the ladies' escape route. Ludmilla would accompany Polahaya, as she often did, while Polahaya retrieved some personal effects she had left behind at Kohl's quarters. Then both ladies would exit by the back door and hustle to the motor pool. Polahaya was a familiar face around the residence, with free access. Hopefully, her return late in the day after everyone was gone wouldn't raise any suspicion. But, anxious and nervous as she was, Polahaya returned to Kohl's quarters too soon that early evening. Major Kohl

was still there, as were several other officers. Everyone was gathering documents or office supplies. Kohl was still wrestling with the details of their evacuation. And into the major's small office, amidst the clutter and chaos, the two young ladies walked in. This certainly was not the game plan. The two women couldn't just unexpectedly walk in, then abruptly turn around and exit out a back door and down to the motor pool. Though shocked and surprised, the ladies quickly regained their composure and delivered some masterful improvisation. They smiled at everyone and exchanged some awkward hellos. Polahaya added a cheerful and nonchalant "Oops! Sorry! We didn't mean to barge in. And this must be some very serious top-secret meeting." She chuckled. The officers did not. She continued.. "I'm the dummy, came late this morning and didn't finish my cleaning earlier. So here I am. Got to do it right, even if it is my last day." That was her job. She also explained she had forgotten to collect a few personal items which might otherwise be thrown out or accidentally hauled away during the evacuation. Kohl helped ease the awkwardness as he in turn hastily wrapped up his staff meeting and hustled the staff out. He paused at the door, then bid the young ladies good night. He also added a cheerful "Good bye, and good luck." He considered, just for a moment, hugging each of the nice ladies, but he decided not to do so. That brief delay at the office lasted only a few minutes. But it felt like several hours for the two women. With the officer staff now gone they exited through the back door and quickened their pace, almost running to the motorpool. The delay was also doubly painful and long because all this time Ivan was hiding, or so they hoped, out in the motor pool, anxiously waiting for his two female escapees.
'

Ivan had in fact succeeded in reaching the motor pool undetected. He was a familiar face around the German headquarters and had free access to all areas. His presence around the motor shouldn't raise any suspicion. The German evacuation was almost complete with very few troops remaining. There also was very little time to gather up all the motor pool equipment or to tackle any much-needed maintenance and repairs. The unfinished, unrepaired motor pool inventory included several jeeps and trucks which Kohl had conveniently declared were not roadworthy and therefore should be left behind. That abandoned inventory would provide Ivan options for their needed transportation out of Borisov And Major Kohl had cheerfully assured Ivan there definitely would be something left behind in the motor pool that would be "roadworthy" for the escapees.

The motor pool consisted of two cavernous garages. One stored and repaired military hardware like tanks, halftracks, and armored personnel carriers. But it was completely empty since any piece of movable military hardware was already headed west. The second garage, equally cavernous, was used for storage and repair of non-combat vehicles: jeeps (two and four seaters), small pickups and huge two-and-a-half-ton supply trucks. The garage was not vacant, as the major had assured Ivan. As Ivan peered into the dark garage, he was excited to see what he thought were silhouettes of several assorted vehicles. But as his eyes adjusted and he stepped further in, his excitement turned into growing confusion and despair.

The garage was difficult to navigate around, littered as it was with spare tires, countless tools, a headlight here, a truck fender there. Gasoline, motor oil and grease were spilled everywhere, all this highlighting the hasty and clumsy German evacuation from Borisov. This is what Major Heinrich Kohl had left for his trusted honor guard: noxious smells, slippery floors, and an obstacle course of useless motor pool parts. This appalling mess also was what his fellow escapees would see when they arrived in the next few minutes. What a disaster! What an embarrassment! Ivan stood and stared and then shouted out, all too loudly and to no one but himself, "You son of a bitch! This is your brilliant master plan? We'll be dead or caught before we even get out of the motorpool."

The garage was large, but its inventory was much smaller than Ivan had seen, or possibly imagined he had seen, when he first entered. And on closer inspection it turned out to be more trash than treasure. Kohl had confidently declared there would be "roadworthy" vehicles. Unfortunately, Kohl's definition of "roadworthy" was very, very charitable as well as misleading. Understandably, the vehicles needed to be in some state of disrepair for Kohl to credibly declare them unsalvageable junk. The half dozen battered jeeps easily qualified as junk, but they were too small for the caravan. One abandoned truck had no front tires, another had no canvas cover over the bed, another had no engine. The last truck had four very bald tires, a torn canvas cover and a cracked windshield. Hopefully, it had a functioning engine. And whether it functioned or not, this motor pool wreck was Ivan's best - and only - candidate for a roadworthy getaway vehicle.

Despite the activity and noise nearby, Ivan was still worried about the attention he would draw by starting up a loud German diesel engine inside the maintenance shed. That's where his friend Volodya hopefully would come to the rescue. Together they could roll the truck out of the shed, enlist one of the women to play driver and then put three strong backs behind the truck to quietly roll it further away from troop activity and possible detection. Two hundred yards was all they would need to push. Then they could power up the diesel and race away. Everyone needed to lend a hand, offer a strong back. But those much needed strong backs! were still missing.

The two women did manage a successful exit out of Major Kohl's home and to the correct motor pool shed. However, Volodya wasn't as successful. He was a familiar enough visitor around the German headquarters. Therefore, he wouldn't be challenged, or at least shouldn't be challenged, as some stranger or threat. However, he did have the bad luck of running into two soldiers who likewise appeared to be wandering around the grounds. The soldiers were visibly nervous and tense, probably worrying about the impending evacuation from Borisov. And both soldiers were armed. They quizzed Volodya as to why he, the camp photographer, was here, and here on a dark moonless night. "Hey, what the hell is our photographer doing out this late at night? You taking spy pictures? Trying to steal some jeep for a getaway? Maybe we ought to haul you off to the Major for some tough questions. Better yet, maybe we should beat some information out of you before you visit the Major? Yeah, that's a better idea." Volodya, usually quick-witted and poised, just stood there, like the proverbial deer in the headlights. But after a few deep breaths he offered a feeble smile and an even more feeble wave of his hand. Regaining some composure and confidence, Volodya stuttered and stammered an explanation about forgetting something, someplace. It wasn't that coherent or convincing. But, just as he was struggling to offer a second, maybe more convincing explanation the two soldiers heard their names called. They immediately forgot about their suspected motor pool spy and off they scrambled into the dark and away from the motor pool area.

With that potential disaster behind him, Volodya hurried to his planned rendezvous with Ivan. Unfortunately, unnerved as Volodya was by that encounter, he hurried to the wrong maintenance shed. Ivan was not there! More panic set in as Volodya feared his three fellow escapees had fled without him. He took several deep breaths, tried to calm his nerves, and rethought the directions Ivan had given him. Two minutes later, Volodya was there hugging his good friend, the friend who had not abandoned him. And, like Ivan, Volodya stood there staring at this wreck that would maybe, just maybe, might qualify as "roadworthy" as Major Kohl had confidently assured Ivan.

With the caravan crew now united the men pushed the truck out of the shed. That task was easy enough as the shed's entry was slightly tilted downward from the concrete floor to the gravel yard. Polahaya took on the role of driver/navigator as the other three grunted and groaned to generate enough inertia to begin a slow roll on the gravel. It was hard work but manageable as they navigated past several large sheds which offered extra noise insulation, as well as distance, from the German troops.

Feeling safe enough, as well as feeling exhausted from the lengthy pushing, Ivan decided they could turn on the diesel and speed away from Borisov. But it was only fitting, almost predictable, that the truck key which should have been under the floor mat was not there. It was a toss-up by all four of them whether they should laugh or cry. So it was a little of both. Who came to the rescue? It wasn't either of the men. Instead, it was Polahaya. She had watched and learned much from her adoptive father, Temofay, who had repaired, as well as started, battered old fire trucks. Polahaya put her hot-wiring skill to good use and started up their motor pool wreck. With just a very short rest break the four climbed into the truck, men in the front, ladies in the bed. Scrambling to escape out of Borisov, the foursome hadn't even taken an inventory of what the truck held, if anything. The foursome had packed only the barest of essentials and very little clothing to minimize any attention. What a pleasant surprise awaited them as they more closely surveyed the escape vehicle. The major had stocked the wreck with several blankets, a week's worth of provisions and water, even a few bottles of vodka. This would be an invaluable stockpile for their upcoming odyssey. Maybe the major wasn't such a son of a bitch after all?

And where, oh where, was the caravan's fifth passenger while everyone was scrambling and stumbling to escape from Borisov? To everyone's collective joy and relief little Tamara was blissfully quiet and cooperative. Polahaya routinely brought her infant, comfortably nestled in a large basket, to Major Kohl's office while she performed light cleaning chores post-delivery. (Polahaya needed the extra pay, modest as it was.) It wasn't that unusual, therefore, that Tamara was present and part of the awkward encounter at Major Kohl's office. The hurried pace from the office to the motor pool wasn't so unusual or unpleasant either. She only whimpered a little as she lay beside her mother while mother steered the "roadworthy" truck out of the garage and down the grave path. Tamara's only trauma was hearing the deafening roar of the battered truck's diesel engine. She cried but her crying noises were no match for the diesel. Mother Polahaya had the magic touch anyway and her daughter was quickly back to sleep. Little Tamara was the near perfect escape artist: calm, quiet, and also unseen.

Chapter 9 - Westward Ho, Westward Ho Again

"A journey of a thousand miles begins with the very first step."

Lao Tzu

Heeding the major's discreet suggestion, the caravan headed southwest to Minsk. The capital of what passed for the Byelorussian Soviet Republic was less than a day away. Hopefully all five caravan passengers, even little Tamara, could just blend into the general chaos, starting new lives, escaping their respective pasts. And, with some luck Ivan and Polahaya could make contact with their old friend and counselor, Stefan, "The Professor."

As Borisov had slipped into greater anarchy, lawlessness and German brutality, Stefan had quietly slipped out of town. There was little for him to contribute in town since schools had been closed for months. There was nothing that even faintly resembled some local government or leadership which might otherwise benefit from the professor's counsel and presence. Certainly the Germans had no need for him either. All they needed was fast or at least functioning vehicles to facilitate their retreat.

Stefan was disappointed to find Minsk was even more chaotic and dangerous than Borisov. The Soviets were more brutal than their German enemies. Increasingly almost anyone could be rounded up by self-proclaimed "officials" of the communist party for questioning, possibly imprisonment. Anyone could be a traitor, a collaborator, an unrepentant imperialist, maybe just an outspoken patriot yearning for an independent Byclorussia. There were even a few rumors floating around about those so-called "honor guards" at the Borisov prison camps.

Stefan and the caravan fivesome did manage to connect with one another on the caravan's second night in Minsk. But, instead of offering comfort, the best Stefan could do was to advise the caravan to head further west, probably completely out of Byelorussia. Stefan would be heading west as well, though precisely where and when was still undecided. He had also kept in touch, discreetly, with Major Kohl. And, despite the logistical challenge it presented in actually traveling several hundred miles to Germany, Stefan believed the caravan's prospects for survival would be far better in Germany. There might even be some support and protection from the major. Of course, that assumed Major Kohl could be located. With the allied advances on the western front, an end to this devastating war was more and more likely. With the increasing possibility of an allied victory, the caravan might become no more than one of countless nameless and aimless bands of refugees from countless countries. And, for Ivan and Polahaya, as well as their other caravan companions, they all might be able to erase old identities, erase old troubling histories and start fresh. That fresh start would definitely be somewhere other than Borisov. With a new plan, with some renewed optimism, the caravan continued on its westward course.

Chapter 10 - Oh, So Many Miles

"Wisely and slow. They stumble who run fast."

William Shakespeare's 'Romeo and Juliet.'

Ivan, ever the opportunist, now head cheerleader, kept promoting a far western exit strategy. And when they first started, the caravan members were upbeat, or at least somewhat upbeat. Sadly, that upbeat attitude quickly changed to more pessimism than optimism. Stefan's warning about the risks of continuing to stay in Minsk upended any initial belief, or hope, that a short ninety-mile escape westward to the capitol would provide them the safety and sanctuary the five members so desperately wanted and hoped for. The renewed course westward, in the comfort of their stolen army vehicle, was also too quickly halted just outside of Minsk. The party had stopped for the night, primarily to rest but also to salvage, or maybe steal, additional supplies for the trip. An abandoned house was their semi-comfortable lodging for the night. But, the next morning, in an ironic twist of fate, their stolen vehicle had itself been stolen.

Ivan was both furious and embarrassed that he'd been so careless in failing to guard their precious escape vehicle. A trek of hundreds of miles on foot was impossible, particularly because of Polahaya's continued poor health and the demands of caring for a newborn. Ivan, the leader, Ivan the opportunist, left the escapees (yes, that's what they now were) to secure some new means of escape westward. As darkness set in, off he went. And, in the middle of the night he returned, waking everyone and insisting on as much silence as possible. Everyone packed up what little they had, stepping out into the night to find their new comfortable alternative to a foot march westward.

The alternative mode of escape could have been, should have been, another truck. Hopefully, it would be less battered and beaten than the Borisov motor pool wreck. Maybe this truck would even have a canvas cover, one that wasn't torn, and one that could actually provide shelter from the elements. Even a sturdy four passenger jeep, again with an intact canvas cover, would work. A decent sized flatbed truck, with four good tires this time, would certainly be acceptable as well. Something, anything that provided them some space, some speed to put Minsk quickly behind them, and maybe even provide some modest comfort.

"Comfortable" would be an overly kind description of what was parked in the front yard. Their "chariot" was a small single bench farm wagon, barely able to fit two adults side by side on the bench. There was a decent sized storage compartment behind the bench. However, the entire bench and compartment were built with what once were sturdy but now very ancient oak boards, bowed and splintered and gray from decades of outdoor use. The bench also constantly creaked and groaned under the weight of its passengers, threatening to disintegrate any minute. Behind the storage box their "chariot" did include an eight-foot-long bed with one foot tall side panels. But, that bed was even more dilapidated and weather beaten than its companion bench and storage compartment. A center floorboard was missing. Another floorboard was badly cracked, ready to break in half at any moment. And, there were countless splintered pieces waiting to attack a careless sleeping or sitting passenger. The four wooden wheels were equally ancient, wobbling with every turn and offering a constant grinding noise. Keeping his thoughts to himself, Ivan speculated, "We'll be damn lucky to move one hundred miles before my late-night travel prize totally falls apart. And out in the middle of nowhere." The one and only reasonably new and sturdy feature of this hijacked wagon was the chariot's horse harness.

And, the power source for this chariot? There was Ivan proudly standing between two horses, their bridles held firmly in his upraised right hand. One horse appeared to be young, spirited and ready to travel anywhere, pull anything. The second power source for their dilapidated chariot was a marginally healthy looking but old horse. "Old" would be a charitable description of this horse, however. "Ancient" would be more appropriate. The horse had a classic old horse swayback appearance though Ivan kept insisting it had "just a very little bit" of a swayback. Its tail was ratty and covered in knots and sand burs. Its mane was no better looking. And its coat had not been brushed in ages. Whatever the condition of that horse and its swayback, this was the best Ivan could do in such a short time, and under the cover of darkness. Young and sturdy, old and swaybacked it would have to be. Needing that darkness to aid their escape with their new "borrowed" wagon, the two ladies hurriedly climbed on board. Small and lightweight Tamara had the privilege of sharing the bench. The two men walked alongside and did so as briskly as they could. By daylight the escapee caravan had put thirty miles behind them, and thirty miles between them and some very angry farmer. The wagon had not fallen apart. Not yet. But the rickety wagon, with its perpetual moans and groans, kept the caravan party perpetually anxious.

Ten days after the acquisition of their chariot and horses the caravan needed to cross a swift flowing but shallow stream. The stream bed was a mixture of river rocks, pebbles and sand. It should have presented a manageable challenge to guide the horse drawn wagon slowly and carefully between the rocks and small depressions. But, with two-thirds of the stream behind them the young horse stumbled and stepped into a depression. Its left front leg buckled. The horse stumbled sideways but fortunately didn't fall, aided as it was by its old companion. The ancient wagon, if it tipped sideways and crashed into the swift stream and its rock strewn bottom, would have resulted in the total demolition of the caravan's very frail means of cross-country transportation. Fortunately, Ivan and Volodya managed to steady the crippled horse and guide it to the solid grass on the other side.

The horse's limp was severe and the leg was noticeably swollen. Ivan and Poahaya were savvy enough about farm animals and determined the horse's leg was not broken but severely sprained and bruised. The horse would need at least four or five days of rest. Then, if they and the horse were lucky, the horse might slowly return to work in another week or two. The emphasis was on a "slow" return.

Unfortunately, the caravan didn't have the luxury of a slow pace on their westward escape. The decision was clear, even if regrettable. They needed to abandon their young horse and press on with their journey. Ivan scouted out the nearby countryside and found a grassy pasture a half mile away. It was currently unoccupied and would provide a comfortable and safe site for their lame horse's recuperation. If a farmer, maybe another wandering traveler, chose to claim ownership of the horse that would be fine. In an ironic twist of fate, the old and swaybacked triumphed over the young and sturdy. And, the caravan's westward odyssey continued.

Chapter 11 - Sightseeing through Europe

"Not all who wander are lost."

J.R.R. Tolkein

Ivan, the caravan's "tour guide", once again painted an upbeat, bright picture of the upcoming westward trek. The Soviets were behind them and preoccupied with consolidating their hold on Borisov and Minsk. The Germans were marching, or rapidly retreating, westward and were countless miles ahead of this motley, hardly very dangerous, band. All that lay ahead for the fivesome was endless miles of abandoned fields and pastures over gently rolling terrain. There must be, Ivan speculated, countless abandoned sheds and farmhouses for rest and shelter. There had to be stray chickens or pigs, maybe a cow or two to capture and add to their food supply. There were plenty of backroads, even if dirty and deep with well-traveled ruts, that would enable them to skirt any cities until they reached the hoped for sanctuary of the German border. And it couldn't be that long a trek from Minsk to that border. After all, the Germans had completed their blitzkrieg through Poland and into central Byelorussia in what must have been only a few days. Little did Ivan know that a westward escape from Minsk to their eventual destination of Hannover would require a grueling adventure over almost 900 miles of central Europe.

Ivan's pep talk was just what the group needed. They had masterminded a clumsy but successful escape from Borisov. They had stumbled through the back streets of Minsk and avoided any entanglements with unfriendly Soviets. And here they were with over 100 miles under their collective belts, plus another thirty miles further away from Minsk. They all were young and reasonably healthy, and blessed - at least somewhat blessed - with their new chariot and noble steed. It would be westward ho, once again, with those blue skies overhead and gently rolling plains, and on an ancient chariot and an equally ancient, but only "slightly" swayback steed. Who could ask for anything more? But, reality set in very quickly. Very soon they would need so much more than pastoral landscapes and blue skies. There would be the recurring shelter to find, plus those elusive chickens and pigs to catch or try to, plus food to find for the horse, plus solutions for several imposing rivers that needed to be crossed.

The collective mood remained upbeat for the first few weeks. The care package from Major Kohl, what remained of it after Minsk, certainly helped. It was pleasant, somewhat pleasant at least, for the men to sleep under the wagon while the women snuggled in the small bed of the buggy. Ivan also had a sizable stash of rubles from his days with the infamous Cossack, which stash could help to buy some basic supplies.

Regrettably, the anxious escapees could only manage between 15 and 20 miles daily, hindered as they were by a steady but old horse and a buggy that could only support two passengers (plus the little one) prudently. This road trip was turning into something far different than their initial naive image of a cheery, peaceful, and very fast paced, excursion through western Byelorussia and northern Poland. Polahaya and Ludmilla kindly, if halfheartedly, volunteered to do some periodic walking instead of riding, The gesture was appreciated. However, the gesture did nothing to quicken the westward snail's pace. The wooden planks of the bed felt increasingly harder and increasingly intolerable at night. The cold, damp ground and the wagon's ugly ,very splintered underbelly became more and more intolerable each night. Shelter. They needed other shelter for a night, maybe even for a day or two.

Their west by northwest route pushed them toward the southern border of present-day Lithuania and then onto the plains of northern Poland. It also kept them at a distance from any sizable towns as well as marauding German forces. The route reconfigured into more of a zigzag than a straight route, however, as their revised daily objective was to find, and then hopefully occupy, a vacant farmhouse or barn. Ivan and Volodya took turns as forward scouts exploring north and south off their dirt road path for some vacant jackpot. They were successful, and with some frequency, in locating small farmhouses which were still structurally upright and without occupants. The former occupants either fled to a safer secret hideout, or they were killed or imprisoned by the Germans. Cruel and sad as it was for the rural population to be forced from their homes, it was a godsend for the weary travelers.

The shelter stops, frequent as they were, did prolong the westward road trip. But they provided a necessary and much needed pause to refresh the bodies and lift the spirits. There was also much to scavenge as well as much to catch, or at least attempt to catch. As Ivan had predicted (or hoped?) the occasional chicken would peek out from a shed, maybe a pig or even a sheep. All had escaped, surprisingly but gratefully, the clutches of a hungry German soldier. A few vegetables were also found which the Germans probably had been too lazy to pull out of a small garden. Though each adult confessed to some reluctance, even embarrassment, in doing so, they all collected extra socks, shirts, pants and blankets which the homeowners left behind. Sadly, but realistically, it was very unlikely the homeowners would ever return for any of their belongings. Or ever return at all.

Their noble steed, aged and slow, was nonetheless still very reliable. But, it, like the five others, needed feed and rest. Garden vegetables helped. So did what few ripe apples anyone could salvage from a tree. Even a rotten apple was a decent treat. There might even be a surprise bonus for the horse with an armful of hay. That scraggly but dependable horse was an invaluable contributor to their progress westward, and it transported its passengers ably all the way to the German border. However, with the daily focus on simply surviving and moving west no one ever thought to give a proper name to their workhorse. It was, and remained, just simply, "the Horse."

This would be the strategy for the fivesome for the next three or four months: travel, rest, scavenge, repeat. The one recurring logistical stumbling block for them was rivers, or more specifically how to cross those rivers. By the time they approached the outskirts of Hannover they would have to cross at least three, maybe four rivers: the Nioman in Byelorussia, the Wisla in Poland, and both the Oder and the Elbe in Germany. Major bridges were either destroyed or in serious disrepair. Ferryboat service was either abandoned or very difficult to find. As they approached a river obstacle Ivan or Volodya set out on a scouting mission. Though with some reluctance, they might ask a local for suggestions or directions. Frequently Ivan also was forced to dip into his Borisov fund to bribe a ferryman for safe passage across a river. Those bribes weren't small or easily agreed upon but they were necessary for their continued safe passage. All that scouting, planning, bribing and crossing were not only expensive but also very time consuming. By the time they completed their last river crossing the north Atlantic fall winds turned much colder and more uncomfortable.

The caravan overcame the challenges of three river crossings reasonably well, despite the varying logistical hurdles at each of those crossings. The Elbe, inside the German border, would be their fourth and gratefully their last river obstacle. But, that German river would prove to be their most difficult crossing, not logistically, but emotionally.

The Elbe wasn't that wide, and it was fairly navigable, serving as a major north/south commercial artery. Having prudently remained on the northern fringe of the countries through which they had trekked, that northern route had put them north of Berlin. If they continued west the occasional road signs would send them to the small German river town of Wittenberge. Since it wasn't a strategic crossroad the ferry crossing was still intact and functioning. Proper timing, the correct fare, plus a strategic extra "thank you" to the ferry master and the caravan would be across the Elbe. That crossing could, and hopefully would, provide a valuable extra sanctuary. And, the river would serve as the important defensive barrier against the Soviet army advancing from the east. Crossing the Elbe would also place them in the very heart of Germany. If local conversations as well as local road signs were accurate, Hannover was also less than one hundred miles southwest of the Elbe's Wittenberge crossing. But, if they crossed, it could be an irreversible crossing with irreversible consequences for all of them.

As they walked down the busy main street toward the ferry crossing Volodya was the first to express his reservations. "Let's walk through this plan before we go crossing over. You know, once we're on the other side there will be no turning back. We'll be Germans, or trying to pass ourselves off as Germans, in heartland Germany. That will be really deep heartland Germany. We've been damn lucky so far playing the part of nomads, looking a little like Germans, talking or mumbling a little like Germans. But again, it's been mostly just dumb luck. Maybe we're better off staying close to the eastern border, blending in with more locals, whether they're German or Polish or whomever from wherever. The war rumors aren't that good either. The Germans are switching to more of a defensive strategy because of the success of those Americans and their allied buddies in northern France. And the Russians keep coming from the east. That means the Germans will be surrounded, we'll be surrounded along with them. We're far better off slipping back east, sidestepping around and then behind our Russian "friends." And then we just disappear among the millions of nameless refugees all over eastern Europe. I say let's not cross."

Surprising everyone, the caravan's undisputed leader, and cheerleader, just stood and listened, showing little emotion while Volodya stated his concern. The ferry was only a few dozen paces away, loaded and ready. It also appeared to be only minutes away from departure. Then with everyone still focusing their attention on him, their hard charging leader nodded his approval of Volodya's position. With that nod he then spoke to his caravan family. "You're right, my dear friend. We'll be deeply inGermany, presumed to be Germans or German sympathizers. And those same Germans, who were once our hated invaders, will probably become our only protectors. How ironic. The battlefield rumors also suggest the Germans will likely be this war's losers. So, we'll be trapped between those Yankee winners on our west, the Soviets on our east. Maybe you're right. We should stop here then sneak back east and just disappear." The logic was simple but persuasive for an eastward reversal and definitely no Elbe crossing. As they drew closer to the tentative game plan of Hannover and the invitation from Ivan's former employer, Ivan also must have questioned the wisdom of that possible reunion. Accepting the protective arm of his Nazi boss? Reconnecting Ivan's wife with her romantic German interest? What was he thinking? Why would he push his caravan across the Elbe?

No one moved. The ferry appeared ready to remove its shorelines and push west. It was Polya, typically quiet and compliant Polya, who finally stepped forward, starting a brisk march forward to the waiting ferry. She had draped her trusty, now thoroughly threadbare, shoulder bag over one shoulder. It contained what few changes of clothing remained, plus her small but invaluable woolen shawl. Baby Tamara was nestled in another threadbare bag over her other shoulder. After a dozen steps she stopped, turned back to her fellow travelers and declared, "I'm going across the Elbe! We've struggled but survived for what must have been ten thousand miles to get this far. I'm far more worried about the Soviets behind us than I am about the Germans around us. And I certainly have no interest in revisiting the endless hell we traveled through in either Poland or Byelorussia. We also know what we can expect if somehow we return, maybe are forced to return, to Borisov. Besides, it's most likely we'll find ourselves in a Germany that will be a defeated Germany, controlled by the winning Allies, whether American or British or French. I'd much rather take my chances as a refugee, even as an Allied prisoner, instead of turning back. So, my dear leader and my dear fellow travelers, are you with me?"

Polya stared at her fellow travelers, smiled at them and waited for a response. She was also smiling at herself, pleased, though a little surprised as well, that she had spoken out. And then, without saying a word, all three hustled up to join her for their last river crossing. It would be a historic and fateful crossing for them. And less than one year later there would be one more far more historic event at a River Elbe crossing.

This crossing, actually more of a river meeting rather than a literal crossing, took place a few miles down river from Wittenberge in the town of Torgau southwest of Berlin. On April 25, 1945 the advancing armies of the U. S. and the Soviet Union met on their respective sides of the Elbe. And, on April 26 a junior officer from the U.S. 6th Infantry Division and a junior officer from the Red Army's 5th Guards Infantry Rifle Division posed for a staged friendly handshake on the bridge spanning the Elbe. It was a brief but very symbolic show of solidarity between the two armies at the River Elbe. A complete Allied victory in Europe was only months away.

Over those hundreds of miles before that fateful Elbe river crossing the caravan made pretty decent progress. Day after day the men walked alongside the horse, the horse doing well despite its years, and keeping up a brisk pace. Though they stayed on small, less traveled roads the Borisov escapees were hardly alone. Even on these backroads they encountered small family groups, solo travelers, the occasional small ragtag contingent of German soldiers. Fortunately, the soldiers showed little, if any, interest in peasants heading east or west or just wandering aimlessly. A small band of partisans infrequently passed them by. The partisans, with ragged attire and ancient rifles, offered no more than a grunt, maybe a brief smile, and then off they headed on some brave but misguided mission to harass German troops. Otherwise, their multi-nation European escape journey was relatively uneventful and free of any serious conflict.

The journey did turn more troublesome as the caravan crossed the Polish border. They avoided contact with the local Polish population as much as they could. However, when contact was made it was quite obvious to any locals that Byeloryssians, or Russians, were passing through. And, though the Germans had inflicted immeasurable pain and suffering throughout Poland, its eastern, now Soviet, neighbor had been just as brutal and destructive. Soviet intruders were not welcome and were not trusted. The caravan prudently tried to stay on the back roads and away from towns of any size.

They deviated from that backroads routine for one brief stop in Bialystok close to the Polish border. It was one of their very few urban stops. Until a few months ago Bialystok had been a sizable Polish city straddling the Polish and Byelorussian borders. An overnight stop in a city was a risk and a major departure from the caravan's cautious strategy of staying off main roads and away from large urban centers. But against their better instincts they collectively decided a stop, a brief stop, would give them a much-needed respite from the monotony of dirty, dusty unoccupied roads and endless farmland. The three-night stay proved to be both terrifying and exciting.

Though Poland was effectively under the control of the Germans from the onset of the war there still were pockets of fierce Polish resistance in and around Bialystok. The German war machine had continued its eastward march and encircled the city. The so-called Bialystok Ghetto Uprising, though fought bravely by Jewish and Polish resistance fighters, was put down after only a few weeks. But that uprising in turn triggered a larger, more vicious German campaign to destroy not only any remnants of the ghetto but to destroy Bialystok's central city as well. Adding to the plight of the Bialystok population, Soviet forces began their push into the region from the east in the early months of 1944 as part of the "Belostok Offensive." Because of that large Soviet offensive the Germans began their own slow strategic retreat from Bialystok. As part of that westward Soviet offensive into the city the Soviet forces proceeded with their own systematic campaign to destroy what remained of the embattled city. This was the geopolitical and military picture in and around Bialystok. Bombs from the east, bombs from the west. Germans retreating but continuing to indiscriminately destroy whatever remained to destroy. Soviet forces advancing but likewise destroying. That final Soviet advance was preceded by an unprecedented nonstop two day artillery barrage of Bialystok. After those two days of destruction the Soviets marched into Bialystok. And on April 26, 1944 the Soviet army proudly declared full uncontested control of what was once a vibrant Polish border town. The Soviets also quickly began to install their own Soviet proxies and recruit Polish collaborators.

As the caravan headed into the city the caravan found itself in a town battered and bombed, with little shelter and mountains of rubble. Disappointed by what they learned and saw as they approached the eastern edge of Bialystok they found some consolation in a large encampment of Bialystok citizens on the northeastern outskirts. They were the fortunate ones who had somehow managed to escape from the wreckage of the central city. The encampment also included other fellow travelers, fleeing from wherever and whatever, heading both east and west, north and south. This encampment would provide the caravan some shelter and a much-needed pause. But it would provide little real comfort. The encampment was a large messy mix of tents, horse drawn carriages, hay wagons, a few elegant carriages, even a few battered trucks and cars. The population was large, diverse and equally ragged looking. There were Poles and Byelorussians, some additional slavic mixes. A small band of Jews had parked on the edge of the encampment as well. Those Jewish numbers weren't that large since they were the fortunate few who had escaped the Nazi effort to either imprison or exterminate what few Jews had survived the Ghetto Uprising. With so many nationalities huddled in the encampment the encampment also became a linguistic Tower of Babel. Even the similarities in Polish and Byelorussian speech were a mixed blessing. An attempt to communicate often produced some badly butchered phrase, some embarrassing or insulting word, though no insult was intended. But despite this melting pot of encampment refugees, there was relatively little conflict or violence. Everyone was in the same proverbial boat, seeking some shelter, however brief, from the ongoing carnage of Germans and Soviets.

The encampment even housed a makeshift flea market and food bazaar. There was little organization, not that much of a selection of anything. But people could nonetheless buy a few odds and ends, if they had any funds. And if one couldn't buy, one could always barter, or at least enjoy the brief entertainment of a time-honored bartering effort. The flea market, the food bazaar, the bartering. This is what drew Ivan and his caravan crew to the Bialystok encampment. They parked their wagon, unharnessed their trusty Horse and collectively relaxed. These Byelorussian escapees were for now just nondescript fellow travelers pausing for momentary shelter and safety from the ongoing war. After securing their campsite Ivan set out to buy or barter a few basics. In particular, all the caravan members, even little Tamara, were in need of fresh, non-holey blankets and new, or if not new, at least less threadbare and cleaner clothes.

While Ivan was off on business the group received its first visit from two young Bialystok hustlers, Pavel and Mikel. The two were roaming the encampment selling a little of anything and everything. The two young men were folksy but very bright, a bit brash but not offensive. They also were quite the jokesters, singers and storytellers. Our Borisov escapees had not enjoyed any of these simple pleasures - a joke, a song, a silly story - in what must have felt like years. And all became instant friends. Polahaya was particularly drawn to the boys, welcoming their lighthearted nature and wit. The two Bialystok Boys, as they were playfully labeled, were also immediately drawn to Polahaya. They were six years younger than her but were captivated by her easy-going personality, her politeness, and especially by her good looks. The Bialystok Boys easily made friends with Ludmilla and Volodya as well. Even baby Tamara looked happy and comfortable as Pavel offered a bouncy knee for her to ride on. Amidst all this cheerful meet and greet Pavel and Mikel almost forgot, though just briefly, why they were visiting this campsite. They were the encampment's undisputed reigning hustlers and vendors. And the Borisov caravan looked very much in need of the Boys' inventory of blankets and shirts. Resourcefully they carried that inventory in two very large, very beaten up, but usable suitcases. And just as they were mixing laughs and stories along with their sales pitches Ivan returned.

He had been roaming the encampment, not yet daring to venture into the heart of the city. He returned empty handed. He then noticed the suitcase "showroom" spread out around the wagon. After his fruitless exploration, Ivan was definitely interested. But he also noticed the attention these two strangers were lavishing on Polahaya, along with the reciprocal smiles and attention Polahaya was directing toward these unwelcome intruders. Yes, chronically jealous, impulsive Ivan only saw them as very unwelcome intruders into his campsite. He stomped over to them, glared down at them as they sat by Polahaya and the showroom, and in a menacing tone demanded, "Who the hell are you? And who invited you to come here and hassle my family?" The Boys were startled and frightened by this very unfriendly greeting from Ivan, a tall very fit man who was standing directly over them. Polahaya came to their rescue. "Ivan, don't be such a bully. They're just two nice young men who dropped by. They're refugees like the rest of us, trying to get by, trying to make a modest living in all this chaos. They're resourceful, they're bright." She paused for a moment and then added, "And, they're hustlers, just like you. Now, sit down, chat, get to know them. Share your jokes and stories, and toss in a few lies, just like they've done with us." Ivan stepped back from the Boys. Looking at these two hustlers he probably saw some of his old self, doing his own share of hustling in the streets and alleys of Borisov. In a few seconds his scowl faded, and before long he and the Boys were exchanging stories and their respective hustling adventures. They collectively recognized a common thread connecting the three of them. All three were hustlers and opportunists as Polahaya had noted. And all three enjoyed the sheer thrill of the hustling or the pursuit of some wild new "opportunity" almost as much as any actual success.

Over a modest dinner and generous pours of vodka the Boys shared more details of their business around the encampment and in Bialystok as well. Essentially, Pavel and Mikel's business was to scavenge around the wreckage of downtown Bialystok for whatever might be of value. It was a risky business wandering around town. Homes weren't always vacant as the Boys assumed. That would result in a very hasty exit. The most fruitful central business district remained a perpetual war zone among Germans, Soviets and Polish partisans. The two major forces also kept up their indiscriminate shelling of buildings and roads. If one side couldn't control a particular strategic sector it would destroy whatever it could and deny the other side any small advantage. Scavenging could be, and all too often was, a very dangerous business. But it could also be very profitable. With a smile Pavel summarized their dangerous daily thievery around town as "borrowing," not theft. Everything would eventually be returned to its proper place somehow, some day. And they presented this "borrowing" sales pitch with a straight face!

After listening to what might loosely be labeled their "business model" Ivan lifted up his vodka glass and declared to his newly adopted friends, "Count me in! We can only stay here in Bialystok for three nights at most. Then we have to keep moving westward. But I can provide you an extra set of eyes and arms, an extra strong back and some muscle if it's needed. Give me a third of whatever profit you make from your so called "borrowing" efforts. Oh, by the way, I will also buy five blankets from you and two pretty shirts for my lovely women. And do you have a pretty outfit for my little Tamara?"

The trio sealed this new business partnership with one more vodka toast, followed by hardy bear hugs. After that brief celebration Ivan looked to Polahaya, as an afterthought, for her approval. She looked first at her own newly adopted little brothers. She imagined either Boy could have been her own beloved Pyotr the Pest. Her Bialystok Boys stared at her with wide smiles. They were silly, smitten teenagers. And they also were clearly excited about adding this clever, tough opportunist to their business. Ivan sat across them, fidgeting in his seat and displaying an equally wide grin, directed at both of them and his wife. He was a hardy drinker and impervious to the copious vodka shots. He was also clearly excited about this new "opportunity," however brief it might be. With this trio of smiles in front of her Polahaya realized there was no way she could undo this partnership. The best she could do was to warn them in her quiet and sweet voice, "You will be shot or blown up. Or maybe you'll be captured and tortured by Germans or Soviets. It won't make any difference which enemy it is. And for what? Some ragged clothes, a few silver pieces, maybe a cute vase? And a few paltry kopeks or marks as the return for your reckless prowling around town. You all are very crazy and very kstupid. And I can't stop you." She fixed her gaze on all three of them and with a smile and a wave of her hand simply said, "Go." Ivan gave his wife a tender kiss and sheepishly said, "Thank you." That very first night in Bialystok Ivan went on his first "borrowing" adventure.

The next three nights were very productive, as was the daytime selling and bartering. Even Ludmilla and Volodya joined on the second and third nights as scouts and lookouts. No one was shot, no one was blown up. And everyone successfully avoided any enemy troops and a cold ugly imprisonment in a damp dark basement. The profits were decent. But after three nights Ivan, with considerable reluctance, advised his Borisov escapees they needed to continue their move west. Leaving this "business opportunity" was very difficult for Ivan. For Polahaya it was particularly difficult to leave her wild, lovable little brothers.

Though the Bialystok stop was brief, Polahaya in particular remembered that stop with some fondness. And, Bialystok would later serve as a helpful "birthplace" for her to list on immigration papers. With a mixture of good luck and sparsely traveled back roads, the caravan's westward travel was largely uneventful. There were no serious confrontations with locals, except for the occasional shouts and glares, as the caravan passed by. Nor were there any military encounters - except one.

Traveling along a large untilled stretch of farmland in the middle of nowhere Poland, the caravan stopped for a brief lunch break. "Horse" was unhitched from the wagon, as was the custom, and tethered to a weathered fence post. The countryside was relatively flat, the flatness altered only slightly by the occasional small hilltop. The sky was clear and bright blue, the luncheon setting peaceful and quiet. Suddenly the quiet was disrupted by a faint but increasingly louder noise somewhere beyond the nearby hill. Polahaya was the first to notice the noise, a very atypical noise since there was rarely any kind of noise at all out here in the middle of nowhere and with no population. "I think I hear an airplane, maybe a big truck, heading toward us," she said. Ivan quickly jumped to his feet and ordered Volodya, "Don't run, don't act nervous, but go to the horse to keep it calm and secured to the post." The noise grew louder and then a black speck appeared above the hilltop. As the speck, now a recognizable plane, cleared the hilltop it abruptly darted upward. Ascending into the sky, the frightened travelers saw its sleek fuselage and a sharp pointed nose. It was painted in deep dark gray, appearing almost black. And under that dark painted nose the plane displayed its distinctive bright yellow patch. The roar of the engine was less a deafening roar and much more so an ear piercing and ominous whining noise. Like the sound of some monstrous wasp or bee from hell zeroing in on a poor defenseless human. After that quick, steep, but short climb the plane's pilot reversed course and pointed that yellow underbelly into a steep downward dive. A dive that was directed straight at the terrified travelers. The picnic party was in the crosshairs, literally so, of a much feared and very deadly German fighter plane.

This was the prized, highly successful creation of German engineer Willy Messerschmitt: the Bf 109. The terrified travelers didn't know the plane's formal name, certainly wouldn't care. All they knew was that it was a German fighter plane, quite evident by the distinct German cross on each wing. And as it continued its downward dive toward them, they now could clearly see the guns positioned under each wing, and aimed directly at them.

Ivan turned his attention back to the women and shouted above the whining noise, "Smile and look pretty. And hold the baby. Make sure they can see the baby." As the plane flew lower and closer Ivan again yelled out to all, "Smile, wave your arms in a nice to see you manner. Don't panic. And don't run. Look friendly" The plane kept descending and its engine continued to deliver its ear-piercing whine. The noise sent Tamara into uncontrollable sobs and screams. And as the four adults struggled to smile and wave, the mystery fighter buzzed directly over the top of them and no more than twenty feet overhead. The caravan foursome held their fake poses, held their breath, then collectively collapsed as the plane gained altitude and flew straight on to somewhere, hopefully somewhere far far away from them. Polahaya unleashed a long list of curses and everyone cheered as the demon plane continued eastward. But the cheers stopped as they saw the plane bank hard quickly to the left and gain altitude. And in what seemed like only a second, the plane executed a tight 180-degree loop and there it was, once again, heading directly at them. "Volodya, hitch Horse to the wagon. Hurry! Polya and Ludmilla get Tamara and get under the wagon. Now!" Ivan and Ludmilla worked hard to keep Horse calm while they clumsily attempted to harness the horse. Ivan instinctively knew that harnessing the horse would be useless since they couldn't begin to outrun or escape from the oncoming plane. But it was something to do instead of just standing there, frozen and paralyzed, on a country road. Shelter under the wagon wouldn't provide any protection either. But it again was better than just standing out on the road. As they all scrambled and struggled, the damnable plane went into a deep dive. And aiming directly at the wagon, the pilot unleashed a terrifying volley of machine gun fire. The volley produced a very long ugly gouge in the field, which gouge ran parallel to the wagon and only about thirty or forty feet to one side. The sadistic pilot clearly didn't miss his target. He simply meant to terrorize the helpless country travelers. And he succeeded. With that cruel gesture the pilot gained altitude immediately. And this time he did continue on his eastward journey.

The two women slowly, cautiously emerged from under the wagon and ran to Ivan and Volodya who had somehow managed to keep their terrified Horse under control. Hugs were exchanged, tears were shed by all and then everyone began to dance and cheer as they celebrated surviving their near-death experience. Ivan, in a trembling but forceful voice, said to the others, "We're leaving. Harness old Horse. We need to gett as far away and as fast as we can from that goddamn crazy pilot."

The women quickly climbed on board, the men and Horse moved double time down the road, and in the opposite direction from the madman pilot. Everyone moved in a near run for about fifty yards and then Polahaya let out an ear-piercing shout, "Stop! Stop! We forgot Tamara!" Yes, there was little Tamara lying on the dirt road swaddled comfortably in a blanket. She was awake and calm and she wasn't wailing any more since that nasty airplane engine noise was now very faint. Polahaya was momentarily frozen in place on the wagon as she stared at her roadside baby bundle. Then she leaped from the wagon and sprinted to check on Tamara. Gratefully Tamara appeared to be perfectly fine and unharmed except for some dirt and dust on her face. Embracing her baby, Polahaya whispered soothing motherly words. Ivan was there just seconds behind her and the two drew into a collective embrace with Tamara smothered between them. As they walked back to the waiting wagon, with Ivan now holding the baby, Polahaya quietly but forcefully unleashed another round of curses, though this time directed at herself, not some unknown pilot. "What a damn fool! Just a damn stupid fool!" she said. "How could I be so careless and selfish to think only about me and climbing on that beat up damn wagon?" Ivan walked by her side, allowing her to vent. Then he paused, offered another collective hug and simply said, "We all forgot. But we're all safe now. Let's go on to Germany." Nothing more was said and the caravan continued westward. Tamara knew nothing of what had happened.

****

It wasn't until decades later that Polahaya, now the American Pauline, told Tamara about her near abandonment in the fields of Poland. Over the years I periodically teased my older sister about being unwanted and being left on a Polish pasture to be picked up - maybe - by some Polish peasant. Or maybe it could have been a gypsy? Then she truly would be Polish instead of just being a fake "Pole" as documented on our parents' immigration papers. Fortunately for me she wasn't left behind. If she had been left I wouldn't have my big tough sister to protect me from the bigger, tougher boys who enjoyed hassling scrawny, loudmouth me during my early years in America

****

Every so often the caravan met some fellow travelers and received bits and pieces of the war. German troops had been decisively routed as part of a massive Soviet offensive in Byelorussia. The Soviets were advancing westward, German troops were continuing to retreat westward as well. For the caravan, for all too obvious reasons, there was no option but to move deeper into Germany and to do so as quickly as possible. But where?

Chapter 12 - German Sanctuary

"The great decisions of human life have as a rule far more to do with instincts…. than with conscious will and well-meaning reasonableness."

Carl Gustav Jung

It was a disappointment to receive orders from German high command directing Major Kohl to evacuate the garrison from Borisov. The ordered evacuation was necessary because of reliable intelligence about an imminent massive Soviet offensive into Byelorussia. Major Kohl, eager and impatient for some real combat, had hoped for different orders, maybe some strategic defense of his garrison. But, he dutifully put together detailed plans for the evacuation.

Under those same high command orders, the evacuation included eliminating all of Borisov's prison camps. Soviet troops entering Borisov from the east a few weeks later would add to the carnage at those camps. Fortunately, because of the rapid Soviet advance Kohl was spared direct involvement in the dismantling and destruction of the camps. For Kohl such direct involvement would have included the extermination of the camps' prisoners. Kohl was doubly fortunate to receive those evacuation orders in time for him and his troops to escape from the bloody military victory of the Soviet army in Byelorussia. Through an ever-changing series of orders Kohl eventually was sent back to Hannover. He had hoped for just such an assignment and was rewarded with a new posting there in October of 1944. Hannover had been his post prior to the reassignment to Borisov. It was also his birthplace. And, though his parents and older brother were dead, all three victims of this ugly war, Hannover still provided many fond memories for the major.

He had shared some of those memories during the occasional visits with his housekeeper Polahaya. Kohl might even have shared a memory or two with his sometimes friend, Ivan the honor guard. In helping Ivan and his family effect an escape from Borisov the major also casually, but not too seriously, urged Ivan to contact Kohl in Hannover. Little did Kohl know how invaluable that offhanded invitation would be to Ivan and Polahaya. Kohl also under appreciated the resolve of Ivan the opportunist, and now Ivan the opportunistic head of his expanded family,

Stefan Mirovich had likewise enjoyed his visits with the major, including the major's childhood memories of Hannover. Mirovich was considered a friend but was also a mystery to Kohl. Mirovich appeared to be neither a collaborator with the Germans nor a Soviet sympathizer. But, the Soviets apparently concerned Stefan enough that he spoke increasingly with Major Kohl about Stefan's need to leave the relative safety of Borisov. As Kohl had invited Ivan to Hannover, Kohl extended the same, and more sincere, invitation to Stefan Mirovich. One day Stefan was teaching at the local schools, the next day he was gone. Where and why, no one knew for sure. But, in the spring of 1944 Stefan vanished. He would reappear in the late fall of 1944 in Hannover, one of countless thousands of homeless, war weary refugees from wherever in Europe.

For the caravan the daily and singular mission was to continue westward. But, where westward? That question took on greater urgency as they approached what looked and felt like German countryside. There were also German road signs, notably those pointing toward Berlin. Collectively the caravan decided Berlin presented too much uncertainty and risk. Heading further into the less populated interior seemed more sensible and safer. The Soviet army was advancing westward, and it was prudent to stay as far ahead of the Soviets as possible. It certainly would be awkward, even dangerous, to explain to Soviet soldiers why Byelorussian peasants were traveling deep into German territory. There also were reports of a huge and successful military campaign by allied forces in France. That massive Allied force was heading east, liberating cities and citizens across the war's western front. Maybe, just maybe, this small band of refugees, even if they were Byelorussian refugees, could also be liberated by those allied forces. Alternatively, by Ivan's calculation Hannover was maybe only 290 kilometers further west. They had struggled and survived through almost 1600 kilometers so far. They could certainly power through another 290 kilometers, prudently taking a wide detour around Berlin, then heading due west to Hannover. Hannover, the city Stefan had mentioned, maybe the city into which Stefan had disappeared. It was also the city to which Major Kohl had "invited" Ivan and Polahaya to escape, if they could. With nothing to lose, plus no better options to explore, the sensible decision was to continue westward to Hannover.

Chapter 13 - Hotel Hannover

"Oh for a lodge in some vast wilderness….
Where rumor of oppression and deceit,
Of unsuccessful or successful war
Might never reach me."

William Cowper

That final leg of their European adventure was even more chaotic. There was civilian and military traffic both east and west. There was a fateful decision to make at the Elbe River crossing. The old but trustworthy Horse was on its proverbial and literal last leg. Though with some regret, the band mercifully released their beloved horse in a meadow on the southern edge of Berlin. They pressed westward, often on foot, occasionally securing a short ride from a kind stranger. Polahaya had regained her strength. But, she could and did put on a sympathetic show of frailty, mixed with charm - and a cute infant - when they met fellow strangers. Fortunately, few cared, at least for now, about anyone's nationality. Ivan in particular had become adept at enough survival German to offer acceptable explanations and pleas for help. Therefore, rides were offered, stories, (maybe lies?) were shared. And, on the first day of November 1944 the 1900-kilometer exodus from Borisov ended as the caravan approached the eastern edge of Hannover. It would be their sanctuary for the next five years. But, it certainly was not a very charming or inviting city that greeted them as they entered.

The caravan found their first temporary shelter, primitive as it was, in an empty tool shed adjacent to an equally empty, and barely habitable home. As the others rested, Ivan ventured out on a cautious foray further into the city. That exploration provided him a more eye-opening and very grim picture of this once important industrial city.

When the war began in 1939, Hannover had been Germany's sixth largest city, with a population of 471,000. By the war's end in 1945 the population would be reduced to slightly over 200,000. It was a major rail hub with two busy east-west routes and two north-south routes. Three massive AG Continental factories produced various military vehicles, aircraft and rubber parts. A multitude of small weapons were built in the Niedersachsen complex. Tracked vehicles were rolled out daily at the sister Hanomag factory. The two sprawling Dawrag and Nerog refineries on the west edge of town supplied gas and motor oil for the ongoing war effort. All that vital military support was scattered in and around Hannover. The military support was invaluable, and every site was operational. But it ceased to be operational once British and American Air power undertook an intensive campaign against Hannover's wartime production.

Beginning in the spring of 1943 that allied aerial assault was relentless, highly effective, and very destructive. Between that spring 1943 start and the last raid on March 3, 1945 the RAF Bomber Command and the U.S. Air Force coordinated 88 raids. The British fondness for bureaucratic recordkeeping at times rivaled that of its German bureaucratic rivals. At the end of that two year aerial campaign the recordkeeping was not only exhaustive but also very informative. 4800 residents, plus 2000 generically labeled "others," were somehow documented as killed during the raids. Fifty-two percent of the central city's structures were either heavily damaged or totally destroyed. And at war's end, as the allies undertook some sort of reconstruction effort, over 7.5 million cubic meters of rubble were removed.

The famous, or infamous, two day "Black Friday" raid of October 8 and 9, 1943 produced its own set of gruesome statistics. Five hundred assorted British aircraft were joined by 200 American planes on the first day's run, whose bombing run lasted only 40 minutes. The aerial ordnance count was extraordinary: 34 thousand high explosives, 900 thousand incendiary explosives, 50 thousand aerial bombs. Fourteen thousand residences were totally destroyed or severely damaged. Hannover's old and picturesque medieval town, thus far unscathed, was now totally demolished. The town's once lively City Center had been leveled just a few months earlier. Factories, residential areas, the commercial heart, even the historic medieval quarter. All were targeted, leaving little that could be considered commercially viable or habitable. This pile of rubble is what Ivan, Polya and their caravan companions would call their sanctuary for the next five years.

Hannover historically had supported a large and prosperous Jewish population. But, the German army forced that unwanted citizenry out of their homes, then forced those Jews into relocation camps into what was once independent Poland. Other local citizens likewise fled from Hannover in significant numbers as the allied bombing continued to turn much of Hannover into rubble. Fewer functioning factories, fewer citizens, whether wanted or unwanted, less and less optimism from the civilians. The same dwindling optimism was evident throughout the resident German army force. And there was less and less certainty about a grand victory for the Third Reich. About all that remained in Hannover was the depleted remnants of the 19th Infantry Division headquarters. And, that headquarters was staffed in part by Major Heinrich Kohl.

One consolation from all that devastation and a shrinking population was that it provided Ivan and his party several options for housing. They left their miniscule shed the very next day in search of something bigger and better. On the eastern edge of town a modest but pleasant neighborhood had suffered considerable damage. But, there were a few nice sized homes, now abandoned, that had suffered only partial hits from an allied bomb. With no occupants, certainly no inquiring neighbors, the travel weary band could set up housekeeping.

Their selection was equal parts desperation and expedience. Everyone was desperate to end their marathon cross-Europe buggy ride which offered only cold damp ground or backbreaking hard buggy boards as their daily sleeping options. Therefore, a home, any home, in any neighborhood, was everyone's fervent wish. As they cautiously explored the neighborhood one lone abandoned house, even if half was demolished by allied air strikes, was still standing right there in front of them. It beckoned them to enter.

The western half of the house was basically a large rubbish pile of wood and shattered glass. There also was a sizable pile of bricks from what must have been, a long time ago, a cozy end wall fireplace. The eastern half of the house was intact including, to their surprise, a completely functioning front door. There was a modest kitchen but no surviving stove or sink. The home included a decent sized living room. There was no bathroom, no bedrooms, but a large assortment of blankets, towels, bedding and discarded clothing. And they had an intact roof, even if only half a roof, over their heads. With a smile they set up housekeeping. Everyone also indulged in the playful daily ritual of formally entering through that useless front door.

This newly acquired mansion, or half-mansion, would be just fine. They huddled collectively in the most sheltered corner. They improvised and built a fire pit along the demolished west wall debris, using the pit for makeshift meals and a little warmth from the increasingly cooler autumn breezes. Everyone improvised as needed when nature called. And no one was forced to spend one more night sleeping - or trying to - on the ground.

Having settled into the new shelter Ivan left his family and once again went exploring. He picked up some news about the army group still housed in Hannover. With that encouraging information Ivan set out to attempt contact with his one-time "employer" from Borisov. Major Kohl might not even be in town, a reunion might not result in friendly greetings or offers of help. Ivan was just as likely to be identified as some enemy "soviet" wandering deep into central Germany. Despite the risks and the uncertainties, Ivan decided he had little to lose, possibly much to gain, by pursuing that hoped-for reunion. Ivan had also honed his language skills along their European trek to such a degree that he might pass for any refugee, from anywhere. Ivan, ever the bold opportunist, did locate the headquarters. He put on a convincing performance of youthful charm, feigned humility, and a hint of desperation about his family's plight. He was rewarded with the news that Major Kohl was in fact here in Hannover.

New shelter was an absolute necessity. Ivan readily acknowledged that. And he also had to admit to himself he couldn't tackle that task on his own. There were entirely too many Germans, civilian and military, everywhere, even in the bombed out sectors. There also was the persistent daily risk of another allied bombing run, anywhere and anytime. Ivan's only sensible strategy was to swallow his pride, connect with Kohl, and ask for his help.

Necessity notwithstanding, Ivan struggled to begin that search, fighting against the very idea of seeing Kohl again. Ivan couldn't say he hated the Major. Though grudgingly, Ivan would even have to admit he admired the Major, just a little. But there was so much to dislike. Yes, the Major had provided security, both financial and physical, in Borisov. Yes, Ivan had to admit to himself, the Major had supplied that ego boosting honor guard uniform and the bragging rights as a "senior" honor guard. But despite those perks and preferences which he provided, Kohl was nothing more than another barbarian, this time a German barbarian, who had invaded Ivan's motherland, and also destroyed Ivan's pre-war comfortable life. And Ivan couldn't dismiss the troubling fear that Kohl's "good deed" recruitment of Ivan as an honor guard would come back to haunt Ivan after the war.(And it certainly would during Ivan's later DP years.) In hindsight Ivan should have said thanks but no thanks to that "honor" position. Kohl had sucked him into that job, not for Ivan's benefit but solely for the benefit of that German invader.

Kohl had also spent too much time with Ivan's Polahaya. She really wasn't Kohl's housekeeper, Ivan knew that. She hardly did any housework. All Ivan could remember was Kohl constantly inviting her to sit down for tea or inviting her to sit on the corner of Kohl's office desk and laugh at his stupid jokes. It was disgusting, embarrassing behavior by the both of them. It certainly was far more than just silly flirtation. And Ivan couldn't rid himself of a nagging suspicion that there was something far more personal, and intimate, between the two of them. With those memories, with that nagging suspicion, how on earth could he even think about reuniting the so-called "housekeeper" and that phony employer?

Pride and vanity made the trek to Kohl's office more difficult as well. "I'll have to look so damn humble and grateful" Ivan kept telling himself. But humility and displays of gratitude didn't come easily for Ivan. Kohl would see him as weak, as some hapless phony. Kohl would expect, probably demand, Ivan to grovel and beg. Then afterward he'd boast to Ivan's Polahaya and paint a pathetic picture of Ivan's groveling, in such stark contrast to Kohl's generosity.

Ivan would also have to endure that humiliating meeting in front of the German barbarian who would be strutting about in his finest military attire. Ivan imagined the uniform, so clean and pressed, and adorned with all those shiny buttons and gaudy medals. And there Ivan would be, very ragged, dirty, unshaven. And with no uniform! What a contrast, and just one more layer of humiliation to which Ivan would be subjecting himself.

How could Ivan go through with this meeting? Several times along the route Ivan stopped to reconsider the wisdom of his plan. Once he even turned around and walked several spaces before admitting, once again, this is what he had to do. With that storm of conflicting emotions inside his head Ivan did continue on. He found the headquarters, introduced himself to the guard at the entrance and asked to speak to Major Heinrich Kohl. As Ivan waited for the guard to return he took a closer look at what passed for a German command post. It was such a stark contrast to the military mansion Ivan remembered visiting in Borisov.

The building was a simple, weathered and quite small storefront. It was located on the edge of the city center and close to one of the major munitions factories. A canopy over the entry door was literally hanging by a few threads and at any moment could come crashing down on an unsuspecting soldier or citizen. Merchandise had been removed, replaced with miscellaneous crates, chairs and tables. And, as could be expected, every piece of furniture was weighed down with papers: orders, messages, requisitions, whatever. A few soldiers constantly scurried around like ants, moving all those important papers. Ivan was ushered to the back of the store, behind what once must have been the checkout counter, and to a doorway. The door itself had been removed. And in a small back room which prior to the war must have served as the shipowner's office Ivan saw his old Borisov employer, Major Heinrich Kohl.

The major's makeshift command post was no more than 12x12. The flooring was old, groaning and squeaking with every step, and with one ancient, dull and small carpet at the entry to the office. Maybe it was there to have everyone wipe their boots before entering. But, soldiers didn't wipe. Maybe it was there to provide one modest decorative touch. The office did have one standard issue office desk which had been requisitioned from somewhere. The desk, just like the furnishings in the front of the store, was decorated with the obligatory mountain of papers. A swivel chair, again an army issue, had been included. The one curious addition to the tiny office's decor was an old stuffed chair. It was clean, only slightly frayed at the arms, and it looked comfortable. Kohl had it stored in the back corner of his office and apparently did not make it available to others. Possibly, and ever so briefly, he might indulge himself and sink into the stuffed chair, escaping from army issued furniture, maybe escaping from the daily grind.

As Ivan surveyed his surroundings, he couldn't help but smile, ever so slightly, at the ironic, almost comical, reversal of fortune for the German major. He had invaded Ivan's homeland and enjoyed a comfortable tour of duty in an elegant mansion. Yet, here was that invader, now having retreated to his homeland, even to his hometown. And now he was commanding his troops from a rundown, abandoned storefront. Ivan also suspected the stuffed chair in Kohl's backroom headquarters served as Kohl's bed.

Ivan walked into the office and found the Major seated at his desk. Ivan approached the desk and politely, if half-heartedly, extended a hand. Kohl remained seated, remained seemingly engrossed in some document, and did not extend a hand in return. Contrary to Ivan's mental image, the Major was likewise unshaven, his uniform was dirty and wrinkled, with buttons only partly buttoned up. And Major Kohl looked tired, very tired. Though it had been only half a year since they had last met, the Major looked as if he had aged years instead of months. Ivan stood at the desk for what felt like hours. Then Ivan, in an angry tone, said, " We need a place to live."

The Major looked up from his papers, motioned Ivan to remove papers from a chair (not the stuffed chair) and sit down. He stared at his former honor guard, still saying nothing. After another interminable period of silence Ivan broke that silence by saying, "Bad beginning by me and I'm sorry, very sorry. The family and I would really appreciate your help in finding us some decent shelter. Something that has an entire roof and four complete walls." With that softened apologetic restart the two men caught up on the last several months.

Major Kohl began. "I know I suggested Hannover as a possible destination. I'm also very impressed, actually amazed, you made it this far. Quite the feat, I must admit, for any man. And it's doubly impressive because you brought a small caravan of family and friends with you. Unfortunately for you, and for me, Hannover is a very unfriendly and dangerous place. We're bombed every day. We're losing this godforsaken war. And it's very likely all of us - you, your family, and yes, even I - will be prisoners of the Allies within a year. We never should have waged this insane campaign to conquer all of Europe. But here I am, still the dutiful soldier, defending this battered city, at least what's left of it. Now tell me about your family and that crazy European road trip."

The proverbial ice was broken, the tension eased for both of them. Then Ivan and Major Kohl settled into recaps of their very different but equally difficult challenges since their respective escapes from Borisov. After he relived the European road trip, complete with rivers and fighter planes, Ivan proceeded to paint a stark and grim picture of their current accommodations, emphasizing the added health risks to little Tamara. Major Kohl, with some hesitation, asked about the health of his favorite housekeeper. And Ivan, to his credit, remained polite and at ease. With all the pleasantries and war stories out of the way, the Major pledged to quickly find a far better shelter. And he would do so the very next day.

Ivan stood up and prepared to leave. But the Major raised one more subject. "Your position as my senior honor guard in Borisov. You conducted yourself well and I sincerely appreciated your service. However, I suspect, and fear, that assignment will cause more headaches and pain than you deserve. And for that I sincerely apologize." There was a long, awkward pause after that apology. Ivan just stood there, uncertain what, if anything, to say. "Thanks." Maybe. Or, "I'm alive but running from everyone here. So, any apologies are hardly what I need right now." But Ivan decided, prudently, not to say a word, just offer a feeble smile and shrug his shoulders. Major Kohl broke the uncomfortable silence, gesturing for Ivan to sit back down. And then the major continued.

"It was with the best of intentions that I offered you that guard position. I placed you in the least troublesome of the prison facilities in Borisov. Its inmates were only the petty thieves, the young, tough talking, tough acting kids who weren't smart enough to keep their mouths shut in front of my German troops. And, yes, there were the assorted Jews and gypsies who stupidly did not escape quickly enough or weren't bright enough to keep a low profile and a closed mouth. We both know they all were either too old or just harmless. But I had to follow orders and, whether old or harmless, I had to put them inside those barbed wire fences that you guarded."

"I intentionally did not assign you to guard duty at any of the military prisoner of war sites. I also did not assign you to the hard labor work sites. I know, from my conversation with other guards and even a few prisoners, that you were not some ugly, violent guard indiscriminately beating up helpless old men and women. Yes, I did watch you strut around in your fancy uniform, thumping your nightstick loudly against the prison fence posts, trying to look tough and scary. But I saw that frequent smile, and I saw the friendly chats with the prisoners."

"Unfortunately, my good intentions and your good behavior won't make a damn bit of difference. Not to any Soviets. Not to any Allied troops. And it won't make any difference to many angry and vengeful Borisov townsfolk. In the eyes of your former friends and neighbors you will most likely be a traitor. And Soviets and Allies might, probably will, label you a Nazi collaborator. As much as I would try to come to your defense, offer an explanation, no one will listen. No one will care."

"Maybe there would have been a better, safer life for you and Polya had we never struck this devil's bargain as my honor guard. Maybe not. But here you are, far from home, threatened from the west, threatened from the east. No place to hide. And I'm the one responsible for your plight. Again, I'm truly sorry."

Ivan sighed, offered more of a smile, and said, "I do appreciate the apology. But it's not really needed nor necessary. I accepted your offer in Borisov and did so freely, so gladly. No coercion, no hesitation. Just me, the young tough guy, a very arrogant tough guy, jumping at the next so-called "opportunity." Explanations, excuses, maybe lies, about my past will come later. Now finding a decent roof over our heads is my sole priority."

"Be careful, be smart, be invisible, if possible." That was all the advice Major Kohl could offer his former employee. With those parting words both men now did shake hands. The next day Major Kohl visited the half-bombed house that had been the caravan's shelter and he undertook the task of relocating everyone to a much nicer and warmer winter home.

An integral part of that critical mission by Major Kohl was to discreetly relocate the group to a less conspicuous neighborhood. Their first half-destroyed home had served them reasonably well.

Their refuge did have a gaping hole in the roof and only half of a wall whose defects weren't that troublesome on a muggy early autumn day or night. But, that hole and the destroyed wall provided no shelter from the approaching cold winds and frequent rain of fall in north central Germany. With winter approaching, old residents of this neighborhood were returning to their homes, bombed and battered as those homes were. The caravan needed better shelter. But it also needed privacy from the returning local German population.

Ever resourceful, Major Kohl searched for new accommodations, complete with an intact roof, hopefully. It needed to be livable, spacious enough for the four adults, plus the baby. Equally important, their new palace needed to be in a completely abandoned neighborhood, and very likely to remain that way. Kohl's researched homesite was nestled in the middle of what had been a Jewish enclave which the locals now considered no man's land and which was of no interest to any non-Jewish German.

The Major led his new home "buyers" down a deserted street and introduced them to not one but two housing options. House number one was an all-wood structure, reasonably intact but very small and very ancient, possibly over a hundred years old. There was a massive pile of rubble next door, the end product of a seemingly precise bomb or artillery shell. Next to that rubble was a large two-story brick/stone/wood home. It was a classic German design, very intact except for a demolished front quarter which appeared to have been a cozy sunroom. The sunroom's wall and windows were destroyed but its roofline was surprisingly intact. A portion of the back north corner of the roof had suffered some sort of bombardment. But the balance of the roof was otherwise intact and stable. This home was truly a mansion, very much a stark contrast to their current half-mansion.

Standing guard in front of their new-found mansion was a German tank. Why or for how long one could only guess. The right tractor tread lay in ruins in the front yard. The tank turret had also taken quite a beating from small rocket and machine gun fire. But here the tank was, abandoned yet still very imposing, parked like some sentinel at this once elegant Jewish home. Adding to the front yard decor, a six-foot marble statue, on its low stone pedestal, likewise stood guard. The statue itself was very ancient, chipped and cracked in several places, but still straight and solid on its pedestal. No one knew, not even Major Kohl, who the ancient Germanic hero was posing so impressively on that pedestal. And any identifying inscription had been weathered away countless years ago. But it, like the abandoned tank, presented quite the impressive curbside image. As some present-day realtor might pitch it, here was some great curb appeal! The statue even had its own low rise picket fence surrounding the ancient marble hero, whoever he was. There was no debate or contest as to which home the caravan would adopt as its new shelter.

The Jewish population which had once enjoyed this quiet neighborhood and its tidy homes had been decimated by mass relocations and senseless killings. Those few who survived the reprisals or relocations faced the endless threat of allied bombing runs. Therefore, escape and disappearance to some rural outpost was better than struggling to survive in urban Hannover. Besides, there was nothing of real value to which a Jewish homeowner could return. Looters had stripped every home of anything that might be of value and also destroyed anything that might be of personal or sentimental value. The one consolation, and a bittersweet irony, for this once tranquil Jewish enclave was that the British and American bombs largely spared it from any significant damage. Whether intentional or accidental, that escape from the bombings was a godsend for our new homeowners.

Their new home had running water, even a functioning toilet and a modest but stocked kitchen. The wood stove could actually provide a hot meal and at a sturdy wooden table for four, or maybe five if everyone huddled just a little closer. There were two usable bedrooms, one for Ivan's family and one for Ludmilla. Volodya, ever the friend and occasional gentleman, volunteered to make a pallet in a small pantry. There was a small wood burning furnace in what passed for a family room. And that, plus Major Kohl's Borisov blankets and the Bialystok bargains, would keep the upcoming winter from becoming too intolerable.

Daily life turned almost normal. Little Tamara grew and stayed healthy. Ludmilla remained a dear friend and aide to Polahaya as well as a loving auntie to Tamara. Volodya generated some income, or at least some bartered provisions, by offering his services as a photographer. Periodically some local, maybe a farmer or a baker, would drop by and leave a small basket of edibles. And, when asked as to why or from whom, the reply was that a nice German officer had paid for this care package.

Major Kohl likewise dropped by every so often. However, he prudently tried to do so while Ivan was out on some errand, hustling or bartering for necessities. Polahaya might even get a short respite from parenting as the major and Polahaya enjoyed a walk in the nearby park that had been spared allied bombs. For Major Kohl he was simply being kind and generous. An old courtship was now just a fond memory. Any contact, very innocent as it was, continued to annoy a perpetually jealous Ivan. But, all contact would end by the spring of 1945 and the major would disappear forever. The marriage would endure for another fifty plus years. However, Ivan could never rid himself of his jealousy and his suspicions about the seriousness of the relationship between Polahaya and Major Kohl.

****

From my early teens, when I was smart enough to begin understanding, I heard - and witnessed - my father angrily lash out at my mother for some perceived mistake or comment. And, it was a predictable part of his ugly tirade to gratuitously toss in the accusation that my mother must have loved "that Nazi" more than my father. His more damning accusation was that she must have slept with him while she was married. It would totally crush her every time. And despite her tearful, and fearful, protests my father was never convinced. In a poignant moment during her final week before death, but with a surprisingly defiant tone in her voice, Polahaya, my mother, told me she never, never was unfaithful to her husband. For fifty plus years she endured those hate filled accusations. But for fifty plus years the two of them stayed married, as that old marriage vow declares, "for better or for worse."

Chapter 14 - Liberation and Relocation

"Change is a great and horrible thing and people love it and hate it at the same time.
Without change, however, you just don't move."

Marc Jacobs

For several months the five Borisov escapees lived in relative comfort and anonymity. All that ended in April 1945. The allied advance continued, and on April 10th the 84th Infantry Division of the American army formally captured Hannover. For the non-military population this capture caused as much confusion as it provided reasons for celebration. There was little organization or support from the U.S. troops. And, after high stakes politics among the major allied powers, Hannover was handed over to the British. But, again it was weeks and then months before any plan was put in place to address the plight of countless thousands of displaced persons. And these were displaced persons not just from Germany but from countless other European countries, including Poles, Ukrainians, and Byelorussians.

For the Borisov foursome (plus one year old Tamara) the liberation of Hannover also meant the loss of the informal, but very valuable, support and protection of their German officer. Major Kohl vanished, and neither Polahaya or Ivan learned anymore about him. He would only live on in their shared memories, more fondly for Polahaya than for Ivan. The liberation of Hannover created a massive round-up of the population. For the Borisov five the roundup resulted in an eviction from their charming, and well-guarded, German "mansion" everyone had shared for the past several months. Relocation of the population, again both civilian and some military, was haphazard and clumsy.

What passed for "DP" camps (the shorthand for Europe's displaced persons) were at first large factories and warehouses. Or what factories and warehouses remained after 90% of Hannover's central commercial hub had been reduced to rubble. It was largely left to the DP's to search out and settle in with their fellow countrymen and women. It should have been a relatively simple task. But for our Borisov escapees this wasn't so simple. Ivan and Polahaya struggled to make a decision about which DP shelter they would, or even could, move into. Despite some hesitation, they chose a factory populated by a combination of Byelorussian/Ukrainian DP's. This would be their new post-war "home."

One week the refugees were lounging in a house with eye appealing brick, stone and decorative wood trim, all guarded by a mystery tank and an imposing Teutonic knight. The next week they were surrounded by cold, rusting gray factory steel, accented only with very unappealing shattered windows. That dreary steel gray mass, populated by hundreds of fellow DP's, was jokingly named by its residents as the "Hannover Hotel." It was quite the haphazard series of relocations in less than six months after the caravan arrived in Hannover: from a shed, to half a house, to a guarded mansion, to the Hannover Hotel.

This new refugee shelter was a massive 200 hundred yard long by 20-yard-wide factory. Somehow, it had survived the bombings, then had been abandoned and subsequently vandalized by looters. What remained was a cavernous, uninviting shell with its twenty foot ceiling, some unidentifiable machine parts, an assortment of rusting axles which the looters must have decided weren't worth hauling away. The factory floor was littered with nuts and bolts and screws, plus grease and oil and sand. There was no visible heating, which wasn't a problem, at least for the time being, because the weather outside was still tolerable.. But the vacant factory also didn't have any visible cooling, except for a sparse array of windows, many of which were rusted shut. Obviously, the factory was designed solely for production, not factory worker comfort. Closed windows, close quarters and periodic late summer heat waves collectively produced an unpleasant and unhealthy, sweaty shop - literally a sweatshop - for the refugees who were herded into the factory.

The refugees were relocated to this and other similar factories with cold efficiency, some semblance of politeness, but not much. After the relocation there was little added support or organization. Despite the debris and the filthy floor, soldiers did manage to mark off 20x20 sections throughout the factory, leaving some narrow walkways among those 20x20 boundaries. Each family unit was provided a supply of poles, rope, at least two, maybe three cots. Each unit was also supplied with the necessary number of blankets, pillows, even a few towels. Most importantly, each family unit was supplied with enough sheets - old, tattered but clean - to fasten however they could to create their own 20x20 "home." These "homes" were literally next to one another with the hanging sheets providing a modicum of what passed for privacy from one's neighbor. The sheets offered no sound insulation and certainly very little opportunity for candid or quiet family conversations. And there certainly was no opportunity for any marital intimacy. Gratefully, everyone, or almost everyone, adjusted to this bedsheet village into which they had been placed. Tensions remained relatively low, as did everyone's voices

The first few weeks in that factory were uneventful. Polahaya was now four months pregnant, Tamara was a healthy, energetic handful, and Ludmilla joined the family as friend and part-time nanny There was a common cooking and cleaning center plus a few, very few, outdoor toilets. Home, sweet home it was not, but it was shelter. Daily management had also changed by late May from the American 84th Infantry to two regiments of the British army.

Unfortunately, those first weeks of relative comfort, plus relative anonymity, were replaced by rumors among this group of DP's about a German collaborator in their factory. Ivan quickly became the number one suspect. The vast majority of the DP's had more to worry about day-to-day than some suspected "traitor" among them. But there were enough meddlesome DP's eager enough, or simply bored enough, to be a daily problem for Ivan and Polahaya. They would pass by the family bedsheet "apartment" and subject Polahaya to hostile stares and glares. Though their apartment received some unwelcome visits from tough talking, hard looking men, Polahaya's fellow DP women were the most intrusive and hostile. One would pull aside a bedsheet and shout out, "Where's your man? What's he up to? Who's he conspiring with today?" Another old crotchety hag would poke her head through the bedsheet and shout, "He was a prison guard, wasn't he. I know it. Others know it. And we heard he was always beating up some poor defenseless fellow Byelorussian." Just idly marking time, these women had nothing better to do than complain, suspect, accuse. And they did so persistently. And they shrewdly and prudently hurled their nasty little comments only while Ivan was not around. There was no reluctance nor fear in their continued harassment. After all big bad Ivan, even if he was around, wouldn't rough up some little old lady, would he? Men showed up far less frequently, prudently suspecting and fearing big bad Ivan's reaction to their insults would not be as restrained. The harassment was taking its toll on Polahaya. And, sadly Ivan could do little to stop the daily verbal assaults.

After five days of this abuse and with Polahaya's growing frustration, Ivan proposed a solution. Within their 20x20 apartment, late at night, and in barely a whisper, Ivan told Polahaya, "I'll disappear completely for a few days. You tell those disgusting, shriveled up old hags we had a fight. I stormed out to who knows where. You don't know when or even if I'll return. And that's just fine with you." Polahaya wasn't happy about the separation scheme or the prospect of being alone and defenseless without her Ivan. But the plan made sense. "After a few days the hags will see only poor lonesome you. Who knows? They might even offer a helping hand with Tamara. I'll recruit Ludmilla as our secret messenger, pick a handy place in the woods for us to meet and share news and notes. And after a week or two all this talk about spies and collaborators will stop. I hope."

The couple hugged, Ivan gave sleeping Tamara a gentle kiss, and off he vanished. For now, there was little policing or control of movement in and among the factory shelters. Ivan found Ludmilla, awakened her and shared his plan. She was willing to be the messenger, showing up at a designated time and place for an information exchange. Ivan easily exited the factory, slipped into the nearby forest and there he remained for the next ten days. He built a decent shelter, foraged as best he could for food and game. Periodically he slipped into the factory complexes at night and "borrowed" some food from a careless or absent apartment dweller. Though he hesitated to do so, "borrowing" was his best practical option during this hideout period. After all, he had to eat. And he certainly could not just casually walk into some factory sheet apartment, unknown and uninvited, and ask for a bite.

On the tenth night at his scheduled rendezvous with Ludmilla she shared good news. "Just as you suspected," she said, "those nasty little old women grew tired of hassling Polahaya and found something new to complain about. Also, and more importantly, everyone's attention is focused on rumors of a major relocation project. We all might be moving out of the factories and resettling in the old German work camps on the outskirts of Hannover. It should be safe for you to come back. Polahaya and Tamara are also waiting for you, especially your little Tamara. See you at the Hotel." The very next morning just before daybreak Ivan quietly slipped back into the factory. He didn't stay hidden though he did keep a lower profile. And what few people saw him didn't seem to care. The family had survived that scare but it became increasingly clear to Ivan that life as a Byelorussian DP was too uncertain and dangerous for him and his family.

As rumored, the British were planning to populate the relocation camp sites with ethnic or national groups, or at least would try to. There wouldn't be disorganized and volatile mixes of ethnic groups and nationalities. And it would be the British who would be making the resettlement decisions, not the refugees.

The huge DP camps around Hannover, in particular Camp Fallingbostel just north of town, were diverse but predominantly Polish. Poland had been invaded and its people horribly oppressed by both Germans and Soviets, not just during the war but for countless decades throughout history. Poles were a very sympathetic population. So, why not become Poles? Furthermore, the Soviets, as one of the major occupation powers, had mandated that all Soviet DP's be repatriated to their respective, supposedly beloved, Soviet republics. Byelorussia was neither a beloved nor safe place to which Ivan or Polahaya wished to return.

Indeed, why not become Poles? This time Polahaya proposed the plan. Again whispering ever so softly, with only the flimsy sheets to muffle her words, Polahaya announced to Ivan, "Let's become Poles. Sure. Poles we will be. And then we'll quietly disappear into that huge Camp Fallingbostel. It's become pretty damn clear that it's neither smart nor safe to be Byelorussians. The language differences aren't that great. I can manage. And you're very quick at picking up everyday speech. People don't ask questions. No one has any documents or identification cards, except for the poor Jews and their tattoos. It will be as simple as saying we're Poles and we want to live with our fellow Poles. I can't imagine the British wil care or question." Ivan had been considering that very plan, but he was surprised to hear Polahaya whisper that plan as well. "You're sure?", he whispered back. "There's just way too much old history, too much baggage from Borisov. Yah, I'm very sure," she replied.

And Poles they became. They definitely could and did look like any nondescript European refugee, whether Byelorussian or Polish or Czech. Their threadbare clothes fit right in with countless other Polish refugees. A cute baby bundle also helped, presenting a sympathetic family portrait. But they needed not only to say they were Polish. They needed to sound much more Polish in name.

First names first. Ivan, once Ivan the Terrible, now became that very common Jan. It would be an easy next step in America to tweak that Jan to John. Polahaya was fairly common, and she might have remained a Polahaya, or a shortened Polya. But, she and Ivan decided a more complete change would be wiser, erasing any past Borisov connection or someone's recollection. So, she became Apolonia, though she still could be a more familiar Polya. That very Byelorussian "Kupraschonik" cried out for a significant change. With a little collective imagination, the new Jan and Polya played with her maiden name (if it was her real maiden name?) and converted "Bekovsky" to a more Polish "Bykowski." They were now Polish in name, needing only to create some details, if asked, about their birthplaces. Hardly anyone in this vast European melting pot of displaced persons had any useful identifying documents such as birth certificates. Jan and Polya would fit right in.

****

Under the relative safety of citizenship in the U.S. I could, and did, in my adult years reveal my parents' Byelorussian roots. But, with that Polish last name I was frequently mistaken for a Pole. Sometimes the mislabeling as a "Pole" or "Pollack" was playful, sometimes that "Pollack" label was cruel. I survived, and I shared that Byelorussian history with whoever was curious. For Jan and Polya the name and nationality changes were indispensable factors in their eventual immigration to America.

****

Movement among the various DP camps continued to be fairly easy, at least for now. Policing was minimal. Rules and regulations were equally minimal. Consequently, it was not too difficult to pack up what few personal possessions the family had, then shop around for a new vacant 20x20 "apartment" in another DP factory. They were lucky and within a few days settled in with a sizable group of fellow Polish DP's. Sadly, that relocation and anonymity among Poles was upended after only a month.

Chapter 15 - Birth and Jail.

"At the end of the day we can endure much more than we think we can."

Frida Kohlo

More relief aid, along with more stability, were welcomed by the DP population as the British assumed formal control of their occupation zone. Polya was now eight months pregnant and British aid, maybe better accommodations, would certainly be welcome. However, the British military was not only more efficient but also more concerned about who was within the sprawling complex of DP encampments.

With some investigation, coupled with an abundance of rumors, Jan Bykowski's name came to the attention of the British intelligence officer, Captain Harold Kelly. Taking an aggressive "better safe than sorry" approach to his duties, Captain Kelly ordered Jan to be jailed. Kelly would investigate further and interrogate at his leisurely pace.The arrest took place one afternoon while Jan was taking a walk around the camp. Unfortunately for him, even more so for Polya, no one except a few British soldiers knew what happened to Jan. Jan did take frequent walks, striking up conversations, trying to hustle or barter for provisions. And, he occasionally didn't return until late at night or maybe even a day later.

For the first few days of "Jan's" absence his very pregnant wife didn't worry too much. In a lighthearted, only slightly worried, tone Polya joked with her dear friend Ludmilla. "Like some village idiot he probably drank too much with some fellow village idiots, passed out for the night and will show up later tonight. Just in time for a meal." It wasn't that improbable, and it had happened before. On the second day, and still with no sheepish and apologetic Jan showing up, Polya turned less lighthearted and more worried. "God forbid he started another fight, took a beating, and ended up in the hospital." Ludmulla did some checking, didn't find Jan, and again he didn't show up for dinner. On the third day real panic set in. Now Polya was conjuring up more serious scenarios. "He's always roaming around the camp, going everywhere, maybe even stupidly wandering too close to the Byelorussian sector. What if someone from the past recognized him? He might be a prisoner somewhere, being beaten, being tortured, maybe killed." Polya blurted out these possibilities with a mixture of dread and anger. Anger at what might have happened to her Jan, but also anger at him. With her tough, reckless and overly confident husband any one of these scenarios was possible.

The unborn child was growing more and more active. And Polya's scheduled due date was only three weeks away. Ludmilla remained the constant companion, comforting and calming Polya as best she could. Ludmilla also continued to be an energetic detective. And in three more days she solved the mystery of Jan's disappearance.

Though a dear friend and very much an integral part of the family for Polya and Jan, Ludmilla was able to enjoy some semblance of a social life outside their family circle. Young, flirtatious and almost as pretty as Polya, Ludmilla developed a budding romance with a young British soldier. She also picked up enough survival English, and she and the soldier, a soldier at the DP camp's jail, enjoyed frequent lighthearted, sometimes serious, conversations. During one of those chats Ludmilla mentioned the plight of her friend, her dear pregnant friend, Polya. Ludmilla deeply cared about her friend's plight, and it was very evident in her voice. "She's my very best friend, a very wonderful mother. And she's also ready to deliver any day," she explained to her attentive, very infatuated young soldier friend. "But," Ludmilla continued, "her husband has disappeared. No word, no clues. She's going crazy and she's fearing the worst. Please, please, can you help her find her man?" The young man was moved by the story and impulsively, though sincerely, promised to find the missing husband. Not just search for him but find him.

He was young, maybe a bit naive. But he wasn't devious or manipulative and he did sound genuinely interested in helping. And offering to help certainly couldn't hurt his budding romance with his "Polish" beauty. Ludmilla had feared she might be prodded to offer some extra "personal" favor to enlist and retain the soldier's aid. But gratefully, that wasn't necessary nor even hinted at. The soldier was on a mission to find Jan Bykowski.

To Ludmilla's surprise and relief her soldier delivered encouraging news the very next day. It was good news and bad. When the two met he shouted out, "I found him and he's alive and healthy. That's the good news." Then with less enthusiasm and almost an apologetic tone in his voice he continued. "The bad news is he's in a jail cell at camp headquarters." Rewarded with a hug and a kiss from Ludmilla, he continued. "I don't have enough rank or connections and I couldn't persuade anyone to tell me why he's in jail. Apparently, there aren't any formal charges against him, not yet at least. And there's no word as to when, or if, he'll be released." The soldier was painting an all-too-common picture of military bureaucracy. Or maybe it was just a picture of general ineptitude, confusion and indecision as the Allies attempted to restore and maintain order out of post-war chaos. If there's a threat, or a perceived threat, jail first, ask questions and sort it all out later. "The jail conditions aren't too terrible. But I was told he can't have any visitors. Period. No exceptions, no explanations. I did have a short visit with the officer in charge of the inmates and I pointed out this particular prisoner had a very pregnant wife. The best he could suggest is that messages could be sent and received though the messages would have to be screened before delivery. I can be, and I definitely want to be, your courier." With another grateful hug and kiss from Ludmilla, they collectively put together a messaging network.

Ludmilla stayed at Polya's side, helping her put together a daily short note for her imprisoned husband. Next morning Ludmillla met with her cheerful soldier courier and handed him the note. The soldier then found an opportunity during his guard detail to visit Jan and deliver the note. Jan reciprocated with his own small note which the soldier dutifully delivered to Ludmilla who then followed up with the expectant wife. Every so often Polya was even able to send a small care package to her jailed husband and expectant new father-to-be. For the next two weeks that very kind soldier, with Ludmilla's help, served as the invaluable messenger between Jan and Polya.

That messenger service was abruptly halted one late afternoon in October as Polya went into labor. Ludmilla had just dropped by, and as was her daily habit, Ludmilla handed over Jan's prison "love letter." They really weren't love letters, and hardly filled with any romantic or polished prose. But they were cute, if simple, "I love you" notes, and they were always a welcome little ritual for Polya. Except not today. This day Ludmilla found her dear friend in considerable pain, frequent contractions, and a very panicked expression on her face. "Forget the note," she moaned. "I need to get to the hospital. Now!" That wasn't so easy a task for poor Ludmilla. No big, brawny spouse to help. A very inadequate Camp Fallingbostel hospital, designed primarily for the occasional cuts and bruises and breaks. The hospital for serious medical attention, including pregnancies, was in Cuxhaven. And Cuxhaven was ten miles away. Nor was there any readily accessible public transit. Whatever was needed had to be arranged through Camp Fallingbostel and it's not so swift, nor very efficient, military bureaucracy.

Ludmilla came to the rescue again. "Lie still, breathe slowly," she instructed Polya. "I'll send Galya from next door to sit with you. And I'll find us a ride to Cuxhaven." Outside she spotted a young British soldier walking down a barracks row. Ever outgoing, and ever resourceful, Ludmilla had put together a large datebook of young soldiers, all glad to chat, glad to share a drink, glad to lend a hand. And it was doubly fortunate this soldier friend happened to be a jeep driver, though currently off duty. She shouted out his name, raced over to him and with teary eyes said, "Oh thank you, you're here. My best friend is going into labor. We desperately need to get her to Cuxhaven." Ludmilla was delivering her most appealing, very convincing, tale of woe. And she put an extra theatrical touch to her "we desperately need…" Not an "I" but a more compelling "we."

There was no questioning, no hesitation from the young British knight, though a knight without any shining armor. He gave no thought to any rules or protocol or any prior permission from military command. His jeep was parked only a few yards away. He scrambled to it and returned in an instant. He gently assisted Polya, plus Ludmilla, into the jeep and off they flew. (Little Tamara remained under the tender care of a neighbor.) It was a fast, frantic road trip. The road to Cuxhaven was barely a road, layered with a combination of dirt and loose gravel. It was also a virtual minefield of countless potholes to navigate around. Our valiant driver drove as fast as he could, dreading the possibility Polya might deliver her child right there in the back of the jeep before their arrival at the hospital. Or, instead of careening around the pothole craters he might careen right into one which in turn would trigger an on-the-spot delivery. Either scenario and the resulting roadside birth of a baby in a British jeep would be difficult to explain. Fortunately for all, Polya arrived at Cuxhaven Hospital just in time. A small but seemingly healthy baby boy was added to the Bykowski household. It was quite the delivery for the record books: a Byelorussian, passing herself off as a Pole, missing a husband, commandeering a British jeep, and delivering a baby boy in a German hospital, under British control.

With Ludmilla dutifully at her side, Polya managed the delivery and postpartum reasonably well. On the third day of her hospital stay she decided she had to leave. That morning she whispered to her friend, "Ludmilla, help me to get dressed and then slip out of here. My boy looks healthy enough, I'm strong enough, and there's my little Tamara back home who needs me. Maybe, just maybe, we'll even have some news from Jan waiting for us." Ludmilla wasn't anywhere as convinced that Polya was ready to be discharged. The newborn was alert but looked undernourished. Polya could use more hospital recuperation time as well. But Polya was adamant about leaving. "I don't trust the British here. They'll ask more questions, wonder about the mysterious missing husband. Maybe they'll try to hold me in the hospital, hold my baby for who knows how long. We have to leave. And now." There was more than enough traffic and confusion in the hospital, very little staffing and almost no security. Consequently, it was a fairly uncomplicated escape plan: put on street clothes, bundle up the baby laying at Polya's bedside, and casually walk out the door. The threesome couldn't risk asking for formal transportation, and there was no nearby British knight, with noble jeep, to chauffeur the threesome back to Camp Fallingbostel. With no readily available options, and despite Ludmilla's insistence that walking was too dangerous, Ludmilla, mother Polya, and baby boy (no name yet) started on the ten-mile trek back to the camp. It was a slow but tolerable pace and Polya was feeling healthier and happier the further they traveled back toward home. No more than a mile down the road an empty truck drove by. In no particular hurry nor any particular mission for the moment, a cheerful, older driver asked if the trio needed a lift. Another British knight, this time a fatherly older knight, to the rescue. Within the hour the family was reunited. Little Tamara also offered her first smile and hug to her little brother. Camp life continued. But Jan remained in jail.

....

Again, all too late in life, my mother shared the details of my birth in Hannover. The hospital was decent, though primitive, from her description. Homecoming for me wasn't that cheerful since I was diagnosed with dysentery just one week after birth. With the severity of that illness, I was hastily baptized in my crib by the readily available priest. No, it wasn't an Orthodox priest which my parents preferred, but at least a priest. That was my entry into post-war Europe. Abandoned, though unintentionally and temporarily, by a father. The offspring of a suspected Nazi collaborator. A sickly kid, complete with bowed legs, growing up amidst the confusion and chaos of Camp Fallingbostel.

....

Ludmilla was able to pass the news of Polya's safe delivery and the arrival of a baby boy to Jan. And, after a quick back and forth the parents decided to name the boy Anton, or Antoni in Polish. Jan, the avid reader, had always enjoyed Anton Chekov. More good news arrived two weeks later as Jan was released from jail, free of any charges or further investigation. Captain Kelly conceded there was an abundance of rumors, plus Kelly's own suspicions. But, there was no hard evidence of any chargeable activity by this so-called Jan Bykowski. Kelly also admitted, with half a smile, that he had more pressing problems that were taking his time and resources. The camp was populated with its assortment of petty thieves, vandals, thugs, maybe a spy or three. Jan left the headquarters jail with nothing more than a documented six week jail term but no formal charges. Four years later Jan would have to revisit that seemingly minor criminal record as he struggled to immigrate his family out of Germany and out of Europe.

Chapter 16 - A Refuge and a Home, a Real Home

"The ornament of a house is the friends who frequent it."

Ralph Waldo Emerson

On April 5, 1945 American forces marched into Hannover and liberated its captive population. And on April 15 British troops entered the vast prison complex of Camp Fallingbostel. Those collective allied victories in and around Hannover would present the Bykowskis with another moving challenge. For a contemporary 21st century homebuyer, whether exploring for the first time or exploring a change, it's all about "location, location, location." If only the Bykowski's were so lucky and had such options. For Jan and Polya there were no exciting locations to explore or select. And instead of "locations" to explore and settle into they endured, more accurately, a recurring and unexciting cycle of "relocation, relocation, relocation." This latest moving challenge out of their previous Hannover "hotels" was unlikely to be a notable improvement from that first bombed out home, to their slightly less bombed out home, to a factory floor with only raggedy sheets for privacy. Nonetheless, their anticipated fourth relocation "hotel" certainly couldn't be any worse. The current rumor was that the relocation site would be that notorious Fallingbostel prison complex. But first the British needed to convert that "Camp" into something far more suitable for DP's than it had been for its war prisoners. The conversion project was daunting.

Bad Fallingbostel had been a centuries old rural village with its main, very traditional focus on raising livestock - primarily sheep - for its large urban neighbor Hannover. In 1937 that changed dramatically as the Wehrmacht began construction of a barracks for workers. The so-called worker camp expanded, the grounds were fenced in, and in 1939 it began receiving its first war prisoners. Poles were its first occupants and French and Belgians were added to the prison population the following year. By mid-1940 the camp housed around 40,000 POW's. As the complex expanded there were at one point up to 90,000 prisoners housed there.

The barracks, or huts as they were called, were of varying sizes. The majority were built to accommodate 150 prisoner cots. But, with the ever-expanding prison population, the barracks routinely housed over 400 prisoners. Then this tightly packed mass of humanity was hauled off daily to over 200 work details in and around Hannover. Though Poles still dominated the prisoner population there was a growing United Nations within the camp as the war continued. Yugoslavs and Ukrainians were added, though the Ukrainians were wrongly labeled as hated Russians. And as the war dragged on the camp added a sizable population of the major allies: more French, then Brits and Americans.

The one consolation of imprisonment at Camp Fallingbostel was that the conditions, though primitive and deplorable, paled in comparison to the various hard labor, non-combatant prisoner camps in and around Hannover. Though not specifically intended or designed for that purpose, those hard labor camps did more closely resemble the notorious concentration camps which German engineers built to advance the Third Reich's "final solution" to its non-Aryan problem.

Though Fallingbostel had been built, and initially maintained, with German efficiency, the entire camp deteriorated to a deplorable state as it strained to house its ever-expanding prisoner population. The historic "Battle of the Bulge" in December/January of 1944-45 compounded the population explosion at Camp Fallingbostel as the Germans captured thousands of American troops. The British who liberated Camp Fallingbostel in the spring of 1945 found a camp with barracks barely habitable, water and sanitation almost nonexistent, and the once much used parade/training grounds completely covered with trash. The Germans had force marched a few POW's out of Fallingbostel prior to the British advance and then left the remaining population to fend for itself. What the British saw as they pushed to the very gate of that dreaded Stalag XIB was a rundown camp with its massive, but extremely grateful, allied prisoner population.

A heartwarming side story to that liberation of this POW camp was the very unexpected "welcome committee" waiting to greet its liberators at the main gate to Camp Fallingbostel. As the British 8th Hussars tank group approached the gate, the group was stunned and overwhelmed by the spectacle in front of the gate. Standing in precision guard formation were twenty British paratroopers. Each one was dressed in a clean, if somewhat tattered, uniform. Many of the tank troops even whispered to each other, with some envy, that the paratroopers' uniforms were far cleaner than their own fatigues. A few of the paratroopers wore what medals they had earned and which medals they had successfully hidden from the greedy hands of their captors. All the paratroopers stood proudly at attention, facing forward, straight and tall and trying their best to look and act stern and serious for their much-welcomed liberators. Three of the paratroopers weren't quite as straight and tall as they wished to be. These three were on crutches. But all three had loudly and passionately insisted on being part of that welcoming honor guard. And as an extra selling point for their inclusion each one had secretly stored away a fine dress uniform, hoping to bring it out of hiding for just such an occasion. The honor guard lineup tried to look stern and stone faced, very proper and British. But the tough soldier facade quickly disappeared as their fellow British liberators bombarded the paratroopers with shouts and cheers and whistles, even a lively pub song or two.

What a grand greeting and what a proud, proud moment for the British soldier who had made this possible: RSM John Lord. He was an ex-Grenadier guard who had been stationed with the British troops fighting on the western front. Unfortunately, Lord was one of 400 paratroopers captured at the Battle of Arnhem in late 1944 and then marched off to Fallingbostel. A tough, no nonsense career soldier who had seen his share of horrors, Lord arrived at Fallingbostel and found the prison conditions far worse than he had feared and imagined. He also found the morale and discipline of the camp's prisoners just as deplorable. Therefore, RSM John Lord took on the personal challenge, starting with his own paratrooper regiment, to change those behaviors and attitudes. For this army veteran bad behavior and bad attitudes were absolutely unacceptable for any proper British soldier. Lord demanded his soldiers rid themselves, and immediately, of their lethargy and lack of hygiene. They would wash and shave every day. They would also schedule some form of exercise every day.

With defeat imminent, the Germans began a hasty and haphazard evacuation of their prison camp, hauling away a few prisoners and leaving the majority of the prison complex to fend for itself. As the Germans evacuated, leaving the camp on the verge of total chaos, the ex-Grenadier enlisted other officers to impose some semblance of discipline and unity. Any day now, or so Lord insisted, the prisoner population would see a liberating allied force, any force, appear at those hated wooden and wire gates. Lord's goal, as well as his crowning achievement, was to prepare for that formal liberation with a welcoming honor guard of his fellow paratroopers. As an extra stroke of good luck it was in fact a British liberation force that stopped at the gate on April 16, 1945. And there was a very proud and proper British honor guard waiting to greet its fellow countrymen.

The British began the enormous task of reconfiguring and rebuilding the multi-part complex into a manageable DP camp. Nazi prisoners were segregated first. Camp Fallingbostel also received its first bureaucratic alphabet soup designation: The DPAC or the Displaced Persons Assembly Center, and it would remain a DPAC until the end of 1949. The DPAC designation was certainly more innocuous and less ominous sounding than the camp's previous, very German designation: Stalag XIB. With a proper bureaucratic label in place, the massive relocation began. There were the additional bureaucratic headaches and hassles. And this newly named DPAC was a massive and very messy United Nations of DP's: Poles, Americans, Frenchmen, Englishmen, Belgians.

There was vandalism and vendettas plus petty thievery as the DP's settled into their new quarters. The British military pursued, initially at least, a polite, hands-off strategy during the relocation. The polite approach, oh so British as one might expect, unfortunately produced little politeness and more chaos. That in turn required the British to conduct its first full sweep of the camp in September to capture thieves and anarchists and to reclaim loot and stolen weapons. A second sweep was necessary in early November. But after that second brief military campaign Camp Fallingbostel evolved into a reasonably safe, comfortable home for its multinational DP's.

Overall, this reconfigured Camp Fallingbostel would provide shelter for over twenty thousand DP's. There was better organization and improved discipline. After all, this was a British camp, and it would be run in a proper, civilized British manner. But, as Captain Kelly had learned so quickly during the initial factory relocation, and which the British high command learned as well, maintaining law and order at Camp Fallingbostel was a difficult and full-time task.

War prisoners had been liberated and a massive clean-up was needed to transform prison Camp Fallingbostel into a more welcoming refugee Camp Fallingbostel. Sadly, what remained after the German exit was a depressing site that was hard to describe. The camp was barely a camp and much more so a vast fenced in junkyard. It was enclosed with a eight foot tall fence interlaced with barbed wire and topped with an additional two layers of razor wire. That ugly razor wire would be an immediate priority to dismantle. There was also a massive two sided twelve-foot front gate adorned with an obscene wrought iron swastika on each door that needed immediate removal as well. The barbed wire laced main entrance was quickly replaced with two less intimidating but still massive wooden gates. But Camp Fallingbostel still was, despite all the welcome cosmetic changes, a guarded, fenced and locked camp for its new occupants. Not quite a prison, but close.

Inside the fence was a huge parade ground. It was covered with dirt and a few seemingly random slabs of poured concrete. There were small green patches of grass struggling to survive, some gravel scattered here and there, and countless potholes of varying sizes and depth. The parade ground was literally a junk yard, covered with countless empty file cabinets, drawers, furniture, small military parts, boxes and miscellaneous articles of clothing. It looked like everything that might be of value had been hauled outside, rummaged through and then discarded right here in the parade ground.

Beyond that main gate was a seemingly endless inventory of massive barracks. An assortment of other buildings was scattered among the barracks: apartment-like structures, small single cottages, warehouses and sheds. Many of the barracks were almost as large as the factories from which the refugees were politely, or semi-politely, evicted. All the structures were wooden, haphazardly painted over in dull olive drab or gray, though many hadn't been painted in years. All too many of the buildings appeared to lean. Some appeared ready to collapse or implode at any moment. And, this so-called camp was scheduled to become the collective home for Hannover's war weary refugees?

The majority of the barracks were two story structures with windows that actually were intact and functional. Some of the barracks had what passed for a more elaborate entryway which opened into a great room or common area. But what might have been called a "great room" was hardly great. Quite the contrary, the area was relatively small. It also was sparsely furnished with an odd assortment of old and barely usable sofas, chairs, plus a small table or two. Whether blessed with a common area or not, the signature feature of every barracks was its dense lineup of beds. They were wooden beds, built from rough hewn pine, unpainted, very primitive in design, but functional.

The beds were tightly aligned, only two feet of space between each bed, each one pressed up against the opposing exterior walls of the barracks. There was a small, equally primitive storage chest at the foot of each bed, barely large enough to store an extra pair of clothes, maybe a small keepsake or toy. The beds did have mattresses, clean looking but very saggy and worn from too many years of use. There was a very primitive set of springs to support each mattress. But those springs, like their companion mattresses, were old, tired, entirely too stretched out over time to provide much support. Consequently, the spring/mattress combo provided its occupant little firm support and an unsettling deep cradle. Once in bed it was a constant challenge to escape out of it.

There were no indoor toilet facilities. There was only one wood burning stove on the first floor, located at one end of the barracks. It offered some modicum of warmth and comfort for those lucky enough, or aggressive enough, to commandeer a bed near that stove. The squatty, potbelly stove was functional, but it was entirely too small for the cavernous barrack. It was a very basic woodburning stove requiring a constant army of volunteers to keep it fueled. But, despite its small size, that potbelly did provide one appealing extra benefit. On top of that squatty stove was a flat surface, roughly a 12x 12 square, designed and located in front of the stove's rear end and its ugly chimney pipe. Consequently, the stove's flat surface offered a makeshift hot plate. The hotplate surface was large enough to support a small tea kettle, maybe a medium sized stock pot, battered and blackened as the pot might be. And, though the hotplate probably wasn't specifically designed for any such purposes, it could also serve as the makeshift cooking surface for someone's equally old and blackened frying pan.

Predictably, there was constant competition for that hotplate: a much-needed pot of hot water for a few vegetables and accompanying broth, a steaming kettle for some equally much needed tea break, maybe a quick fry for a rare, very greasy sausage. And queuing itself for a turn at the hotplate provided the semi-patient person waiting in line added fringe benefits. That DP was rewarded by the proximity to that warm potbelly. He or she, and maybe an accompanying toddler, could also enjoy the intoxicating aroma of someone's bubbling vegetable pot, or that sizzling sausage. Simple pleasures in a simple, and very primitive, setting.

Overall, the competition for the hotplate was polite, and there were usually no more than eight or ten DP's waiting at a time. There was some occasional shoving. But, the shoves were more apologetic than aggressive. Everyone was just trying to get by, trying to get along. The barracks had no partitions, no family configurations. This was simply one massive communal bedroom. And if one wasn't quick enough to claim the first-floor bed, a steep narrow staircase waited for its second floor occupants. That staircase, just like the barracks' mattresses and springs, was old and grossly overused, with sagging and groaning stair treads.

Unfortunately for some refugees, they were herded over to the dreaded St. Barbara barracks. This was a large cluster of buildings, similar in structure and with equally drab colors. However, these barracks were four story structures, not two. Therefore, they presented its occupants with double the population, double the noise. And for some of the unlucky refugee occupants it presented the added daily challenge of tackling four floors of old, wobbly, creaking and groaning stairs. Adding to the deplorable conditions of those St. Barbara barracks, only the first floor was furnished with a usable stove. Those additional two or three groaning stairways also presented an extra challenge, as well as an embarrassment, for those who had to answer that urgent call, in the middle of the night, to the outhouse. No matter how hard anyone tried, those dreadful stairs moaned and groaned doubly loud in the middle of the night. Those moans and groans in turn generated a loud chorus of shouts and curses from fellow refugees. A sound night's sleep was a rare treat in any Fallingbostel barracks.

The accommodations were primitive, the communal sleeping arrangements were uncomfortable. And there were the challenging stairways at St Barbara. Nonetheless, the barracks at Camp Fallingbostel, any barracks, were a vast improvement for those refugees who had endured cold, rusting factory walls and equally cold concrete factory floors. Wooden barracks were definitely more inviting. And the communal sleeping arrangement wasn't much worse than the frayed, thin sheets which marked the 20x20 boundary of a DP's factory "home."

Because they had two small children to care for, the Bykowskis fortunately were spared the barracks life. Instead of communal sleeping quarters, they were pleasantly surprised to learn they had been assigned an old, shabby, but sound - and very dry - standalone home for the next four years. And, they settled into what would be a bland, but relatively safe, daily routine. Get up, get in line for rations, perform some periodic camp-wide chores, try to eventually secure relocation to some better place, maybe a job, outside of the camp.

This latest relocation home was in fact a home, an intact, unbombed home. It was a much welcome improvement from their previous communal factory living arrangement. And it definitely was an improvement from the dreaded St. Barbara barracks and those terrifying stairways. Everyone, even the youngsters, had fond memories, however short-lived, of their stay at the "German fortress." That's what Jan and Polya had named the abandoned Jewish home, complete with its imposing Germanic stone sentinel and his/its front yard tank guardian. But here they all were, just the four of them, under one sturdy protective roof.

The home was small, just 35 feet by 25 feet. It was a simple functional design, built as an officer's quarters. Yes, it was a decent house, but definitely not some bachelor's party house. As one entered the house there was a combination living room and kitchen, what might today be labeled an "efficiency" apartment arrangement. The common area was furnished with a worn but comfortable sofa, an ancient rocker, a small collection of books, mostly German, but with a few English titles as well. In the middle of the common room there was a small 12x12 rug. The rug was dull, mostly brown and green, badly faded and badly frayed. But it was a welcome addition to the cracked and splintered wood floor.

The house included a small separate bedroom, barely large enough for a double bed, a cot, or maybe if they were tightly squeezed together, two cots. Drawing on his brief but useful carpentry experience, Jan salvaged scrap lumber and built a bunk bed for the two children, with older Tamara commandeering the lofty upper bunk. After some well-placed pleas from Polya they managed to obtain two additional decent mattresses for the bunks. With wood supports for the mattresses instead of worn-out box springs, the children actually enjoyed a comfortable resting place. And they were spared the ordeal of climbing in and then struggling to climb out of some deeply curved and very uncomfortable barracks bed.

The typical bedtime routine was for the children to play in the common room on that small but still slightly fluffy rug, and in front of the home's potbelly furnace. Dad and mom would watch them play, let them fall asleep by the warmth of the potbelly. Jan would carry them off to their respective beds. And then Jan and Polya could enjoy the modest comfort, the much welcome privacy, of the common room, its potbelly, and it's warm rug.

The back quarter of the common room also functioned as the kitchen. The centerpiece of that kitchen area was a large stove. The stove's four ornate, stubby legs appeared out of place, designed more for show than function. But, the stove's large three burner cooktop surface was quite the functional extra feature. Polya could either work over a small exposed open flame or on top of a grated cover. It was a wood fired stove, but it was large enough to hold an additional small bed of coal which could offer a more consistent source of heat.

Only three feet from that elegant stove Polya had the added luxury of a sizable prep table. It was sturdy, with a smooth butcher block top. There was also a useful sink built into the prep table, large enough to hold a bowl or a small kettle. And, for added convenience the prep table included a small hand pump. It was firmly anchored to the table and positioned over a five-gallon bucket stored under the table top. What a luxury for Polya: a large stove, workable prep space, and a water pump all at her fingertips. The only downside was the need to empty the sink bowl (no plumbing or a garbage disposal) and to replenish the pump's water reservoir. But, the children could help with those chores, or at least try to.

This was far more kitchen convenience than Polya was accustomed to. And, it had been months, maybe years, since she had seen and enjoyed what truly was a kitchen. And a fine, elegant kitchen at that. She whispered a thank you to the German craftsman who had designed these amenities into their small but oh so comfortable quarters. She wasn't a gourmet cook, didn't want to be, and wasn't that creative. But, she would utilize that kitchen every day and keep everyone as well fed as she was able.

Water could be boiled, soup could be prepared, what modest protein the family was provided - or what Jan bartered for - could be fried and hopefully not burned. The family was provided a weekly ration of food, mostly potatoes and/or rice, plenty of vegetables, and a scarce amount of dairy products. Sadly, there was nowhere near enough milk to support two young children. There was plenty of bacon provided. However, there was very little meat and an excess of fat on the slices. The one weekly ration that was generously supplied was German sausages, an understandable commodity in this German encampment. Those sausages were, like their bacon relatives, far more fatty than meaty. But for hungry refugees, whether young or old, it didn't matter. The bacon and sausage provisions were meat, so fatty and salty and often gristly, but oh so tasty. Healthy eating wasn't a concern. Just eating something, anything, was the family's only real concern. And occasionally the weekly ration included a sizable package of ground beef or ground pork. This extra treat was likewise fatty, too fatty, and coarsely ground. But who cared? Polya wasn't a gourmet cook. But she created countless combinations of vegetables and soups, garnished sparingly with some scarce but precious protein. No one was ever stuffed after a meal. The children were skinny, but they were not emaciated. And no one starved. No one except that whiney little boy who always cried out, even after an extra potato or an extra sausage, "I'm starving! (a big, loud protest for a little boy) Give me more! Please give me more!" He didn't starve. Everyone survived and remained reasonably healthy during their Camp Fallingbostel refugee years. Jan, ever the opportunist, worked tirelessly to ensure the family remained comfortable, decently dressed and reasonably well fed

This officer's quarters was among a cluster of other quarters. Consequently, there were some neighbors. There might be other refugees to meet, maybe with whom adults and children might even socialize. But, socializing was infrequent and friendships weren't much more than the occasional hellos. Almost every refugee had a history, often a complicated or uncomfortable past, which a refugee didn't need to nor want to share. Consequently, conversations typically were polite but superficial. One's personal history remained just that, unspoken and ancient history. Additionally, friendships were difficult to build since the entire camp population was a transient one. If one made a friend that friend could quickly, often unexpectedly, be gone. There might be a mandated relocation, for some unexplained bureaucratic reason. Or it could be that much anticipated news that an immigration request had finally been approved and a newly acquired friend, maybe an entire family, would be gone the following week. That was the ebb and flow of a refugee camp. A family is relocated, a new family is relocated , and a stranger is your new next door neighbor in some officer's quarters.

The disruptive transience of the camp was difficult on the two youngsters as well. But at their young age they learned to adjust fairly quickly. They had each other. They had a vast parade ground as their playground, even if there was more dirt than grass to play on. And every new young neighbor, whatever the background or complicated history, was willing to say hello, kick a ball in the dirt, play tag, climb what few trees remained at the camp. Camp life was simple.

For the two youngsters the DP years were forgettable, and fond memories were few and far between. They grew from innocent infants to curious and energetic toddlers, to footloose explorers wandering throughout the vast campgrounds. They awoke, they wandered, they returned to what passed for a home, tired and dirty and often hungry. Antoni had even improved his very predictable "I'm starving" routine. Running into their shelter, falling on the floor, he immediately released a pathetic, and well-practiced, combination of tears and sobs. Playing along with the ritual, Polya dutifully and tenderly lifted him up, wiped the tears and the runny nose and asked, on cue, "What's the matter" Antoni whimpered and replied, "I'm starving, and you didn't give me anything to eat!" Polya, with patience and a sympathetic smile, always replied," But, Antoni, you didn't ask for anything to eat." His reply was always a tearful and simple "Oh." She then found a slice of bread, maybe even a piece of cheese, and all was well. Yes, the family was never well fed, was occasionally hungry but no one ever starved. Except for Antoni.

Despite the uneventful, forgettable daily routine there was one weekly event the children looked forward to and thoroughly enjoyed. They waited at the front door, despite any rain or shine or blustery wind for their field trip every Friday to the "elegant" neighborhood in the southeast corner of the vast, otherwise dreary and nondescript, Camp Fallingbostel. In that corner there were a number of cottages, much larger than the modest Bykowski hut, and certainly far more elegant and inviting. The cottages were all painted a bright white and were decorated with a small but lush patch of green lawn. Each cottage was also decorated with a small picket fence, again painted a brilliant white. Even the streets throughout this cottage enclave were almost white, paved with crushed rock and gravel. This was in stark contrast to the ever-present dirt, and occasional mud, throughout the rest of the camp.

These larger cottages were occupied by senior military personnel, or so Polya suspected. During their walks the family met a few residents. There was little interaction but there always were polite smiles or waves of the hand. For Polya and the children it was a pleasant escape from the browns and grays of Camp Fallingbostel. And even at their very young ages, one could see the children's joy, plus some innocent envy, as they wandered around this pristine neighborhood.

However, on this day the joy, and their smiles, ended abruptly as they turned a corner. There on that bright paved street, and amidst all those bright white cottages, stood a tall, thin someone, or something. On closer inspection, it was a tall, very slender man, not some scary "something." And he was dressed entirely in black. He wore a tight-fitting shirt, tight fitting pants, long and bulky boots. A long black satchel was draped over his left shoulder. Protruding out of the satchel was an assortment of brushes and odd tools. A lengthy bundle of rope was draped over one of the brushes. A long twelve-foot ladder rested precariously on his right shoulder, pointed forward and wobbling up and down like some sideways teeter totter. He wore a tall black skinny stovepipe hat, but there was no visible hair protruding around that stovepipe. And in his right hand, already encumbered by the bulky ladder on his shoulder, the stranger carried his trademark tool: a long, jet black chimney sweeping broom. How can you be a chimney sweeper without a proper, even though very ancient, broom? With all that bulky weaponry it was a wonder the man could move. But he appeared to be very comfortable, and balanced, as he proceeded down the street. Even Mary Poppins might have been startled on first seeing this tall black figure.

He was no more than thirty feet from the family as they rounded the corner. On seeing the black clothed stranger all three of them almost tripped and fell as they abruptly stopped their leisurely stroll. When they stopped, the blackclad stranger stopped as well. Then he slowly turned his head, showing our startled strollers a soot covered face, basically black, but with occasional small patches of whitish skin. They also saw two large bright blue eyes among all that soot. He stood and stared back at all three of them. Then he flashed a large smile. Along with the smile he raised his broom into the air and waved it at the startled strangers like some playful battle flag. Having offered his greeting, he turned back down the cottage road, took an abrupt right turn and disappeared between two cottages.

The threesome stood there on the street, momentarily paralyzed by this black apparition. With equal parts curiosity and dread, the kids slowly released their mother's hands. Then they cautiously walked over to where the black man had stepped between the two cottages. But he was nowhere to be found. Maybe he had climbed up some cottage roof and they hadn't been alert enough to look up. Maybe he had entered one of those cottages. Maybe, just maybe, he had simply vanished. The black faced, soot covered stranger was gone. But, there on the ground, neatly placed among a small patch of flowers, was the stranger's stovepipe hat. It lay upside down and inside the hat were two small daisies. With those two small daisies placed inside the hat it was evident the hat had been left there purposely. The children inched closer to the hat, stared down at the flowers nestled inside. There was the temptation to pick up the hat, maybe try it on for size. Big sister inched a little closer and bent down for an inspection. But fear trumped any further curiosity or courage. The kids ran back to their mother, clutched her hands all the more tightly. They asked nothing, said nothing except to ask, in unison, "Can we go home? Right now? And can we run?"

That night the children still asked no questions, didn't even mention anything to their father. Polya considered talking to the children about their encounter, explaining to them who that black broom man was. Local folklore also said a handshake with a chimney sweeper brought you good luck. He wasn't some mysterious "something", just a friendly, hardworking chimney sweeper. But she decided to let the children imagine, or maybe just forget, that encounter with the mysterious man in black. They did resume their "elegant" neighborhood walk the following Friday. But they never again saw the chimney sweeper. Nor did they find the intentionally abandoned stovepipe hat.

Ludmilla relocated to a group cabin with five other young women. But, she remained a steadfast friend and auntie, now splitting her time between the two children. She also continued her budding romance with the good Samaritan British soldier, at least for another six months. Then she was off on another romantic adventure with some other young soldier, maybe an officer this time around. She was perfectly happy with this carefree lifestyle, dating and flirting when she wasn't working at the camp cafeteria. Ludmilla did secure passage to Australia in 1950. There were tearful good-byes, letters back and forth with the two old friends for almost a year. And, then mail stopped, and sadly Polya never heard anymore from her fellow Borisov escapee.

Another member of the Borisov escape caravan left soon after Jan and Polya left their first Hannover "mansion." There had been enough room back at their mansion for the four adults, including Volodya, the aspiring photographer. However, with the forced relocation of the DP's to various factories and warehouses Volodya was placed in a factory separated from his friends. He remained in contact. But, the separation, though very understandable, did provide Volodya some prudent distance between him and Jan, formerly "Ivan," the Camp's suspected German collaborator.

Volodya also made his own tactical decision to become a Ukrainian instead of a Pole. That in turn created further distance and fewer contacts among old friends since the Polish and Ukrainian sectors in Fallingbostel were at opposite ends of the vast camp. Jan initially was angry and felt betrayed by his former friend Volodya. After all, it was Jan, the opportunistic Ivan the Terrible, who had single-handedly rescued Volodya from Borisov. But, Jan slowly, even if grudgingly, began to appreciate and agree with Volodya's decision.

There were some meetings during the Camp Fallingbostel years. Volodya easily blended into the Ukrainian camp population. He also built a decent cottage business as a camp photographer, accepting bartered provisions and the occasional hard currency. Rubles, marks, zloty, he was not particular, and it enabled him to survive comfortably enough in Camp Fallingbostel. Ivan did learn, second hand, that Volodya was able to evade the forced repatriation of Ukrainians back to the Soviet Union. Instead of Ukraine, Volodya was able to slip into France. Maybe he was aided by some British officer, grateful for photos he generously received from Volodya? Maybe there was a generous bribe to an immigration official? Volodya could be just as opportunistic as his old friend. And he did manage to immigrate out of this post-war refugee camp while Jan and family were still in immigration limbo. There were a few letters back and forth with invitations to join him in France, when and if they could. But, as was the case with fellow traveler Ludmilla, the friends slowly lost touch with one another. Maybe, just maybe, Volodya became the photographer of the rich and famous in Paris.

The loss of friends was doubly painful since both Volodya and Ludmilla had served as surrogate aunt and uncle to the two infants. The two youngsters sorely missed the visits, the occasional small treats, the opportunity to make faces for the periodic camera shot. But, one day out of nowhere an old friendly face appeared at the family's hut to cheer up not just the little tykes but Polya and Jan as well. It was Stefan, their old "Professor", counselor and dear friend from Borisov.

The surprise reunion was warm though a little puzzling for the youngsters. Neither child knew who the stranger was at their door. But it was quite obvious, even for these very young children, that he was no stranger to the parents. Maybe he was some long missing family member? The kids watched and smiled as hugs and kisses were exchanged among the adults. But they still were puzzled as to who the stranger was. They tugged at their mother's dress for information. Polya replied with a large smile and a tear or two, "Children, this is your Dyadya Stefan." He really wasn't their uncle or "Dyadya." But to the parents he was a very real relative, connected and supportive, ever helpful. And it was an uncle-like connection that extended back to Ivan and Polya's early teenage years. A dear uncle is what Stefan was to them. And that's what Stefan became to these two young children: "Dyadya Stefan."

Both children were just beginning to explore and expand their speech skills. They talked more, learned more words, constantly blurted out undecipherable words and sounds. But one word, actually two words, they mastered and shouted out clearly and often. Those two words were "Dyadya Stefan," their beloved, newly discovered "Dyadya Stefan."

The children were too young to ask questions as to where this newly reunited uncle came from or what he had been doing for half a decade or more. But Jan and Polya were very eager and curious to learn more about their Dyadya Stefan and his adventures. Polya, Stefan's childhood pupil, took the lead, rattling off a number of questions. "Where have you been? Why did you go to Minsk? Why did you leave? How did you get to Hannover? How did you find us?" And on and on she went with questions. It was quite apparent that their uncle was doing quite well, probably eating quite well and living quite comfortably also. He had aged, as all of them had. But Stefan did not have that weathered, weary appearance of someone who had trekked several hundred brutal miles across war torn Europe. He also didn't have the bland, drab, all too often threadbare attire of a refugee struggling to get by in DP Camp Fallingbostel. Quite the contrary, here was their uncle looking trim and very healthy and clothed in nice, almost elegant clothes.

Though pressed for details, Stefan was either vague or very short with any answers. "I stayed in Minsk longer than you did and longer than I should have," he answered. "I spoke a little too much, complained a little too often, and found myself on the unwanted/unwelcome list of some self-important Bolsheviks. Apparently, I wasn't revolutionary enough for them." Though pressed again for more tantalizing details, Stefan's only response was, "So I prudently, and quietly, left Minsk for friendlier places and friendlier faces." Recalling their own difficulties as well as the several hundred mile trek from Borisov to Minsk to Hannover, Jan and Polya asked for more details about Stefan's European escape route. Stefan's short, cryptic response was, "Some friends helped me. No one you would know or want to know." That short answer shut off any further probing as to who helped. But it didn't stop them from asking how Stefan made that several hundred-mile trek. Stefan's reply was, "I received a very kind and generous offer of a car, not fancy but reliable, for the trip. And it took us only six days to reach the German border." Jan and Polya noted the "us" reference but resisted the urge to ask about "us." They wanted to but resisted asking more about the mystery car and how Stefan had been able to travel in relative ease and speed throughout the European countryside. And apparently it was an easy and uneventful roadtrip without any confrontation with soldiers or nasty fighter planes. "And here I am in Camp Fallingbostel, just like you and countless other thousands of refugees." Stefan offered no more information on how he had arrived in Hannover, what, if any, contact he had with his old

Hannover friend, Major Heinrich Kohl. And he offered no further details as to how he arrived in this DP camp or what he did day to day. He simply deflected any further conversation about him. "But enough about me," he said. "How's my lovely star pupil? And tell me all about these cute children of yours."

Before he left that first afternoon Stefan did disclose that he also had assumed a Polish identity though he was housed among a large band of Byelorussian DP's. Not surprisingly, Stefan had also built a strong working relationship with several senior British officers running, or trying to run, Camp Fallingbostel. And, though Stefan again was vague on the details, he did volunteer that he'd heard some rumors about a suspected collaborator from Borisov. So, with a combination of curiosity and old memories, Stefan did some searching around the camp. And, here he was at their doorstep, reuniting with Ivan the Terrible and Stefan's favorite childhood pupil, Polahaya.

The decades-long friendship among the three of these Borisov refugees/escapees remained deep and unwavering. But despite the friendship, Stefan, their Dyadya Stefan, remained a mystery to Jan and Polya. He helped and advised. He appeared, disappeared and reappeared. He had mysterious connections and provided counsel to those who were powerful and influential, and often mysterious as well. Those connections were seemingly everywhere, from small town Borisov to Minsk to Germany, even to America. Stefan Mirovich was clearly far more than just an amiable small-town professor. But what he really was, who he really was, remained a frustrating lifetime mystery for Jan and Polya.

Stefan was obviously doing well as a DP, occupying a nice cabin near British headquarters. And, though he didn't flaunt his comfortable existence, he was very generous to his reunited friends, and especially the two children. Their Dyadya Stefan regularly delivered an extra basket of produce, a larger slice of ham, some cookies and a rare piece or two of candy for the little ones. What Stefan observed, however, and couldn't immediately relieve, was Jan's frustration and anger at his inability to improve the family's daily life. This was Jan/Ivan, the ever-resourceful opportunist and tough guy, searching for something to do with both his mind as well as his body.

With a little investigation on his part, Stefan found two promising solutions for Jan to explore. The huge, sprawling camp complex had countless frustrated, healthy men who needed outlets for all that pent up energy. The British command, along with a few well-respected DP residents, was organizing various sporting clubs. There was even some discussion about paying DP's, however modestly, for their participation. Boxing, football, even table tennis were among the various sports being considered. Stefan shared the information with Jan, and Jan was more than willing to try any and all sports, however organized - even unorganized - they might be. Ivan the Terrible, then Jan the DP, would soon become Jan the athlete.

....

In my adult years I've been asked countless times what memories I have of my five plus years in Camp Fallingbostel and our modest home. Though it's not that uncommon for people to have vivid memories of their very youngest years, I have none. Except one. It's that chimney sweeper, in total black and with his flag waving broom. He's there in front of me, only feet away, flashing a smile and then sauntering along the gravel road among those bright white cottages and their bright white picket fences. And then just vanishing.

There are no memories of childhood playmates, if there were any, no mental images of playgrounds or communal sandlots. There are no memories of adults, whether in shiny military uniforms or drab Camp secondhand rags, dropping by to offer a small sweet treat or a ride on a bouncy knee. There is no recollection of any barracks or huts, or soldiers, or dusty parade grounds. Except for that chimney sweeper, there are no memories of Camp Fallingbostel. None. Sad, or maybe not so sad.

Summer Research, Summer Memories

For over a decade during our adolescent and early teenage years the Gillette Cavalcade of Sports was a Friday night television ritual. Our father was glued to the small screen, with our mother politely putting on a decent showing of interest. We three children actually joined in, innocently cheering and jeering. We even learned the difference between a welterweight and a middleweight. The heavyweights were easy to identify. We didn't know too much more about this brutish sport, and we didn't choose many favorites. We simply mimicked the enthusiasm and often the intensity of our father. He even took us to a few amateur bouts at the local YMCA, treating us to ringside seats. And every so often there was an additional Wednesday presentation of that Gillette Cavalcade. No one could recall with certainty, but each of us vaguely remembered that our father occasionally brought out a pair of those ancient, very tattered boxing gloves he had brought across the Atlantic. He routinely placed the gloves on the coffee table, watched our evening bouts and then returned the gloves to their old wooden storage chest. We were awash in boxing. Looking back, we collectively did enjoy that Friday ritual. But we did wonder why it was such a favorite with our father.

Adding to that interest in, almost an obsession with, boxing our father forced all three of us into our basement to learn boxing fundamentals. We hated it initially, but we later learned to tolerate the basement lessons. We eventually thanked our father for those lessons as we grew up in the tough streets of our hometown.

Chapter 17 - Boxing and Bruises

"I coulda had class. I coulda been a contender. I coulda been somebody."

Marlon Brando as Terry Malloy in "On the Waterfront"

Fallingbostel had an overabundance of bored, frustrated, angry and energetic young men. Boxing could and did provide an ideal outlet for those varied and pent-up emotions. With the camp's diverse ethnic population, boxing would also provide an outlet for settling old resentments, old feuds in a somewhat sanctioned way. Poles could take on Ukrainians, gypsies could settle grudges, maybe with Jews, maybe with anyone. There were countless combinations to match up, and there appeared to be no shortage of willing combatants. And, it was extremely fortunate for the British command that the perfect officer for this project was right here in Camp Fallingbostel.

Robert Fisher was born and spent his early formative years in the mean back streets and alleys of Manchester, England. Childhood was forgettable, his parents were rarely seen, and his five siblings constantly fought with one another. Robert, a middle child, didn't grow as tall as he would like, but he was stocky and strong. And, in those mean streets, as well as in their crowded home, Robert developed into a savvy street boxer. He was noticed by the manager and head trainer of what passed for a local boxing club. Robert was invited to join and became a very avid member. He had quick hands, quick feet, and pursued a grueling training regimen. And, though he didn't have the height or weight of a heavyweight he could be an imposing welterweight, maybe a middleweight.

Robert became obsessed with boxing. The club trainer pushed Robert forward into an English version of a golden gloves competition, and Robert easily won the regional championship. He continued to improve his skills, developed more finesse, and won far more unanimous decisions on points instead of knockouts. Robert took pride in his boxing style which was in stark contrast to an all-too-common thuggish style, a style that today might be labeled a "mixed martial" something or other. With a healthy ego, a dedicated trainer and a continuing string of victories, as it was spoken in a memorable old movie, Robert "coulda been a contendah" for a professional national championship,

Robert turned pro, took on the crowd pleasing, ringside name of "Bob the Bruiser." He also took on the title of husband, marrying his long-time sweetheart he had met on those same mean streets of Manchester. His wife Lilly was very supportive, and they were starting to live more comfortably with his boxing prize money. They were even beginning to talk seriously about a baby. Maybe it would be a little girl to soften the tough guy exterior of Bob the Bruiser. Regrettably, after the nation's longstanding reluctance to do so, Britain finally declared war against Nazi Germany. Bob's boxing passion, Lilly's and Bob's future plans were all put on hold as duty called and Bob enlisted.

The Fallingbostel boxing project was a godsend for Robert. He tackled his new assignment with the same passion and intensity he had tackled his early boxing career. He also willingly provided training tips to any DP who was interested. He emphasized and taught the finesse aspect of boxing which had served Bob so well. Not everyone caught on or embraced that style. Unfortunately, there were more than enough thuggish, no finesse, DP boxers throughout the camp.

Despite the enthusiastic endorsement from Fallingbostel command to develop a camp-wide boxing competition, Captain Fisher had almost nothing to work with. There were no boxing rings, no spectator stands, no training facility. All he had were vast acres and acres of parade grounds which British Command, with a straight face, generously donated to Fisher's project. Command wouldn't agree to the construction of two raised platforms for his rings, and gravel, especially tons of gravel, weren't the ideal surfaces for maneuvering about or for falling down during a match. So, the ever resourceful captain requisitioned several truckloads of sawdust and wood chips from a local mill to create a slightly friendlier ring floor. Sawdust in the mouth or splinters in the feet were still far more tolerable than gravel. Fisher also requisitioned several yards of heavy rope from the Bremerhaven naval post, plus weather treated oak posts, which enabled him to create two crude but sturdy boxing rings. Just as the British had civilized, at least slightly, the ancient blood sport of boxing, they had also changed the original primitive boxing rings into boxing squares. But, they continued to be called boxing "rings." And Captain Bob, true to his British roots, built two 16 X 16 boxing "rings" right in the center of Camp Fallingbostel's parade grounds.

Other equipment was either scarce or non-existent. Fisher had his own two pairs of gloves and was able to locate two other pairs which he volunteered for formal bouts. For practices and sparring matches boxers were required to wrap their fists with strips of naval canvas. There was considerable grumbling about that fist wrapping requirement. These were tough, macho men who wanted nothing less than a real man's toe-to-toe, naked fist, no holds barred battle. But, this was Captain Fisher's stern rule, and everyone complied, even if reluctantly.

Captain Fisher's one other "equipment" innovation was potatoes, more specifically fifty-pound bags of potatoes. There were literally tons to spare, and the commissary didn't mind some softening of the potatoes which were a daily staple of camp life. The captain, now more often addressed as "Captain Bob the Bruiser", recruited some camp engineers to construct one dozen stands from which those fifty-pound bags hung and now became punching bags. And, oh how every aspiring boxer loved those potatoes! Minor brawls even broke out periodically because a boxer was taking too much time, enjoying the demolition of those potatoes too much. Besides the limited supply of gloves - and they were "one size fits all" gloves - Captain Fisher's one other equipment regret was the absence of any boxing shoes. Every DP was provided a pair of boots or shoes. They weren't fancy, they might have holes and paper-thin soles. But, they were very functional and wearable for anything and anywhere. Anywhere except a boxing ring. The hazards of plodding around a boxing ring with boots were obvious. At times it was even comical to watch two opponents lumbering and stumbling when they should have been bobbing and weaving. One solution was simple, if primitive. Every boxer went barefoot, enduring the occasional bruised feet and splinters along the path to becoming the Camp Fallingbostel boxing champion.

For Jan boxing was a natural fit. It wasn't grudges or resentment that drove him to boxing. It was more simply a much-needed return to those days as a charismatic, brash bully from Borisov. Jan was just right for the ring as well, standing 6'1" and at a lean but muscular 175 pounds. He wasn't that quick on his feet, but he had good reflexes and very quick hands.

Stefan had shared the rumors that there might be prize money distributed to participants. And, though this was a huge camp of displaced persons, there were pockets of wealth among the DP's. There might be prize money not only from the British administrators but also some unofficial "incentives" or bonuses for a talented boxer representing some particular ethnic group. For Jan, ever the opportunist, he might be able to provide a little bit more food to supplement their DP rations, maybe buy a few luxuries from the camp store or from its growing black market.

Jan and Stefan took a brief tour of the small, partly constructed boxing complex. It wouldn't make any aspiring boxing champion overly excited about stepping into what passed for a ring. But Jan didn't care. A boxing career it would be, wherever and in whatever ring he had to enter. The two new boxing partners walked back to Jan's hut to share the good news. But the closer they came to home doubts crept in. There weren't doubts about Jan boxing or his certain success. The growing doubts were about how Polya would react to this new "business" venture. He could hear it all now. "You're doing what? You are a fool. This won't be boxing. It will simply be those barroom brawls I remember from Borisov. There are hundreds of thugs and lunatics all over this camp more than ready to fight. Maybe they'll love to mutilate some suspected spy or collaborator. The British sure won't care about some play nice rules, won't enforce them even if they promise they will. They'll just watch all you tough guys beat each other's brains out and thoroughly enjoy this blood sport." Though this was what Jan suspected Polya would say, he couldn't help but think those same thoughts himself. But, despite his own misgivings, the allure of becoming that big time tough guy champion was too powerful. To break the news and possibly soften Polya's reaction Jan and Stefan agreed Stefan should take the lead in presenting their plan. Stefan had that calm demeanor, the polished words that would turn Polya's possible, very likely, initial outrage to acceptance and support. Yes, that was their clever strategy.

It was their seemingly clever strategy until both men stepped into the hut and found Polya seated at the kitchen table. Before Stefan uttered a word Jan excitedly blurted out, "Polya, you won't believe this great idea Stefan dreamed up. The British are organizing boxing competitions throughout the camp. They'll offer prize money to winners. There definitely will be betting and more money to collect. I can do it! I can be the big, bad Polish champion! And our dear professor Stefan will be my manager. We'll be rich! Well, maybe not that rich but I'm absolutely positive we'll make lots of money for you, for the kids and for Stefan." Like some foolish, giddy adolescent Jan struck an intimidating boxing pose, shadow boxed and danced around an imaginary ring, and then raised his arms - with imaginary gloves - triumphantly in the air. It was Jan's tough guy opportunist persona on full display: vain, arrogant, and supremely confident. It could have been a bad attempt twenty plus years later at some triumphal victory scene from a Rocky Balboa movie. But despite its silliness it was a joyful, innocent performance by Jan the champion. Stefan stared at Jan as he performed. He was angry and disappointed with Jan's impulsive speech, a speech which had undermined their prudent strategy. But, despite the disappointment, Stefan couldn't help but smile at Jan's youthful enthusiasm as well as his obvious self-confidence in seeing himself as that successful, and maybe rich, Camp Fallingbostel champion.

As for Polya, Jan was absolutely correct. She didn't believe a single word of what he was saying. Polya was neither excited nor amused by the new "business opportunity." And normally meek, quiet Polya lashed out at both of them for concocting this insane scheme. She repeated, almost verbatim, what Jan had imagined earlier. She continued, "With those barroom brawls you so politely call boxing matches you will also collect a lifetime of beatings and bruises and scars. If you're lucky, maybe, just maybe, you'll escape some permanent crippling injury. And when you're injured or crippled who will take care of me and the children? As for you, my supposed wise and caring professor, what the hell were you thinking? That I'd look forward to my handsome, if stupid, husband returning every week with more cuts, more stitches, more black and blue marks all over his body? He'll probably have permanent black eyes also. No, that's not the Ivan the Terrible I want to see. And it's not the father I want my children to see."

After the uncharacteristic tongue lashing Polya paused, then took a long, slow breath. She saw that silly sheepish smile on Jan's face. She mentally re-lived that equally silly but exuberant victory performance by Jan. She faced both of her silly but charming troublemakers, offered just the slightest hint of a smile and ended with her trademark "oy, oy, oy!" She left the small kitchen, the two men sipped a little contraband vodka, and the next day Jan signed up for his first match.

****

As kids growing up in America we saw and heard that "oy, oy, oy" time and again from our mother. It was a cute, endearing gesture delivered to express her disappointment or anger at something stupid we had done or said. This was as forceful and angry as she became. And, as adults we occasionally would toss out that playful "oy, oy, oy" to each other and even to Mom. She would scowl and then we all would laugh.

****

The British captain in charge of the boxing competition took Jan under his wing immediately. Jan was brash, arrogant, definitely a bully, but it was hard to dislike him. He was also a quick learner and rapidly turned into a formidable camp heavyweight. The captain also provided Jan with two pairs of boxing gloves, mysteriously requisitioned, as permanent loaners if Jan wanted to pursue some unsupervised training and conditioning. Jan tackled the new opportunity very seriously. He lost his first few bouts by the primitive refereeing standards in place, but he wasn't knocked out or knocked down. With more experience Jan began winning matches and increasingly did so with knockouts.

The British prize money wasn't that large, but it did add up as Jan won more and more. There was also a small bonus for knockouts which Jan was more than happy to deliver. DP's had brought some of their own rubles, or marks, or whatever to the camp. And those DP's set up some spirited betting pools as well. A few of the deeper pocket DP's even became avid supporters and unofficial sponsors of their man, "Big Jan." As Jan won his bouts so did his sponsors, and he was rewarded with a cut of those sponsors' winning bets.

There was more food on the table for the Bykowski family. There was a little walk about, showing off money in Jan's pocket. There were some cute little toys for the kids, even though toys were fairly scarce. Scarce, unless you had some extra cash on hand and connected with the appropriate black marketeer. The family enjoyed the extra luxury of fancy, well-made party clothes. Sadly, there weren't many parties to attend. Nonetheless, the kids had elegant outfits, and Jan and Polya could and did frequently appear in tailored suits. Polya also had one additional, very extravagant luxury: a small but stylish fur shawl.

Boxing was good, despite the initial misgivings, and Jan suffered only the predictable bruises and aching ribs. To Jan's credit, he also resisted the temptation to throw a fight despite the periodic financial bribes that enticed him to do so. He was an opportunist. But, he was proud enough, and vain enough, to win, or to lose, in a fair and honest fight. Success continued for eighteen months. Stefan attended all the bouts, but Polya refused to see even one bout. That was her defiant threat when this mad so-called "opportunity" had first been presented to her and she was true to her word. She hated the primitive brutality of those bouts that had very little refereeing and even less rules. And, she constantly feared her tough Jan would return one day battered, bloodied and permanently injured.

It was inevitable that day would come. As a heavyweight Jan faced a growing number of bigger, tougher boxers. Bob the Bruiser continued with his self-imposed role as the Camp Fallingbostel boxing "commissioner." But he also devoted an increasing amount of time grooming Jan.

On a more personal level Bob had also developed a deepening fondness not just for Jan but for the entire family. He was as much a loving if unofficial uncle to Polya and the children as was their other "uncle" Stefan Mirovich. Additionally, Stefan served as a very active collaborator, grooming Jan with his boxing career. Stefan even served as a ringside trainer/coach/cheerleader. He also acted as Jan's money manager, prudently placing bets on his young champion while also prudently protecting those winnings from Jan's occasional impulses.

Jan was not just a tough heavyweight slugger. Trainer Bob was adding a new element to his slugger skills, training Jan to become a skilled boxer, with not only power but finesse. After a few initial losses, though none by knockouts, Jan was currently undefeated through 21 bouts. He was the prime target of every young contender. But the match everyone expected, and loudly demanded, was against the other highly successful heavyweight, Vlad the Giant. The label was a fitting one for this Lithuanian who stood six feet six inches and weighed in at 215 pounds. By those vital statistics the Giant was five inches taller than Jan and over thirty pounds heavier. The Giant was also undefeated through his last 20 bouts, seventeen by knockouts and all within the first two rounds. The only loss had been at the hands of a boxer who had finessed his way through seven rounds and handily won by a unanimous decision. Sadly, for that victorious opponent, there had been a rematch which the Giant decisively won in the second round by a thundering knockout. The Giant had brutally advanced, not allowing his opponent to stay away with finesse and footwork which he'd so strategically employed in their first outing.

With growing public clamor for the marquee match, Bob, accompanied by Stefan, visited Jan at his home after a strenuous but productive afternoon workout. The mission was not to obtain Jan's agreement to such a match. He was more than ready and committed to that match, actually any match. The two managers' mission was to solidify a winning fight strategy. With Polya quietly listening at the table, Bob laid out their plan. "We've reached out to the Lithuanian's manager and we're on for a match in a week," Bob cheerfully announced. Bob prudently and strategically did not call their upcoming opponent the "Giant" as everyone else did. "Giant" was too intimidating a label and the mere sight of the boxer would be intimidating enough, even for brash and confident Jan, without adding that descriptive label to their conversation. "There's a match two days from now and we, you included, need to go on a scouting trip. He's big, he's strong, but he's not that agile as you'll see." Jan was eager to watch and eager to fight. "Here's the key to your success," Bob continued. "You can beat him. We know you can. But you can't beat him in a slugfest. You need to be, and remain, a finesse boxer, bobbing and weaving, jabbing and annoying the Lithuanian. You follow that strategy, keep away from any clinches. And no slugfest! Do you understand? Do you agree?" Jan did agree. Polya, still quietly, silently listening, was also relieved to hear the cautious strategy and Jan's encouraging acceptance.

The scouting trip was productive. Jan was not that intimidated, though he was impressed by the sight of his Lithuanian opponent. The team was upbeat, a final light workout was scheduled, and Polya even considered attending her very first match. A massive crowd gathered at Captain Bob's not so fancy, but functional, "championship" ring. The gambling was intense with Jan being the popular favorite though the bets were evenly split between the two heavyweights.

At the last minute Polya passed on attending ringside. As Jan left their home, she gave him a long hard hug and whispered, "I know you'll win even though I hate this whole boxing business. Just keep your promise to be a smart boxer, not a slugger. I want you back here, bruised just a little, but not battered and crippled." With a smile Jan casually replied, "I promise." If only he had kept that promise.

Accompanied by his co-managers, Jan entered the ring. There was a polite, if stiff, exchange of handshakes at the center of the ring, and the bout began. The first round produced little more than circling around and tossing a few exploratory punches, a predictable mutual effort to assess one's opponent. The Giant did land a few glancing punches, but they had little effect on Jan.

Back at their corner, Bob sensed impatience by the Lithuanian and reminded Jan to continue to be the savvy boxer. "Jab, dance, frustrate this so-called "Giant" and he'll become more and more reckless and clumsy. He'll beat himself." However, the crowd was shouting wildly, loudly for Jan. Regrettably, Jan, despite the ringside advice, let his vanity and impatience trump the sound advice. "I can beat this slow big man. I can hit him harder, move faster," he thought to himself as he rose from his corner stool. As the boisterous crowd cheered ever more loudly, if that was possible, Jan turned his boxing advantage into a slugfest disaster. He didn't dance. He stood his ground as the Giant advanced and heavy, unsophisticated exchanges began. Bob leaned into the ring as far as he could and bellowed out, "Dance, you fool, dance." Maybe Jan heard his manager above the deafening roar, maybe he didn't. At the end of the round Jan staggered, and definitely did not dance, back to his corner. The third, fourth and fifth rounds weren't any better. What defense Jan could offer wasn't effective, he took an eight count twice, and the Giant kept up his punishing blows. Before the sixth round began Bob looked at his bloodied boxer and said, "You've done well, my dear friend. You've been knocked down but not out. The crowd still loves you. Stay on that stool when the bell rings. Please." Jan said nothing, rose up from his stool and then looked back and said, "Just two more rounds. I can do it." Jan did manage a few powerful punches which put the Giant down for his own eight count but Jan could barely stagger back to his corner at the end of round six. Whispering, and with both eyes nearly swollen shut Jan muttered "Ok." Bob immediately grabbed a towel and tossed it into the ring. The fight was over.

The crowd did cheer politely, though not very loudly, for the Lithuanian Giant. He was clearly the better fighter this day, and he would continue to inflict pain and quick knockouts on future opponents. To his great credit the Lithuanian Giant, on this day, was also a gentle giant. Jan sat on his corner stool, barely able to move. In a classy gesture of sportsmanship, the Lithuanian crossed the ring, lifted Jan firmly but politely under his arms and said, "You are one hell of a tough fighter. You hurt me. And I have no interest at all in meeting you another time." He smiled and returned Jan to his stool. Then he offered a double fist - or glove - bump, another smile and a helping hand as Jan hobbled out of the ring.

Back at their home Polya could only gasp and weep. Fearing the worst, Polya had tactfully hustled the children to the bedroom before their battered father arrived. She cleaned up the cuts, his bloody lip and bloody nose. She applied a cool, wet and soothing towel to his badly swollen and nearly shut eyes. His entire face was swollen, black and blue and barely recognizable. But she couldn't shelter the children in the bedroom forever from this scary face. She went into the bedroom and offered a brief explanation and a warning as to what they should expect. "Your father was brave and good, but he was badly beaten in a boxing match. He's not very handsome right now. But, don't be frightened. He's not that hurt, and he will get better soon, real soon. Now go say hi." As they entered the room and saw their father Polya feared this might be too traumatic and they would become hysterical. To her surprise and relief, the children just stopped and stared for a few minutes. Then without uttering a word, but with copious tears running down their faces, they went over to their father and each one gingerly embraced a leg. The children sensed hugs and kisses would have to be postponed for a few days.

That ended Jan's string of twenty straight wins and sixteen knockouts. That beating also ended Jan's boxing career. He was vain and proud and oftentimes foolish. But, he was honest enough with himself to realize it was time to walk away from this "business opportunity" while he was literally able to walk away. There was money in his pocket, more and better food at their table, fancy dress up clothes for the whole family. And, there were two pairs of boxing gloves, in less than perfect shape, but still very usable, which the British captain gave to Jan as a parting gift.

Stefan also provided one other parting gift. Two days after the bout he visited the Bykowski home and dropped off an eye-popping bundle of money on the table. With a sheepish smile he explained. "There was so much betting! And, so much of the bets were on you, the crowd's hero. Initially on you, that is, through the first two rounds. Then your fickle fan club started turning on you. And, I have to confess I could understand the turn as you boldly, but so stupidly, decided to change the boxing match into a slugfest. So, I made the decision to turn on you as well." Stefan paused, waiting for some explosive reaction. But there was none, to his surprise.

Stefan continued. "Yes, I did bet against you. But, they were bets with a twist, a shrewd and potentially very profitable twist. I took bets that despite the beating you invited from the Lithuanian Giant you would not get knocked out and you would last at least six rounds. I also took bets you would put down the Giant for an eight count at least once. High stakes, high risk, but I had faith in your ability and your stamina. People thought I was crazy, and they swarmed all over me to take the bets. The odds were great. You were great. And, my foolish but oh so brave boxer, we won a mountain of money! I'm taking forty percent because I put up the cash. You get sixty percent of this huge pile. I also heard it from countless bettors, as well as from many around the camp, that they were very proud of your effort. Well done, my dear friend! And I sincerely hope with this cash on the table you will forgive me for betting against you."

Jan rose from the table, slowly and gingerly, and walked over to his friend. He scowled at Stefan, though it wasn't a very serious or threatening scowl. Then he clenched his right fist, though again slowly and gingerly, and shook it in front of Stefan. He demanded, "You bet against me? You actually thought I'd lose?" There was a long pause. Then the scowl turned into a broad smile as Jan replied. "Bold! Shrewd and brilliant! Of course, I forgive you. And, yes, I'll take sixty percent. My face says I deserve it!" The vodka flowed, hardy hugs were exchanged. Even Bob the Bruiser dropped by later that day to join the celebration. And the dream of the Camp Fallingbostel heavyweight boxing title came to an end.

....

Growing up in a tough part of town in America, my father gave me boxing lessons at a very young age. Our little brother was schooled in boxing a few years later, and it served him equally well in the tough back streets of our hometown. Though our father thought it was a skill only for boys, my older sister insisted on getting boxing lessons as well. Father relented, grudgingly, and we spent many afternoons in our tiny home's basement learning to bob and weave and punch and jab. We tried repeatedly to learn about our father's boxing career, begging and prodding him for details. But, time and again he offered very few details. All he grudgingly volunteered was that he was "pretty good." One day as we, once again, nagged him for more details he, once again, told us he was "pretty good." But, then with a smile, and a touch of humility which he didn't display very often, he said he was "pretty damn good." Or as he told us, with that uncharacteristic smile, he was pretty damn good until he was almost killed by a cheerful Lithuanian giant. The end, no more boxing. And no more details.

The boxing lessons were invaluable in helping both of us, especially scrawny me, in our poor and tough neighborhood. I was the better student than my older sister, with more finesse and better footwork. However, when our father forced the two of us to spar in the basement my sister consistently won. All this took place decades before Smoking Joe Frazier came onto the boxing scene with his relentless, charging style. My sister, though short on style and finesse, just charged into me just like a Smokin' Joe, fists flying, head down, feet constantly moving toward me. And, I could do nothing but endure a vicious, and very embarrassing, beating until our father, laughing heartily, pulled my sister off me. Sometimes, after the basement beating, I wished those two pairs of gloves had never made that trans-Atlantic trek.

……………………………………………

Jan hobbled around for almost a month, with Polya dutifully nursing him along. She tossed in the periodic "oy, oy, oy" in a gentle, caring voice, almost a whisper. But, she said no more. The two infants had problems recognizing their father for the first week or two, hidden as Jan was behind swollen and blackened eyes. But, everyone survived the ordeal, and Jan suffered no permanent injuries, except an injured pride. And, with recovered health Jan, once again the opportunist, went in search of another adventure, another "business opportunity." Captain Robert Fisher, good old Bob the Bruiser, once again came to the rescue.

Chapter 18 - Fallingbostel Football and Fame

"See, the conquering hero comes
Sound the trumpet, beat the drums."

Thomas Morell

Fallingbostel's DP population provided an enormous pool of raw talent for this very universal and very popular sport called football. (Universal and popular almost everywhere, that is, except for the United States where it was called soccer.) Several club teams were being organized, as well as a number of unofficial national teams. The British administration heartily encouraged the sport. It involved far larger numbers of players than individual sports like boxing. The European brand of play was rough to some degree but there was a fair amount of tactics and finesse. Overall, Fallingbostel football was more than just brutish pushing or tripping or elbowing. And, sixty minutes of nonstop scrambling up and down a football pitch certainly provided a useful outlet for all that pent-up male testosterone that otherwise would need a release around the campgrounds or the resident barracks.

With sports being a logical outlet for Jan's energy, strength, as well as his outsized ego, Bob approached Jan with the idea of joining a football team. After a nice dinner at the Bykowski home Bob presented Jan, with Polya in attendance, the rewards, and only a few risks, of club football. "You're a natural for the game, especially as a goalkeeper," Bob began. "You have good quick reflexes, particularly with your hands. You're not a flashy sprinter with blazing speed. But you don't need to be. You have decent stamina even after your recent retirement and recovery. You have good size and a sizable wingspan to cover the net. And your size will give any player second thoughts about charging headlong toward you near the goal. Let's do it, and I'll help you connect with a team. Tomorrow. Oh, and there's lots of money to be earned." Jan listened intently and nodded his head approvingly as Bob painted the flattering picture of Big Jan the Goalkeeper.

Polya was the first one to speak up. With a look of concern, but with the hint of a smile, she asked Bob, "Did you by chance consult, or possibly conspire, with that former friend of ours, Stefan? He's the one who presented us with Jan's last "business opportunity." The opportunity that made some money but almost got my Jan mutilated and crippled for life? That so-called opportunity also resulted in Jan coming really, really close to losing what few brains he had before he began slugging it out with thugs and giants. I've actually watched a few football matches and I've seen bodies tripping, sliding, colliding, funny flags flying everywhere, lots and lots of fist fights. From my amateur's viewpoint there's plenty of bumps, cuts, bruises, even broken bones on a football pitch. It's not much of a football pitch either but much more like a large patch of dirt and a few clumps of grass. There are several more people involved, not just two stupid guys beating each other up in a dirty sawdust and woodchips ring. That's a plus. But you're planning to put my man at the goal, staring down at fifteen or more players kicking and shoving right in front of that same goal. So, my Jan can have the fun of being kicked and shoved, maybe hit in the face with a rocket ball, maybe smashed in the face with a rocket foot. It sounds like boxing in a mob, but a mob without gloves. What do you think, Jan? Does any of this sound like fun?"

Of course it sounded like fun, with his boxing career and his brutal final bout now just a distant memory. But Jan prudently said nothing for the moment, just smiled, and looked to Bob for support. Bob responded. "Polya, you paint too harsh a picture of the Fallingbostel football program. I personally know the British officer who's in charge. He was, and is, a talented football player who fully appreciates how the matches should be played. He's also recruited several other players, officers and enlisted men, to volunteer as referees and linesmen. They're fully committed to seeing that the matches are played fairly and properly. They won't hesitate to call fouls, issue those funny yellow flags, and throw out a player with a red card. They are also fully committed to ensuring the safety of a goalkeeper. Jan will be safe. And I'm very confident he will be good. I believe you might even enjoy watching a few matches. And your handsome hulk will not come home bloodied and crippled."

With his charming and oh so reassuring smile directed at her, Polya smiled back at salesman Bob. And that night Jan, the former heavyweight contender, became a football player. There was no "oy, oy, oy" from Polya this time, only a resigned shrug of her shoulders. However, she still silently wished for some more ho-hum, no contact business opportunity for her ever energetic, ever ambitious Jan.

Bob's upbeat picture of polite, civilized club football was somewhat accurate. But it was only somewhat. Polya was relieved that Jan did not return from his matches battered and crippled. There was a little blood occasionally. But it was only from a bloody nose as Jan found himself on the receiving end of a violent shot on goal. Jan also did receive his share of bruised ribs, black and blue shins and forearms. Captain Bob's benign picture of Fallingbostel football was most starkly inaccurate in suggesting there was little physical contact. Quite the contrary, there was non-stop pushing and holding and tripping. Cards, both yellow and red, were constantly pulled by the conscientious but overworked referees. The frequent red cards all too often left a team woefully short of manpower on the pitch. That in turn left Jan all too often at the goal with little defensive support against a swarm of opposing players charging directly at him.

.

Yes, there were some collisions, but not many, and there were those bruising shots to the chest and head. But, in contrast to the no holds barred bouts in the boxing ring, goalkeeping was quite the welcome new sport. Polya was also ecstatic with this relatively more civilized new outlet for her husband. She even made it to every match, cheering wildly though she knew very little about either strategies or rules. And, she always closed her eyes when her Jan was forced to stand on the goal line awaiting that dreaded penalty kick. Polya also brought the children to every match, and the kids cheered just as wildly as their mother. They likewise knew almost nothing about the game. All they knew, and needed to know, was that their father was the huge man, with the funny colored jersey, guarding a big net. And, he guarded it quite well.

Dozens of teams were formed, many of them populated by a non-descript mix of fellow DP's who just wanted to play together. But, there was a growing number of teams put together by barracks location. Barracks X. recruited its best and toughest to take on other teams from other barracks. The fiercest team rivalries, however, developed among so-called "national" teams or distinct regions and ethnic backgrounds from some European nation. With national pride, or some ethnic pride, playing such an important role in the composition of a team's lineup, the competition among these teams was extremely intense. And, all too often the matches included the inevitable brawl or brawls, along with an excessive number of yellow and red cards.

Because of the intense rivalry among the "national" teams, the football matches generated a large, and equally intense, amount of gambling. The Poles delighted in betting against almost any team, be they Ukrainians or Serbs or whomever. And, so it was with almost every other national team. There was national pride to be restored, old grudges to be settled. There was some modest official payment to the winning players at the weekly organized tournaments. But, that winning prize amount, parceled out by the British authorities and divided among a team's 15 players, was indeed very modest. Unauthorized gambling and payouts among the winning players provided a far more satisfying reward. There were bragging rights as well, huge bragging rights. There were also a handful of spectators, armed with that secret stash of funds brought along to Camp Fallingbostel, who gambled heavily on a national favorite. And, with a team winning its match, some of those wealthy spectators were very willing to reward a winning team with a portion of those sideline bets. There were hearty handshakes with a hearty wad of rubles or kopeks included with those handshakes. There also were generous quantities of vodka to add to the celebration. Everything to keep teammates happy and to keep those teams winning.

Jan had the added luxury of being a talented and very sought-after goalkeeper. His background was conveniently vague, and he spoke several languages. Consequently, he was recruited often during his two years in camp football to switch from one national team to another. And, that switch would include some generous "thank you" bonus for the negotiated switch. Boxing, despite the physical toll on Jan, had been profitable for Jan and his family. Football turned out to be just as profitable, and far less painful. Here he was again, Jan the opportunist, doing that which he enjoyed while he collected a few pounds, dollars or marks as well.

………………………………………..

During those early years in America we three kids (my little brother would arrive seven years after me) explored and enjoyed some success with very traditional American sports. It would be thirty plus years later that football (or now American "soccer") finally became fashionable, and we pursued the sport through our children. But, only then did we first learn about our father's soccer playing past. Our mother shared those long-forgotten memories of us children watching and cheering our father. But regrettably, as was too often the case, Jan Bykowski, the star goalkeeper of Camp Fallingbostel, shared very few details of those football years. Lost stories, lost opportunities for us children. Had we known this history much earlier we might have enjoyed some playful dribbling and shots on goal with that Fallingbostel goalkeeping star.

Chapter 19 - Friends and Family

"Family not only need to consist of merely those we share blood, but also for those whom we'd give blood."

Nicholas Nickleby by Charles Dickens

Jan continued to be successful as a breadwinner and popular athlete. That, unfortunately, too often left little time to devote to either Polya or the children. Shy by nature and fully devoted to her children's welfare, Polya didn't build many camp friendships at first. But, she began to regain some of that self-esteem and confidence from her early Borisov years. She also slowly, but steadily, did cultivate some friendships which would prove invaluable when immigration out of their DP "home" became a possibility.

Most important for Polya was the continuing friendship and mentoring from Stefan Mirovich. He remained that loving father figure as well as the jovial, often generous, uncle to the children. Polya still deeply regretted her childhood failure to continue in school. And, here Stefan was most valuable. He supplied her with a small mountain of continuing homework. He supplied her with an equal sized mountain of quizzes which oftentimes she was forced to retake. She struggled, she resisted, but eventually Stefan declared she had met all the requirements for her "graduation" from the Borisov equivalent of junior high school. Stefan even enlisted a friend to create a suitable diploma for his proud graduate. Stefan was also an invaluable tutor for Polya in mastering day-to-day Polish. With her limited contacts outside the home, she didn't get much practice in or exposure to what was supposedly her native tongue. And, when she did get out Jan typically dominated the conversation and sheltered her from too much interaction, if any at all. However, Jan, Polya and Stefan knew the Bykowski's would need to present themselves as far more authentic Poles when they began exploring immigration with British authorities. Again, Stefan undertook this language challenge with the same enthusiasm and energy he brought to Polya's schooling. There was reading and writing and constant conversations. And, again Stefan produced a competent, and very proud, graduate.

Another friendship, and a very unexpected one, arose out of Jan's boxing career. The entire DP population loved the competition, and everyone liked and admired its creator and boxing commissioner, Bob the Bruiser. He didn't need nor expect to be called a "Captain Bob," though he didn't object. But he very much enjoyed the "Bruiser" label.

Jan was certainly one of Bob's favorites. He was disappointed but very supportive when Jan decided to retire. They had trained together extensively, and Captain Bob was a frequent visitor to the Bykowski household. Even after Jan switched from boxing trunks to football shorts Bob continued to be a frequent visitor. The British officer had a devoted wife back in England, but they had no children. Polya gained a kind, caring, oftentimes very funny, older brother. The children gained another jovial uncle with that equally funny and at times incomprehensible British accent. Bob taught both Jan and Polya a few survival words and phrases in English. More importantly, that growing friendship would prove invaluable in the early months of 1949. Britain, along with its allies, was developing the administrative framework for the resettlement of its vast DP population. News also spread throughout the camp, and throughout Europe, that President Truman had signed a historic Displaced Persons Act of 1948. Immigration to America, viewed by almost every immigrant to be the new promised land, could now be not just a pipe dream but a reality. It certainly couldn't hurt to have an ally, as well as a true friend, in the British command to help navigate around the immigration obstacles.

Though Polya, along with Jan and the children, loved and enjoyed their surrogate DP family, Polya's deepest fondness was for the zany Bialystok Boys, Mikel and Pavel. It had been only a brief encounter in Bialystok during the family's escape from Borisov. But, here they were,l equally shocked and surprised and ecstatic, as the two cousins spotted Polya one sunny afternoon in the stands cheering for Jan (the former Ivan) at a football match. She now had two children to wrestle with, and it had been almost four years since their Bialystok encounter. But, the boys were just as starstruck as they had been back then. Polya was less shy and more poised than the young beauty they had first met in the back streets of Bialystok. But, she still was a beautiful young lady. And, the boys instantly made themselves the newest additions to the Bykowski family.

Mikel and Pavel were cousins born and raised in the small Polish town of Baranovicz. The boys were the respective oldest children from two closely knit families on adjoining plots of farmland. Their fathers were hard working but also very fun loving. A simple farm life, including some livestock, should have been perfectly fine for these two cousins. Additionally, each household had six children to share farm chores. Completing the family portraits, each household included a loving and ever cheerful mother and wife. What else could a young, healthy Polish boy want or need?

 The two cousins worked hard, were good big brothers to their siblings, and were very much like their fathers with their silly jokes and pranks. But both cousins dreamed about and schemed about escaping the comfort and the boredom of farm life. Though bright enough, they were terrible students, always slow with their homework and constantly disruptive in the classroom. They weren't mean spirited or cruel with those jokes and pranks. They were simply young and dumb and bored. They also were very well acquainted with the ever present and the frequently used switch their one-hundred-year-old school teacher nun enjoyed administering to the boys' knuckles. (Maybe she wasn't quite one hundred, but close).

Mikel and Pavel were born only two months apart. And at their sixteenth birthdays their fathers grudgingly released them from their roles as senior farm hands and big brothers to find the elusive fame and fortune in the big city. Off they went together after the fall harvest and connected with some distant but friendly cousin in Bialystok. It was a medium sized industrial town of 25,000. And, there were some added opportunities, along with some risks, because of its proximity to the Byelorussian border. With free lodging offered by their distant cousin, the country cousins, now the Bialystok Boys, went job hunting. Their fathers would not have approved of, nor applauded, their sons' choices. But here they were hustling on the streets, and more often in the back streets and alleys, of Bialystok. There was some day labor in the factories and warehouses, providing enough pay to get by and splurge at a dingy bar. But, there were more profitable opportunities in smuggling anything and everything back and forth across the border. There were black market goods to buy or sell or barter. There were the occasional unguarded or carelessly unlocked warehouses with merchandise the Boys would "borrow." That's what the Boys jokingly labeled their burglaries: warehouse goods which they were "borrowing" but would return some day. Besides, the Polish military guarding the warehouses was just as corrupt as the Soviet military counterparts across the border. There was rarely any violence or vandalism, just quick grab and run. And, even if some scheme or deal blew up on them, hardly anyone could resist the irrepressible smiles, the slick, partially believable excuses the Bialystok Boys delivered.

These were the young, reckless but very likable cousins Ivan and Polya had met in Bialystok on their westward passage. The caravan gang, plus little Tamara, and the Bialystok Boys had spent two days laughing, scavenging, and even "borrowing" together. "Borrowing." That was the creative label the Boys had used in Bialystok: "borrowing" whatever they needed or wanted. Mikel and Pavel also quickly learned back then at their first meeting with Jan and Polya in Bialystok that the caravan members were Byelorussian. But it didn't matter to the Boys. Here, reunited in Camp Fallingbostel, it still didn't matter to them. Though their respective motives were different, and their goals were different, all six adults were simply struggling to survive back in those tough streets of Bialystok. And, here they were together again, in Camp Fallingbostel, still struggling to survive.

Mikel and Pavel had traveled a very different, even more troublesome, road from Bialystok to the heartland of Germany. After the Bykowski's left Bialystok, semi-comfortable in their "borrowed" wagon, the Boys were rounded up by German soldiers. Then it was a combination of overcrowded trucks and overcrowded railcars that hauled the Boys and countless other Poles to forced labor in Germany. Hannover was their new place of employment with housing at labor camp Fallingbostel. Fortunately for them the labor and imprisonment were relatively brief as the British liberated Hannover less than a year later.

It was freedom, and freedom so gratefully welcomed. But, it was only partial freedom. The boys were no longer prisoners at the once dreaded Camp Fallingbostel. Nonetheless they remained at the camp, now as homeless DP's. It wasn't much of a home. But there was almost nothing of Bialystok or Baranovicz to which they could return even if they were able to leave the camp. They were simply DP's from a country that now barely existed after its collective destruction by both the Germans and the Soviets. These Polish refugees, the Bialystok Boys, did what they did best, easily making friends and finding opportunities throughout the Polish population. Their chance reunion with Polya at the football pitch provided them one new group of friends to offset the monotony of camp life.

Having reunited, the Bialystok Boys enthusiastically watched and cheered at Jan's matches, visited the home frequently, entertained everyone with their silly stories and childish roughhousing. There still was that deep infatuation with Polya. But, the Boys were now smart enough, and prudent enough, to hold their emotions in check. For Polya they became the fond and very protective siblings she never really had. And, they would do anything for her, anything. In 1949 as immigration activity increased Polya would present them with a severe test of their loyalty to her.

Chapter. 20 - Immigration Games

"Success is a collection of problems solved."

I. M. Pei

With the war's end the Allied powers were confronted with an estimated six million displaced persons within Germany's borders. There was a complex mix of concentration camp survivors, prisoners of war, enslaved laborers and political prisoners. Fortunately, the Allies were able to repatriate a large number back to their home countries or resettle many others to somewhere outside of Germany. Despite this herculean effort, by the end of 1945 there still were over one million DP's remaining in Germany.

Repatriation became an ever more urgent priority for the Allies. The ongoing administration of the DP camps, largely under American and British control, was presenting a larger economic strain on government budgets. The camps also added to the military's ongoing massive task of maintaining order among a large, diverse, and increasingly restless population. Polish DP's were singled out as the high priority for repatriation since they were the largest ethnic group of the one million plus DP population still residing in Germany. This repatriation priority should have been an added blessing for Jan and Apolonia. But it also presented them with some competing and difficult options.

It was universally acknowledged by all the Allied powers that DP camps housed countless numbers of Nazi sympathizers, collaborators, spies, soldiers, and war criminals who had managed to slip into the DP safe havens. Sympathetic lies were easily offered, fake papers were obtained, army uniforms were buried or burned and replaced with nondescript peasant garb. It was the Allied mission to identify, prosecute and definitely not allow them to slip away out of Germany and Allied hands. A quick repatriation to their claimed Polish "homeland", if offered, would enable Ivan to avoid any close Allied scrutiny. Or so he hoped. And Jan sensed that even though he had survived his initial six-week jail episode a threat of another investigation, maybe jail, was possible.

Unfortunately, repatriation could put him at risk with Polish authorities as well. The risk really wasn't from Polish authorities. Poles had little if any authority. Poland was under the control of an assertive communist regime and was now a post-war Soviet puppet "Republic." And communists were likewise hunting for those same Nazi collaborators and sympathizers who had betrayed their Soviet motherland. Jan, the former Ivan of Borisov, could very likely appear on some Soviet wanted list.

Stay in Germany and possibly be identified and prosecuted. Repatriate to Poland and maybe be identified and prosecuted. The old cliche of "damned if you do, damned if you don't" fit all too perfectly for Jan and his family. And the British and Americans added to Jan's predicament by their collective push to repatriate Poles.

The pace of repatriation was aggressive and impressive, at least initially. A push began in earnest in October 1945 and resulted in almost 120,000 Poles returning to Poland from the camps. Another 106,000 repatriated the following month. But by January 1946, as a brutal winter set in, Polish repatriation completely shut down. The initial surge was probably a mix of euphoria and the exciting prospect of freedom from any camp, no matter how benign the camp had been. But the enthusiasm for many changed to growing indecision about returning home. Homes and cities and small villages where they had lived were reduced to rubble. For some, their Polish village had been annexed and now was within the newly proclaimed border of Soviet Russia. The Polish government was no more than a puppet regime, run by Russians. And many DPs, if pressed to choose, admitted they preferred the German occupation over a Russian occupation. Maybe it wasn't such a bad idea to delay or even refuse repatriation? Maybe more immigration options, not just repatriation, might become available? Possibly to Canada or Australia or the biggest prize, America?

Repatriation versus non-repatriation was hotly debated among the DP camp population. And this debate added to Jan's own indecision. Numerous fellow Polish DPs frequently asked Jan about his relocation plans. The questions weren't mean spirited or combative, usually. But the questions, along with unsolicited advice, were all too frequent. Some DPs urged him to repatriate and badgered him to explain why he appeared hesitant to do so. Others urged him to stay within the comfort and stability of Camp Fallingbostel and questioned why he felt so uncomfortable when asked about his Polish roots. Jan could only offer weak explanations or just shrug his shoulders and walk away in silence, hoping to preempt any longer and awkward streetside conversation. For Jan there were no good choices, no convenient and safe answers.

President Truman's Displaced Persons Act of 1948 provided a much-needed additional avenue for resettlement out of Germany, at least on paper. The Act's long title read "An act to authorize for a limited period of time the admission to the United States of certain persons for permanent residence." The legislative history behind the bill indicated a strong desire to prioritize immigration visas for Polish DP's. Call it a brilliant strategy. Call it serendipity. Call it simple dumb luck. Whatever it might be called, Jan and Polya's early decision to assume a Polish identity improved their immigration chances, at least on paper. The legislation also identified an "eligible displaced person" as one who was in Germany as a DP between 1939 and "on or before December 22, 1945." The Bykowski's, with their late 1944 Hannover arrival and their "residence" first in Hannover and then at Camp Fallingbostel, definitely qualified. That "residence" was in the British zone, this again satisfying another legislative prerequisite for an "eligible displaced person." The American zone would also qualify as an acceptable "residence. The Russian post-war occupation zone was not included.

Sadly, that well intended, humanitarian legislation provided very modest tangible relief. Immigration visas could not exceed two hundred thousand for the first two years. Furthermore, the law was scheduled to sunset in 1952. These legislative restrictions, coupled with that narrow legislative sunset window, underscored the prevailing anti-immigration sentiment in the US. America had more than enough problems, more than enough of its own to feed and clothe and shelter after this terrible war. America did not need any more foreigners. With the Act's June 1952 expiration, President Truman's humanitarian effort resulted in a modest total of 393,542 DP's resettling in America. Of those fortunate few, 34 percent had listed Poland as their country of birth.

Through the Camp's informal news network, Jan and Polya heard about the inaugural transport of Truman's DP's to America on October 30, 1948. A refurbished troop transport, the USS General Black, departed from Bremerhaven harbor with 883 grateful and very jubilant passengers. Almost half of them were Poles, with half of them scheduled to make New York City their new home. What an exciting resettlement possibility for any DP. Jan and Polya, Poles, with their two cute little Poles, could be on that next transport out of Bremerhaven. Maybe, just maybe, that most sought-after goal of resettlement in America wasn't that impossible. But, after some brief euphoria, imagining the four of them on board the USS General

Black on its second trans-Atlantic passage, the two DP's had to return to and contend with real life Camp Fallingbostel.

Added layers of bureaucracy and paperwork became the daily norm in the spring of 1949. German authorities had joined with the allied occupation command, notably the Americans and British, to restore some order to the massive postwar population. "Resettlement" was the fancy bureaucratic label for the campaign to close all the camps and release all DP's. The campaign's simple strategy was to send DP's to wherever they wanted to go and to what country would accept them. But, as with every bureaucracy, particularly one driven by the military, someone, any DP, couldn't just say "I want to go there," wherever "there" might be, and go there. There had to be paperwork. Lots of paperwork.

Jan and Polya were no exceptions to the common desire to leave Germany. But, they had two major obstacles to overcome. First, they had no documents whatsoever to provide to anyone. No birth certificates, no marriage license, no childrens' birth certificates. The absence of any documents was actually somewhat of a plus since any authentic documents would identify them as Byelorussian nationals, not Poles. Their second obstacle was to create some credible documentation to support their claim of Polish citizenship. Poles were receiving extra support and priority during this resettlement campaign. Soviet nationals, from whatever republic, were not. And Byelorussia was certainly the last place to which Jan and Polya wanted to return. President Truman's 1948 Immigration Act opened an additional, even if small, door to a new exodus of DP's, Poles in particular, to America. So America it should be, and Poles they definitely needed to be. But, how could they navigate through this immigration maze?

The more difficult initial question that needed answering was not how to navigate the immigration maze but if they should even attempt to do so. The American president, Harry S. Truman, was presenting a tremendous opportunity for these two displaced "Poles." How could this ever restless, resourceful opportunist pass it by? Immigration, and quite possibly to that most sought-after America was an opportunity not just for Ivan, that all too often self-centered Ivan. He saw this as an opportunity for his wife, an opportunity for their two children, to find a new home, to solidify their new identities, and to leave their troublesome European history behind, and hopefully behind forever.

Despite the allure and excitement of immigration, Ivan hesitated. He and his family were living comfortably. Certainly, they were not wealthy, but they were comfortable. More importantly, they were invisible within the vast confines of Camp Fallingbostel. There were no threats. There were no current investigations. That one awkward and uncomfortable period in jail was almost ancient history. Almost. Immigration applications, probably related background checks, could again generate renewed inquiries into Jan's past. Fallingbostel's population was shrinking. But, the DP population was still sizable. Maybe there might be some volunteer role for Jan or Polya, maybe some modest supervisory position. Or maybe Captain Bob the Bruiser might pull some bureaucratic strings and secure a more permanent position for Ivan, whether in England or Germany. Yes ,even post-war Germany, outside a DP camp, might not be such an unrealistic possibility. Here was Ivan, the opportunist, seriously considering doing nothing, just kicking that prized immigration can down the road. It certainly was easier to do so. It also was safer not just for him but for his wife and children.

Uncharacteristic as it was for Ivan to discuss rather than decide, one night after dinner and with children in bed, Ivan asked Polya to sit down and discuss the immigration pros and cons. He spoke slowly and patiently, and it was a frank and lengthy exchange, with Polya saying little but nodding her head periodically to convey her understanding and her support. With nothing more to explore, Ivan offered some semblance of a smile and said, "It will be one hell of a challenge. And there are huge risks. I'm willing to take on those risks. But, I want you to be comfortable and prepared to go forward. Not just me alone. I want it to be and it needs to be the two of us. Are you willing?" Polya rarely spoke forcefully. And, any profanity or crude language from her was even more rare. Ivan provided more than enough of that every day. But, Polya reached across the table, firmly grabbed both of Ivan's hands and declared, "Hell, yes, let's go for it!!!"

Their first step in moving forward was to consult their old friend and mentor, Stefan Mirovich. Stefan was likewise committed to exiting Germany, ideally immigrating to everyone's promised land, the U.S. of A. He was also well aware of the documentation obstacles. Stefan's advice? Create your own history, enlist friends and witnesses as necessary. And, then deliver that history with as much humility, sincerity and conviction as possible. Ivan was ever the resourceful, successful opportunist. Polya had matured into quite the capable opportunist as well. They could pull it off.

The critical hurdle for the two of them, and for any undocumented DP, was to complete the somewhat ominous but very necessary "Statement on Oath." That Statement, submitted before some "resettlement officer" in Hamburg, sworn to that officer and dutifully notarized, needed to present the vital "personal status" of the Bykowski family: birth dates and places, parentage, childrens' birth information. All those vital personal "statements" could be created and then packaged as a combination of fact and fiction into the all-important big "Statement." That was the easy part. But, and a big but at that, the Statement needed two witnesses to attest - under oath - to the truthfulness of the Bykowski declarations.

There were countless resettlement applications to process. And the marching order was to move applicants as quickly as possible with minimal bureaucratic paper pushing. There also were few, if any, background checks. Yes, there still was some risk in submitting a false statement. There was also a significant risk for someone to assume the role of a documented, very public, witness to a false statement. For Jan and Polya there was no question, certainly no hesitation, as to what needed to be done. A witness, and more precisely, two credible witnesses were their critical stumbling blocks.

Polya addressed that stumbling block by volunteering to recruit her dear, fun-loving Bialystok Boys, Mikel and Pavel. At dinner that night Polya laid out her recruitment plan. "We can enlist my Bialystok Boys to serve as our authentic Polish witnesses," she proposed. Polya enjoyed using that playful affectionate Bialystok Boys label. During their collective, if brief, time together in Bialystok they literally had become her "Boys", following her everywhere, responding to her every request, however serious or silly. She continued. "They're very real, native Poles who have traveled everywhere. They can give us first hand background on towns and villages we can talk about and claim as our birthplaces. They'll be our longtime friends, maybe our childhood playmates, to better convince others about our Polish roots. They're clever and quick on their feet. I'm confident they can stand up to any tough questions or hassling from any dimwitted British officer. I know for certain the Boys are very loyal and devoted to us and will do anything we ask them to do."

Jan listened, didn't interrupt, and did offer the occasional supportive smile and nod of the head as Polya laid out her plan. But he had his serious reservations. "Yes, I'm sure they are loyal, and they are devoted. But that loyalty and devotion are directed just to cute, lovely you. They spend all their time tripping over each other trying to get your attention, trying to get a smile. They don't give a damn about me," Jan replied, and with some bitterness in his voice. Jan was always too quick to become jealous of any man, especially some young man who offered a few words or a smile to Polya. And these Bialystok Boys had offered more than their fair share of flattering words and big smiles. This jealousy would remain a lingering, lifelong problem for Jan. "And despite your glowing picture of their talents," Jan continued, "your so-called "Boys" are best known around the camp for their stupid jokes, their equally stupid pranks, and their black market salesmanship. With their reputation for always hustling for some quick money - any kind of money - they could be easily bought or bribed. Or even with their supposed loyalty, they might simply decide to turn on us. They are the true Poles after all. We'd be ratted out as phony Poles, and not just phony Poles but phony Soviet Poles. And these are the two you're expecting us to trust with our future, maybe even our lives?"

Polya had likewise listened in silence to Jan as he made his compelling counter argument. " I hear you. I do understand and share some of your concerns as well," she said. "And, yes, they are more devoted to me. But I truly believe they will stay loyal to me. And they'll be loyal to you as well, and they won't betray us. And they will wholeheartedly and happily commit to the game of outwitting any British interrogators. Also, and unfortunately for the two of us, they're not just our best option. They frankly are our only realistic option." And with that last comment both Jan and Polya agreed to enlist their Bialystok Boys. But before Polya went to meet the Boys, Jan tossed out the idea of a sizable bribe, he'd call it a generous "thank you," to hopefully solidify their commitment. Polya's response was swift. "Absolutely Not!" she replied. "They are loyal, they will remain loyal, and they don't need, nor will they expect anything. A bribe will be an insult to them. No, I'll go to them, ask for their help, and they will deliver." And deliver they would.

Polya met with them the next day. She alternated between playful flirt and damsel in distress. She laid out the plan and their vital roles. As she spoke, she could see the Boys' growing enthusiasm and excitement. They were delighted to join in this high stakes game of deception. They could and would outwit the Brits and secure that all important Statement on Oath for Polya - and for Jan as well.

Mikel and Pavel built a convincing background for not just Jan and Polya but for the Boys as well. There were small town birthplaces for Jan and Polya, and the Boys provided detailed histories of those towns should the resettlement officer be curious or suspicious. Mikel and Pavel also built a credible back story as to why these four knew one another. Mikel had a girlfriend who in turn became a friend of Polya. Pavel and Jan went back several years as school mates and friends. The Bialystok Boys, formerly the Baranovicz Boys, were close cousins and all four had met and became friends in Bialystok. The Boys provided detailed histories of the "big" city as well, just in case.

With all the raw data in place Mikel and Pavel drilled the two nervous applicants on their stories. The drilling was relentless and intense, and there was no timeline for the as yet unscheduled Statement on Oath interview. It could be weeks away. It could be days away. Every morning the foursome rehearsed their "Statement" stories. They reconvened at dinner every night as well to continue rehearsing. The Boys knew their core stories, the birthplaces, the childhood villages. Jan and Polya needed to learn and memorize the most and be the most convincing. To their credit, Mikel and Pavel fully embraced their roles as teachers and taskmasters. A present-day attorney would have been impressed as the Boys prepped their two witnesses for their time on the witness stand. Together they bombarded their witnesses with questions. "Where were you born? Describe that village. You're not really a Pole are you? Where was your spouse born? Why did you go to

Bialystok? Where and how did you meet this Pavel character?" The Boys alternated between polite and rude, between good cop and bad cop, trying their best to unnerve their witnesses or catch them in some contradiction. No one knew what to expect, therefore the Boys drilled Jan and Polya to expect the worst.

The intense drilling was all the more important for Polya since she still struggled to master conversational Polish. She needed to know her script, needed to comfortably recite her script, but do so with good conversational Polish. Polya also reminded the coaching staff that she couldn't provide an actual birthdate. She had to admit, with embarrassment, she didn't know that date, nor could her mother help. With her imperfect command of Polish the four of them came up with a convenient solution. They gave Polya a birthday, numerical birth month, and birth year which were collectively easy to remember and even easier to recite anytime and anywhere to whoever asked. Every day at both rehearsal sessions Polya was ordered to recite her vital birth statistics thirty times, and to do so quickly. That quick fix proved to be invaluable. So what if it was pure fiction? No one would know and no one would really care. Except Polahaya.

Whether good news or bad, just five days after the deception plan was conceived and rehearsals began, Jan received word the two of them, plus witnesses, were expected the next day for their "Statement on Oath." In those five days Jan's initial skepticism had quickly turned to enthusiasm and optimism and great admiration for his Polish cast members. Those real Poles had schooled and harassed and cheered on their students and turned Polya and Jan into credible Polish applicants. Nervous? They were definitely nervous. But, they were also eager to go forward, to have this last immigration hurdle behind them.

A battered British army truck transported the four to Hamburg the next morning. The two children were left with a kind, grandmotherly neighbor. The foursome was directed to a nondescript building with a large wooden sign propped up by the front door identifying this to be the "501 Sub-Area Office" of the International Relief Organization. The entire operation was under British supervision, neat and orderly and precise as to who went where, did what. Everything was oh so organized and oh so terrifying to the foursome. It also didn't ease anyone's nerves to see a heavy military presence along with an estimated 400 other applicants queuing in classic British fashion for their interviews.

The Bykowski name was called, and the four entered a small room. There was a British military person who identified himself as the Resettlement Officer. There was also a non-military German official with an unintelligible title and a young lady who spoke in a whisper and identified herself as the International Relief representative. And, most ominously for all, there was a mousey, wrinkled old woman, barely visible behind her sparse desk and her large typewriter. . She said nothing, never made eye contact, just slowly and methodically typed every single word that was spoken.

The two applicants, plus their accomplices/witnesses, fully expected an intense interrogation, skeptical questions, maybe some surprise document to debunk their so-called statements they were making "on oath." Instead, the Resettlement Officer was surprisingly pleasant. Technically he was a non-commissioned officer in the British army, a veteran Master Sergeant as was evident by the bars and chevrons on his uniform. He was an older soldier, with a grizzled face, even a little facial stubble. Master Sergeant William B. Hammond was past his combat prime, but still very fit, except for a slight limp as he walked across the small office space to greet his next group of interviewees. The foursome was taken aback by their interviewer. They had expected a high-ranking military officer, maybe some stern looking captain or major to interrogate them. However, the entire camp was overwhelmed by the ongoing immigration exodus, and it was woefully short of senior officer personnel to process the never ending line of applicants. Therefore, the master sergeant was reassigned from field duty to desk duty.

The master sergeant extended a hand to the men, offered a casual nod to the ladies. After brief, polite hellos he slowly ambled over to a very weathered office chair and comfortably slouched in it. He gestured for everyone to sit. With his casual gesture and his relaxed pose behind the desk he conveyed an unspoken but clear message: "Relax, don't be nervous or scared." It was quite evident Master Sergeant Hammond didn't take himself or his desk duty too seriously. Maybe he was bored. Maybe he was growing weary of the endless, nameless stream of applicants waiting their turn. Maybe he wanted the interviews to be quick and friendly and over, allowing him to limp over to that much needed stop at the non-com club. And maybe, just maybe, he sympathized with this endless stream of DP's who were desperately, and very understandably, trying to escape this "paradise" in search of a better future. And maybe Master Sergeant William B. Hammond, an anxious DP's final immigration gatekeeper, simply believed he should not and would not be an obstacle in anyone's pursuit of an escape from Camp Fallingbostel.

With formal introductions out of the way, the master sergeant explained he could address any of them in English or German or Polish. Turning his attention to Jan and Polya his questions weren't much more than rudimentary "name, rank and serial number." There was a predictable inquiry as to their respective birthplaces. But then the master sergeant asked them how and when the two of them managed to end up in this "paradise" called Camp Fallingbostel. Jan was caught off guard by the question. Everyone was here because they all were liberated ex-prisoners. End of story. The foursome had hardly given the question any attention during their extensive rehearsing sessions. Jan stammered a little, briefly lost his trademark poise. But he quickly recovered. In fluent Polish he replied. "Ours is the same journey, Sergeant Hammond... My apologies, Master Sergeant Hammond. Our journey is the same as every other Pole in every Polish town and village. The Germans came, destroyed, killed, captured. We managed to escape at first. We ran, we hid, we eventually were rounded up, where and when I can't say. Then there were forced marches to Germany, forced labor, where and for how long I again can't say. And with the Allied liberation we again were rounded up and dumped here in what you have so kindly called a "paradise." Jan offered a half-hearted smile, shrugged his shoulders as if to say "I have no more details or information to offer." Master Sergeant Hammond smiled back and didn't probe further. He then turned to Polya and asked if she had anything further to add. Prudently, Polya only smiled and shook her head. She had been coached well to keep her conversation to an absolute minimum to avoid highlighting her poor command of Polish.

The master sergeant abruptly shifted his focus to Mikel and Pavel, the Bialystok Boys. They were the all-important witnesses to that all-important Statement on Oath. That was the document that would validate the Polish nationality of these two nervous immigration applicants. Master Sergeant Hammond probed more thoroughly into the Boys' background, their relationship to Polya and Jan, the Boys' own refugee odyssey from Bialystok to Hannover and Camp Fallingbostel. It was a critical, lengthy probe but it really was much more a curious inquiry by the master sergeant as to how this foursome had connected. And Pavel and Mikel, the very talented Bialystok Boys, delivered their storyline masterfully. If anything, they were maybe too smooth, too glib in recounting the foursome's friendship and their childhood adventures. It was quite evident Master Sergeant Hammond was thoroughly sold and entertained.

Though he had some mixed emotions about doing so, he eventually had to politely cut the Boys short with their enthusiastic storytelling. The visit to the non-com club was long overdue.

There were no more questions to ask, no documents that needed further examination. And with a firm handshake from the Resettlement Officer to Jan and Polya, and a thank you to Mikel and Pavel, the Statement on Oath was formally signed by all. The Bykowskis were ushered out, a new applicant or couple was ushered in.

Between the continuing exits and entries at the interview room there was only one immovable constant. It was that wrinkled old woman. She never looked up from her ancient typewriter, apparently never took a break, never said a word. She just typed history. Maybe she was typing historical facts, maybe she was typing historical fiction. For the wrinkled old woman, it probably didn't matter. She just typed. For the Resettlement Officer this might have been his hundredth interview that day, maybe his three-thousandth that month. With few exceptions all the interviewed applicants were understandably nervous but believable. They came from small towns, led simple lives before the war, now had nothing. And, now they were looking for that ticket out of that former prison work camp, Camp Fallingbostel, to somewhere better. This Resettlement Officer was more than willing to listen to any "oath," accept that oath in good faith, and help an immigrant move forward toward that sought after resettlement "somewhere, anywhere."

During the drive back to Fallingbostel in the battered truck, now packed with twenty other passengers, the foursome said little, did not engage others with their respective application histories. Maybe there was a British spy on board. Maybe one of the four had made a fatal error in their rehearsed stories. Maybe someone might actually be from Bialystok or Baranovicz. The four survived the trip back, an hour drive which felt like ten hours instead of one. But, once they returned to the Bykowski house, retrieved the two children, and closed the door they broke into a collective chorus of cheers and screams, and an endless stream of tears, celebrating their successful "Statement on Oath." Pavel excused himself, returned sweaty and winded fifteen minutes later, and started their celebration with not one but two bottles of vodka, expensive Polish vodka. Jan and Polya were now officially registered as Poles, so why not celebrate with good Polish stuff.

The paperwork went forward without any questions or delays, it now serving as a universal application for immigration to whatever country was willing to accept these four Polish DP's. Everything was going forward nicely. Almost everything. There still was the problem of "bad blood."

The immigration application routinely included a perfunctory medical exam, complete with a blood test. There was some truth in the slogan about America, and other generous nations, welcoming the poor, the downtrodden, those yearning to be free. But, the open arms weren't quite so open for immigrants with serious health problems. Countries like America, Great Britain, Australia had their own share of the ill and disabled already. An exam and blood test would, or maybe could, identify troublesome histories such as typhus or polio or tuberculosis. It could also identify, and possibly disqualify, an applicant with a history of dysentery. And, Jan had struggled through, but survived, a nasty bout of dysentery in his first year in Hannover.

The risk of detection and disqualification was too great, the stakes too high for Jan. He had to come up with a Plan B. In theory the plan was pretty straightforward. Jan would recruit someone to impersonate him and provide the necessary - and clean - blood sample. As he had already discovered, the entire immigration process was massive, very loosely organized, often chaotic, and not very well policed. Jan had several friends who had a passing similarity to him. They were good, trustworthy friends, willing to lend a hand. Jan was also shrewd enough to secure someone's support, as well as the necessary silence, with a generous bribe. And, like it was for the Bialystok Boys, this presented another opportunity to outwit the British authorities. Jan's friend succeeded; the blood testing was benign. And, with another hurdle behind them, Jan and Polya, plus children, were placed on the immigration rolls. But, there they remained for the next eighteen months.

Summer Research, Summer Memories

An old, very sturdy wooden chest had been hauled off to the curbside a dozen years ago when the parents relocated to Ohio. At that time there was no sentiment, no nostalgic farewell to the European relic that had served as the family's one and only piece of transatlantic luggage. But as we continued our summertime research that old long forgotten chest now brought back old memories. It also generated additional questions and its share of historic contradictions.

The most noteworthy contradiction was the chest's prominent Tennessee street address painted on a chest that had never been to Tennessee. Our father, presumably the chest's creator, must have found the bottom of an old paint can, probably an equally old paint brush, and salvaged enough paint to crudely print out the vital statistics of street name, house number, and a mystery American state with its baffling array of double vowels and double consonants. The decades old explanation/myth was that the family was booked for an American settlement in Tennessee. Only after our father's death did our mother debunk that myth. We were never scheduled to become Tennesseans or Volunteers or whatever else those American locals called themselves. A fictitious Tennessee "sponsorship" was simply part of a common and effective scheme to enable European refugees to secure transatlantic passage. Our one and only Tennessee "home" was our weather beaten wooden chest.

That long forgotten chest had also provided its share of fond memories. As youngsters that chest was off limits, or at least its contents were, until we two oldest siblings were declared old enough to learn the fine art of boxing. With that decision two pairs of well used boxing gloves were pulled out of the mystery chest. And boxing lessons began.

Though we weren't allowed to explore the chest's contents, we were welcome to sit on it, use it for whatever. We two brothers put it to heavy use as our exercise bench. Our father found or bought or maybe bartered a basic set of dumbbells, a bar and a set of weights for bench presses. A few thin pillows and a folded blanket provided a modest cushion on the hard wooden lid. Five years later we were provided with a new, bona fide weightlifting bench. But during those five years the chest held up, literally so, and served its purpose well.

The chest also served as a durable laboratory table for one elaborate high school science project. The chest suffered through test tubes, several of which broke. It supported a smallish, makeshift aquarium that was supposed to grow some exotic underwater plants, very unsuccessfully. That plant growing failure certainly wasn't the chest's fault. The chest also served as the home for a half dozen petri dishes, all containing creepy, unidentifiable contents. The entire science project was a disaster though, gratefully, it was not an "F." That sturdy, tough old oak chest survived all that abuse. And if we had the foresight to hold on to that chest, instead of carelessly discarding it at the street curb, it very likely could still be some grandchild's sturdy workbench, maybe even a fun hiding place. And that old, crudely painted address might still be there to confuse innocent and curious minds.

Chapter 21 - Anticipation and Preparation

"The scariest moment is always just before you start."

Stephen King

Family names were called, countless DP's boarded transport ships to new homes. America was the universal first choice for everyone. On Jan's and Polya's applications they listed several desirable destinations. Any destination, except Byelorussia, would be just fine. But, they didn't list America. It was the most sought after, definitely. Consequently, with so many applications the odds of acceptance were less favorable. Background checks by the American immigration officers were also rumored to be the most extensive and thorough. Jan certainly did not want that kind of probing. Despite all these prudent, cautionary steps the Bykowski family name did not get called, not by France, or Canada or Ireland. Not by any country. Disappointing weeks turned into disappointing months. That disappointment was compounded by Stefan's announcement in late 1950 that he was shipping off in a few days to America. Even the Bialystok boys got the joyful news they were heading to Canada.

Hope turned to increasing despair. There was even a growing fear that somehow the family's true history had been discovered. Jan the Pole was not a Pole. Jan was a gangster, having spent his early years working the streets of Borisov as "Ivan the Terrible." Jan was a despised collaborator. It wasn't even Jan's blood sample. With increasing despair, and with few options, Jan turned to his old boxing mentor, Captain "Bob the Bruiser." He wasn't directly involved in the British immigration efforts. But, the captain was well connected with the senior personnel, and a good word from Captain

Fisher certainly couldn't hurt. Fisher did reach out but learned British applications were currently on hold. The captain was also a good friend of an American immigration counterpart. He painted a sympathetic picture of Jan and his family, stressing they had been in immigration limbo for eighteen plus months. And, the family included two very cute children Captain Fisher absolutely adored. To the captain's great surprise, the American officer urged the captain to bring Ivan and Polya, and definitely the children, for an application and for an interview. Shocked, delighted, even a little confused, the family scheduled that visit the very next day. And what a great day it was.

Lieutenant George Cooper was a 30-year-old artillery officer now assigned to processing immigration applications. He had been loaned to the British sector to help power through the stockpile of applications from the sprawling, overpopulated Camp Fallingbostel. Cooper was efficient, thorough, and hardworking. He had a pleasant, no-nonsense style in interviewing applicants, particularly those pursuing a "resettlement" to America. He had also conducted a quick background check into this Polish applicant, Jan Bykowski, and learned about Jan's brief stay in jail.

The interview was long but pleasant enough. It was less of an interview and more of a polite, if occasionally stiff and awkward, conversation. But, despite Jan's fears, it was not a hostile interrogation. Lieutenant Cooper invited Jan to sit down and began by asking Jan about his name. "Jan Bykowski. I assume that's your real name and that's how I'll address you. But, as you may know, that's a very, very common name. In this camp there must be several hundred Bykowski's, most of them Polish, but many Russians as well. Jans, Ivans, Igors. You Bykowski's are everywhere. Are you all related? Or is Bykowski some very convenient, common alias to replace some less convenient, maybe more troublesome name?" The lieutenant paused, smiling and waiting for a reply. Jan stared back at his interviewer, smiled, and replied. "Common, yes, and sometimes it's as much of a problem for me as it might be for you and all your paperwork you need to deal with. But that's me, just a common Jan along with hundreds of Bykowski's. For all I know I might have dozens of cousins I've never met, might never meet. I've heard there are hundreds, probably thousands of Smiths and Joneses in your America. They might also have the problem of too many unknown cousins. Maybe too many of your American uncles as well." Jan smiled. Cooper couldn't help but smile back at Jan. And Lieutenant Cooper moved on.

Jan's Fallingbostel history came up next, sports in particular. "I've heard about your boxing exploits here at the Camp. In this rough, crude, cruel DP camp I'm impressed, yet also surprised, you'd take on such a hobby. Yes, it's no secret there was plenty of betting, probably some fixed fights. And the rumor is you did well financially. But it is a vicious and dangerous way to make dollars, or marks, or whatever you made. Surprisingly, you don't look too beaten and battered, except for that scar on your cheek. Any other boxing scars, or should I call them "trophies", from your time in the ring? I do need to provide a medical summary and general description of our applicants." Jan sat up straight and tall and stiff and replied, "No, I'm here healthy and without any lasting boxing scars or broken bones or some crippled body. Other than that bloody beating from the Lithuanian which I'm sure you heard about. I have to confess, however, that I barely lived through the repeated lectures and curses from my wife for taking up that "hobby" as you called it. Her tongue lashing was far more painful than any punches I collected during my boxing days." The lieutenant smiled again at Jan's brief but candid comments and shifted the conversation to football.

"My friend, Captain Fisher, or "Bob the Bruiser" as many know him, tells me you also did quite well on the football pitch. Well indeed for a former boxer who had never played football before arriving at

Camp Fallingbostel. I suspect you again received a few of those dollars or marks or whatever for your goalkeeping efforts. So, tell me which of those hobbies did you enjoy more here at Fallingbostel?" Jan hesitated for a few moments then leaned closer to the Lieutenant and almost whispered, "Since it's just the two of us here, I would choose boxing over football. I can't say I enjoyed all the body blows and shots to the head I received. And I certainly wouldn't make such a confession if my wife was present. I can't explain it, but there's something special, despite the pain and risk, about that one-on-one matchup in a small ring and with a fanatic crowd screaming against me, or hopefully for me." Cooper replied with a half-whispered, "I appreciate your candor and honesty. And I can understand, even if just a little, the pull of that one-on-one battle. I also promise you I will not say anything to your wife about your preference."

Lieutenant Cooper switched topics again and focused his attention on the distinct scar on Jan's cheek. "Accident, battle scar, unknown?" Cooper asked, pointing to that scar. "You don't mind me asking?" Jan quickly, calmly and with a sheepish smile replied, "Just young stupid behavior by me, before marriage, before children. It was a barroom brawl, two fools with quick tempers, sharp knives, going at it. Luckily no serious injuries by either of us. My only defense for all that stupid behavior is that I came to the defense of a beautiful woman who was being hassled by a drunken loudmouth." The lieutenant smiled back at Jan and asked, "Was that beauty you defended by chance your wife?" "Yes," Jan relied. "Not my wife back then, but yes, that was the beauty I needed to defend." Cooper asked no more questions about wounds or scars. This saved Jan from possibly needing to disclose and explain his other notable jagged scar on his chest. That chest scar history, if more fully and honestly described by Jan, might not be so sympathetically glossed over by the curious interviewer.

Jan was relaxed and was almost enjoying the interview. Then Lieutenant Cooper dropped the gotcha question. "Why did my British colleagues throw you in jail for six full weeks? That certainly can't be because of some petty crime or stupid brawl. I know my British counterparts have far more important business, far too many crises to manage each day. They don't throw someone in jail for nothing. So…….?" Jan was caught off guard with the probing, very direct question. He visibly stiffened in his seat, tried to maintain that casual smile, but not very successfully. A few beads of sweat also trickled down his neck and back.

Several months earlier Jan had prepped extensively for this type of question at his "Statement on Oath." But the question gratefully never came up. He'd almost forgotten what he planned to say, how much he had rehearsed a smooth convincing reply. Regaining some of his poise, Jan matter-of-factly replied, "I don't know why the British jailed me. They never told me." That was an honest answer from Jan. When he was jailed, he prudently didn't ask any questions, offered no resistance or complaint. He did, however, tell his British jailers that his wife was expecting and only a few days away from delivering their second child. Obviously, the British didn't care. Jan was simply a quiet, almost invisible inmate among dozens of other inmates. But he had no doubt in his mind why the British were interested in him and his activities prior to Camp Fallingbostel.

"I find it hard to believe you asked no questions, didn't protest," the Lieutenant replied. "But I'll accept that answer, at least for the moment. What I did learn from my British counterparts about your imprisonment, even if you chose not to ask, is that they suspected you were a German collaborator. You worked somewhere at a German prison camp that housed and brutalized Allied military prisoners. And there's a rumor you're not even Polish."

Jan took another deep breath, paused for several seconds to again try calming his nerves, and offered the reply he'd rehearsed time and time again. "I'm sure you've read my Statement on Oath that tells you who I am and where I came from. I am Polish. I never worked as a guard in any German prison camp that housed Allied soldiers. And I never, never mistreated any Allied soldiers. Were it not for Allied soldiers I wouldn't be here today. There will always be rumors. And I can't defend, or even try to defend, against every rumor about me, or about my family. And, Lieutenant Cooper, you know, and I know, the British never filed a complaint or any kind of criminal charge against me. Just six weeks in jail, unable even to be at my wife's side at childbirth. Six painful weeks and no formal charges or complaints." Everything Jan said was true, except for the Polish ancestry. He was very specific, very narrow and very precise as to what he said. Nor was Lieutenant Cooper in any position to challenge or contradict what Jan had so carefully stated. Cooper also had to admit to himself he was developing a grudging respect for Jan Bykowski, or whoever he was, during their interview.

The lieutenant paused for a few minutes, and the interviewer and interviewee just sat across from one another and exchanged awkward smiles. During that silence it became clear to this lieutenant that all those rumors and suspicions were now just history, very ancient and increasingly irrelevant history. Across the table from him was a confident, hardworking father, a father who had received more than his fair share of beatings and bruises while providing some income and provisions for his family. Jan had earned the respect and friendship of Bob the Bruiser. And, as an extra emotional plus there were those two cute children seated on the respective knees of lovely, smiling Polya who was impatiently waiting in the hall for her Jan to appear. This soldier had no desire nor any intention to delay or derail this family's immigration. An immigration to America. Lieutenant Cooper approved the application on the spot and promised to move the process forward as quickly as he could.

The family was notified that they were listed on the passenger manifest of the USS General Harry Taylor, scheduled for departure out of Bremerhaven on August 21, 1951. This was only 30 days away which was great news. But, there were additional administrative details to address before that departure. First, an immigrating family had to present some financial ability, however modest, to support themselves for the first few months of their arrival in America. That wasn't a problem for Jan. He had prudently stored away a comfortable fund from his earnings, legitimate and otherwise, as a boxer and goalkeeper. The second detail was to secure a sponsor who would support and advise them on their arrival.

Such sponsorships were coordinated through a variety of voluntary organizations. Relief groups might be created and managed by civic groups, charitable foundations, and religious denominations. There were dozens of groups very willing to help. And, there were numerous volunteers willing to serve as those welcoming stateside sponsors. The regrettable downside to all this volunteerism was that there were countless more anxious applicants than there were able sponsors.

Lieutenant Cooper stepped forward, once again, to assist with the sponsorship problem. He was acquainted with a Baptist missionary group with a large network of churches throughout the American heartland. And, after a few days the lieutenant excitedly announced a stateside sponsor had been confirmed. He advised Jan and Polya the sponsorship was through a church. And, it was a Baptist church though the lieutenant knew the Bykowskis' religious affiliation was Russian Orthodox. Were they comfortable, did they object? Of course not. They were simply overjoyed that a sponsorship, any sponsorship, had been finalized, and so quickly. The sponsor was in fact the local pastor at a church in Tennessee. Gallatin, Tennessee to be more specific. Tennessee, Texas, Iowa, it again didn't matter to Jan and Polya. Any state, any city, any local church willing to embrace them was perfectly fine.

With the departure date rapidly approaching, Jan and Polya scrambled to organize what modest possessions they had. They learned space on the transport ship was very limited, and the transatlantic passage could be, and probably would be, rough. The family's possessions would need a sturdy storage container. And, though there were few possessions, the possessions were priceless: two pairs of well-used boxing gloves, one set of fancy dress-up clothes for all four, two pretty playground balls from the Professor, one elegant fur shawl, and a handful of studio portraits of family members during their Hannover stay. Jan went to the camp's woodworking shop and in one afternoon built a sturdy wooden chest. With great pride he also painted on the top of the chest the family name and an actual street address in Gallatin, Tennessee. The chest easily held everything the family needed and cared about. And, it easily survived the wind, rain and banging about on its maiden voyage to America.

....

I remember that rugged chest hauled around and carefully stored in the seemingly endless apartments and homes we occupied in our first two decades in America. The chest's hand painted street address, though a little faded, was still quite readable: a pleasant-sounding street in Gallatin, Tennessee. As I grew older and more curious I wondered and then asked about that address that was hundreds of miles from Davenport. As with so many questions asked, very few answers were offered. It wasn't until those emancipation years that our mother revealed the true story or, more accurately, the myth of Gallatin.

The story, recited repeatedly over the years, was that the sponsor had backed out of the pledge to serve in that capacity. We didn't receive that news until we reached the port of New Orleans. Then it was back onto the USS General Taylor to New York to explore a plan B. The real story was that there was a Baptist relief ministry, and there was a Gallatin connection with that relief group. But, there never was any kind hearted Baptist church goer the ministry or Lieutenant Cooper had located. There was no official sponsor. There was only a phantom sponsor dutifully identified on the requisite paperwork. An immigrant was provided the sponsor's name. The immigrant then attempted to connect with that named sponsor upon landing in some American port. But the phantom sponsor never appeared. No sponsor? No problem. As this immigration game was routinely played, an immigrant rarely was placed back on a transport and returned to a European DP camp. Instead, something was rearranged, a bonafide sponsor was located, and a very grateful immigrant eventually found a new home in America. My parents knew this, as this was confidentially disclosed by their good samaritan lieutenant before they boarded the General Harry Taylor. But, Lieutenant Cooper was very confident Jan Bykowski, ever the opportunist, would solve this nuisance sponsor problem. In an ironic twist, our family developed a neighborhood friendship with a devout Baptist family a few years after settling in Davenport. From the Gallatin myth we might have become part of a Tennessee Baptist minister's family and his congregation. In real life there actually was a Davenport Baptist connection. It wasn't that long lasting or that influential for us two boys. But it proved to be an important and lifelong religious and social connection for our sister.

The August 21 departure date was only two days away. All the paperwork was in order. Everyone was very nervous but very excited. The two children didn't wander outside. Instead, they planted their scrawny little selves on top of their chest and spent most of the day just sitting, and smiling, and waiting. There were few good-byes since almost all of everyone's friends or playmates had already boarded ships over the past four or five months.

Finally, after a seemingly endless wait, August 21 arrived. They boarded a bus early in the morning for the two-hour drive to Bremerhaven. They arrived at the port by nine a.m. though General Harry Taylor wasn't scheduled to ship out until 2:00 p.m. It was classic military hurry up and wait, and that wait was agonizingly long and tense. Precisely at noon, a sloppily dressed, clearly bored, junior officer appeared at the head of the gangplank attached onto the transport ship. Trying to sound important and look important, the officer began shouting out, ever so slowly, the names of immigrants who could begin boarding. "Immigrants," that's what he called them in a tone of voice that was condescending and arrogant. "Immigrant X, hustle up, get on board." Frankly, the men, women and children boarding the ship couldn't care what they were labeled or how they were called out. They were boarding, and they were heading to America. That's all that mattered.

The slow, deliberate roll call, nonetheless, was taking its toll. The trek up the gangplank was long, and everyone had a heavy chest or a huge suitcase to haul up that gangplank. And, like a predictable script from some grade B movie, the roll call was winding down. Over 700 passengers had already boarded. But, sadly no "Bykowski" name was called out. There were no more than a dozen passengers (not "immigrants") left on the loading dock, including the four Bykowski's. A family of three was called out, then a married couple. Only just ten minutes remained before the scheduled departure. And, then the smug, arrogant officer slowly, ever so slowly, shouted out "Polish immigrants Jan Bykowski, Polya, Tamara and Antoni, hurry up on board!" During the past thirty days Jan had feared something, everything, would fall apart. All the deception would be discovered, and the four would be left standing on the dock, humiliated and heartbroken, as the USS General Harry Taylor headed west across the Atlantic. Of course, the children knew nothing, but they sensed their parents' tension during those last few days and those long hours at the dock. And, then no more tension, just huge smiles, along with some tears, as all four hurried up that gangplank. Off to America!

Chapter 22 - The Passage and the Detour

"A ship is safe in harbor, but that's not what ships are for."

John A. Shedd

The "General," as its passengers referred to it, was a reasonably new, well-traveled, navy ship. It had been built in 1943 as a troop transport, capable of carrying up to 3000 soldiers. It and countless other transports saw considerable action until 1946. After three years of transport duty the General was decommissioned and stored in a huge graveyard in upstate New York. It was reactivated and refurbished, ever so slightly, in March 1950 to help transport refugees from Europe to America. The transport was clean, sturdy but hardly luxurious. This workhorse served as the new home for the Bykowski's on their twenty plus day trans-Atlantic passage. Accommodations were what one would expect from a troop transport. There were over 700 passengers on board, including dozens of children of varying ages. Of those 700 passengers, there were almost 200 family groups. However, there were no facilities to house those families together. Men and boys were bunked in the aft quarters, the women and girls bunked forward. There were a few cabins reserved for the elderly as well as mothers with small children. Unfortunately, Polya's children were considered too old. Therefore, the family was relegated to separate sleeping accommodations. Despite that mandatory bedtime separation, the family was free to gather, maybe wander just a little, and enjoy meals together. Food was decent and plentiful, even for perpetually starved Antoni. For many it was the first time in their lives to taste an orange, trying to salvage and savor all that sweet, messy juice. Bananas were also a first time treat as were nickel Cokes from a magic, never empty machine. In the evening, the ship's crew even offered old black-and-white American movies, mostly lively musicals with equally lively dancing. Every adult who was able was assigned daily duties, with the women providing kitchen help and the men handling clean-up assignments on deck or in the engine room.

The passenger population was very diverse, the living quarters were tight and overcrowded. However, everyone, whatever his or her nationality, cooperated and smiled and helped their fellow travelers. They were all in the same boat, literally so. Every one of them was just a nondescript "alien" as the ship's manifest officially labeled them. Their only enemy was the weather.

It was continually cold and rainy, with rough seas that refused to calm down. The middle passage also included a two day violent storm which forced everyone to stay below deck. Food remained decent and plentiful. But, with such ugly weather and the never-ending pitch and roll of the transport, food wasn't a high priority on anyone's mind, or anyone's stomach.

Decades later I asked our mother if she had any memories of that passage. The one memory she offered was of lying in her cot below deck for the entire crossing. She did also recall once, just once, taking both of us children to the base of a long, wide stairway which led to the ship's deck. We kids were scared but curious enough to see how terrible the weather was outside. The view from the base of the stairway was all we needed. It was indeed frightening and ugly with thunder and lightning. There was also a frightening amount of saltwater bombarding us from the deck and rushing down the gangplank. That was it. We scrambled and stumbled back to our cots and didn't do any sightseeing again.

I've been asked often what memories I have of the lengthy ocean passage and our much-anticipated arrival in America. Regrettably there are none, except one. It's that frightening view up from that stairway looking out at the angry Atlantic storm.

Except for all too frequent visits to an overwhelmed sick bay, every "alien" survived. And, one dreary morning the General navigated the last bend in the Mississippi delta and the port of New Orleans was in sight. There was no flotilla of tugboats to greet the transport, no inspiring statue in the harbor. It was just a drab, very busy port with its mix of freighters, barges, tankers and a few other transports. New Orleans wasn't the busiest or the best-known port of entry for immigrants. But, it was busy, nonetheless, and it served as a major disembarkation point for European refugees. Roughly one third of the General's passengers were scheduled to end their transatlantic voyage here. This included the Bykowski's. Maybe.

The disembarkation rules were fairly simple. Everyone packed their belongings, moved to the topside and waited for their respective sponsors to announce themselves. That same smug, disgusting little officer was again positioned at the top of the gangplank calling out the names of his pathetic "immigrants" and commanding them to come forward and introduce themselves to their respective sponsors. Eighty sponsors shouted out their names. Just eighty and then there were no more sponsors on the bottom of the gangplank. Sadly, there were more than fifty immigrants still standing, still waiting for their names to be called. Jan, Polya, Tanya and Antoni were there, next to that smug officer, and part of that still uncalled crowd.

Sounding very disgusted, the officer said, almost in a whisper, "Here we go again." It was very evident this game had been played before, and probably often. The seemingly abandoned immigrants were ordered back to their quarters to await further news and moving orders, if any. For some, not being called and not being able to finally take that first step onto American soil in New Orleans was heartbreaking and unexpected. The Bykowski children were sad and confused. Jan and Polya, on the other hand, took this apparent setback in stride. They hugged their children, nudged them back down that wide stairway. And, with a smile and another warm hug they assured the children everything would work out just fine. They didn't want to be "Volunteers" anyway, and Tennessee was too hard to spell. An hour after that last roll call a far more pleasant young officer contacted every one of the abandoned immigrants. In stark contrast to the previous officer, this one was polite and sympathetic to their setback. But, he reassured them that not a single one of the General's "guests" would be shipped back to Europe. "That is not the American way," he proudly advised them. Instead, they were politely instructed to rejoin their fellow passengers on board the General and continue on to New York. The U.S. government's commitment was to find them a new sponsor and a new home, somewhere in America. It might be someplace easier to spell than Tennessee, maybe a simpler Iowa or Ohio. That very afternoon at 5:00 the General Harry Taylor left the port, wound itself through the twists and turns of the delta and headed back onto the Atlantic and toward the port of New York.

Chapter 23 - Coming to America

"Give me your tired, your poor, your huddled masses yearning to breathe free, the wretched refuse of your teeming shore."

Emma Lazurus

The second leg of the family's journey was uneventful. Weather was kinder, there was some coastal scenery to break the ocean monotony. Nonetheless, the passage was depressingly long, or so it felt to all four of them. The parents had given a decent theatrical performance of their joy, followed by sadness, on their New Orleans arrival and non-departure. And, now they were bound for that real port every immigrant had talked about, everyone had seen in photos and brochures. But, how long would this second leg of their journey take before they arrived?

It must have been weeks, or so they believed, when in fact it was only 5 days. And, then one morning, appropriately with a sunny sky, the Statue appeared in the distance. There were cheers and tears, a deafening mix of oohs and aahs. Some just stared in silence, amazed and ever so grateful to be arriving in America. The pace now was slow as the General navigated around the Statue of Liberty and toward the piers of Ellis Island. All four stood on the top deck of their trusty General, staring in awe at that magnificent, welcoming statue. And, then the chaotic cattle call began as several hundred "refugees" (that was the official label for this ship load of passengers) scrambled to get in line and begin the anticipated inspection ritual.

The typical disembarkation point in late 1951 was at one of countless piers in lower Manhattan. Ellis Island was receiving fewer and fewer incoming immigrants, and more and more passengers proceeded through an expedited arrival and inspection ritual on the mainland. Then they quickly and joyfully scattered wherever. Regrettably, the Bykowski's were not listed as first class or second-class passengers. Instead, they were identified with that nondescript and somewhat humbling "third class steerage" label. And, "steerage" was redirected to a waiting ferry and then off to Ellis Island.

Off the ferry and up an imposing dockside stone stairway they were herded. There at the top of that stairway was the impressive main building and its magnificent Great Hall. It truly was a great hall: a grossly exaggerated two story cavern, beautiful but not overly ornate, with a very tall vaulted ceiling and a dual column of pillars supporting a second floor balcony around the perimeter of the cavernous first floor. Rumors were circulating that there was a sizable reduction in the number of immigrants actually passing through Ellis Island. But, when Jan and Polya and the children entered the Great Hall they were startled and overwhelmed by the mass of humanity crammed inside the Hall. The processing line appeared to snake back and forth endlessly. Metal pipe partitions separated those snaking lines, but the partitions were entirely too narrow. They barely provided little more than a shoulder's width of room, if one had narrow shoulders. Adding to the discomfort and near chaos among this mass of bodies, the snaking lines moved ever so slowly, with a rumored average journey through this processing line lasting almost four hours. There was no designated place to sit, no elbow room, very little space between one sweaty body in front and one behind.

Before the family could join that serpentine processing line Jan had to do something with that once creative, now damnable, storage chest. During the Atlantic passage he had resourcefully found and then attached two small wheels to one end of the chest. Not four, but two, but better than none at all. He also scavenged a length of two-inch-thick braided rope plus some straps of old but usable leather. He used the leather straps to secure the frayed edges of the rope, aided by a few nails. Now he had a primitive but usable rope handle by which he could pull his two-wheeled chest. Not fancy, still cumbersome, but an improvement over the alternative of carrying the chest around Ellis Island. Improvements notwithstanding, it still was a major nuisance.

There was a loosely guarded luggage station in one corner of the Hall. It offered no guarantee that one's luggage, or a storage chest, would be safe from vandalism or theft. But, who would really be interested in this crudely constructed, walnut stained, crudely lettered and now very weathered wooden chest? Hardly a chest treasure for anyone, except for the Bykowski's. Off in search of the luggage station they went. Upon arriving at the station the plan was to leave the children there. Jan and Polya would then hustle back to the processing line.

With the agonizingly slow pace of the processing line the youngsters would have struggled to stay up and keep pace, even at that snail's pace. The wooden chest would be their far friendlier resting place, even though Jan and Polya were uncomfortable in leaving them there alone. Their one consolation was that other children were left there by their parents. Additionally, there were four elderly volunteers available to offer some assistance.

Before they maneuvered themselves to the luggage station, all four took a brief walk to the Great Hall's signature landmark. Actually, it wasn't that much of a physical landmark, and only slightly more ornate than posts around it. But it was noteworthy nonetheless. This was the all-important "kissing post" known to both immigration authorities and countless thousands of incoming immigrants. The tradition had started in the early 1920's for incoming immigrants to meet and reunite with family members at that post. And at those heartfelt reunions, at that Great Hall post, countless kisses were exchanged. Big, lingering kisses, cute little kisses, multiple kisses, passionate kisses, countless different styles from countless ethnic traditions. Consequently, and quite properly so, this was designated the Great Hall's "kissing post." Hopefully, nothing would happen while the parents queued in line. But, if the children, for whatever reason, strayed away from the luggage room and got lost in the sea of immigrants they were instructed to look for and head to the well-known post. There would always be a kind stranger waiting at that kissing post to reunite with a family member. He or she would surely help the children find their way back to the luggage station. Strangers helping strangers reunite or relocate back to a safe place.

As Jan and Polya prepared to leave their children, Jan lifted both of them on top of the chest. But it was Polya, in her soft, soothing voice who gave the children their orders. With a stern face, but with an added wink, she told them, "You know we need to leave you here, but just for a little while. We know you will be safe, and we know you will be careful. We are also leaving you with the very important job of guarding our family's valuable chest. We are certain you will be courageous and brave." With that short speech Jan and Polya gave the children a huge smile and a salute. The two newly appointed guardians, with the most serious look they could offer, saluted their mother and father as well. Then smiles, hugs and kisses were exchanged, after which mother and father went off in search of the end of the line for their stockyard journey. Left alone now but cheerful about their important mission, the two guardians sat down on the chest, dangled their feet over the edge, and watched the faceless crowd in front of them. Other children were there but the only exchanges were with a smile or a wave of the hand. Occasionally one of the two children stood up, straight and as tall as possible, and literally stood guard. Then the guard sat down next to the sibling and the two watched and waited. And waited. And waited.

The Bykowski family was listed as "third class," meaning they had no stateside family connections, no marketable skills, and only the barest of documents with their "Statement on Oath." As Jan had planned ahead, he was able to present the requisite $25 per person which demonstrated to the immigration officers that a person wouldn't land on these shores destitute and unable to provide at least a meal or two. The easy first part was behind them. Next came the mandated two part processing ritual which took a painful three to five hours to complete. It was common knowledge among the immigrant population that there were two relatively simple and straightforward requirements to the processing ordeal. Simple in theory but not always so simple in real life. First, one had to be disease free. Second, one had to look and sound as if she or he was capable of finding and maintaining some type of gainful employment. Satisfy those requirements or else the Great Hall becomes, as many immigrants fearfully labeled it, a not so great "Hall of Tears." The Bykowski's capably satisfied the first set of requirements, providing short, confident yeses that they were disease free. With one checkpoint behind them, they marched on to the next station in the ritual.

 An officer asked a number of perfunctory questions: "Where are you from? Why are you here? What did you do?" Etc, etc. Regrettably, this officer - maybe every Ellis Island immigration officer - sounded like and acted like the abusive little tyrant on the gang plank of General Harry Taylor. But, Jan, with Polya silently by his side, kept his composure, and they passed the interrogation. Despite the unimaginable good luck they had enjoyed over the past two years, and despite being literally on American soil, Jan still felt that inner dread that everything would unravel. With so much troubling history which they brought with them across the Atlantic, the dread wasn't that far-fetched. Nor was it that easy to dismiss.

There had been five long years of constant planning, scheming and deception that could be uncovered. All of that effort would then be lost and the Bykowski's would be unceremoniously hauled back onto a transport heading east. However, the odds of successfully remaining in America, somewhere, were definitely in their favor. From its creation as a port of entry in 1917 until its closure in 1954 Ellis Island received over 7 million immigrants. Of those arriving immigrants only two percent were denied entry into the United States. Passing the inspection ritual was the key, of course. A two or three hour wait in line and then the dreaded "inspection" must have felt like an eternity (maybe hell?) for everyone. But, overall it functioned like a reasonably fast, well-conceived assembly line, even if the line did turn chaotic at times. The immigration authorities were far more interested in moving that human assembly line forward as quickly as possible. Identifying undesirables such as thieves or assassins, maybe spies, was not a high priority. Neither was it a high priority to interrogate someone about his or her country of origin.

Nothing unraveled, another arrogant bureaucrat was now just an unpleasant memory. All that remained was a medical exam. The examinations were conducted in a smaller room adjacent to the Great Hall. Jan pointed Polya in that direction, and as she headed to the exam he scurried as fast as he could to collect their two small guardians. As always, there were countless bodies to navigate around, to shove aside, though semi-politely, before Jan arrived at the luggage room. It had been hours, though it felt like years, since he and Polya had deposited them there alone with the chest. But, he was relieved and delighted to see them seated on the chest, feet dangling and arms waving as they spotted their father. He swept them up, one in each arm, enjoying a hearty hug from both. There would be time for stories and explanations later. Right now, he was off, racing to rejoin Polya at the exam center. Racing would be a gross exaggeration of his pace and progress. There was still the endless sea of bodies to push, to prod, to dance around. He succeeded with no serious mishaps or confrontations. The children simply laughed and cheered as their father charged on through the crowd. The four reunited and then, as it is said in the military, they once again had to "hurry up and then wait." They waited. And they waited.

The inner dread returned as he waited Jan relived his bold but very risky "bad blood" episode. To his great relief, the medical exam was surprisingly brief with a doctor only asking about general health, asking everyone to say "aah" as the doctor made a very quick exam of teeth and throat. The only unpleasant part of the exam was the mandatory combination shot of vaccines against contagious diseases. As one final, very unwelcome parting "present" on leaving the Ellis Island Great Hall everyone went through a small exit and was fumigated.

As they boarded a ferry to mainland the Bykowski's said their final good-byes to their dear host, the General Harry Taylor. The transport had served them capably, and it would continue its trans-Atlantic refugee missions until 1958. It was decommissioned, then reactivated in 1964 to carry out various military missions until a final, well-deserved retirement in 1993. In a fitting final mission in 2009 the General became a host once again. The ship was sunk off the coast in the Florida Keys National Marine Sanctuary to be used as an artificial reef. Countless millions of marine life would now make the General their new home.

With no sponsor to greet them, the family was directed to a side building which housed a number of relief organizations. Their logical stop was at the desk of the Polish-American Relief Fund. To no one's surprise there were several dozen fellow refugees, maybe some actual Poles, needing a helping hand. The line to the help desk was very long, the pace very slow. But, the family had no other useful strategy and nothing but time to kill. They stood in line, again, for another three hours. The kids parked themselves on an empty bench during the wait, just dangling their feet and feeling ever so relieved to be off that heaving ship. The bench was also far more comfortable than their wooden chest. While they waited in line Jan and Polahaya quietly rehearsed their "abandonment" story, putting together a credible and, hopefully, a sympathetic tale. This was Jan, the ever-resourceful opportunist, and Jan would deliver food and shelter for the family. He was confident he would do so, though he hoped he would only need to do so temporarily. Having experienced and survived the overwhelming crowds and chaos of New York's Ellis Island, the family was more than ready to leave this big, messy and scary metropolis.

As that long line inched ever so slowly forward Jan had a revelation. The revelation, or maybe the family salvation, was that their old Professor friend, Stefan Mirovich, had settled somewhere in the states. Stefan had successfully immigrated out of Camp Fallingbostel a year or more prior to the Bykowski's own successful exit. Their Professor had even written a few letters to the family, had glowingly described his new home. And, as would be expected of kind and thoughtful Stefan, he had urged Jan and Polya to apply to America. Stefan would help them in any way he could, be it a formal sponsorship, or money or train tickets, whatever. His letters were always cheerful and upbeat and sincere. Could Stefan, once again, come to their rescue? Or was this just naive wishful thinking on their part? Their doubts notwithstanding, here they were, yes, actually here in America. Their Professor was here as well. And, with the hours ticking away and nothing but an unpredictable Polish help desk in front of them, Jan and Polya mutually decided they had nothing to lose.

When they reached the help desk, they proudly announced they had a Plan B after their Gallatin, Tennessee disappointment. They had met a fellow Camp Fallingbostel refugee with whom they had stayed in touch. He remained a dear friend, and was successfully settled in the U.S. More importantly, he was willing, as well as financially able, to help with their American resettlement. All they needed to do was to contact him, and they had an address to make that contact. Jan stated he would send a letter immediately, assuming he could enlist the support of a volunteer to tutor Jan through the in's and out's of the U.S. postal service. A positive response would come quickly, they were certain. All the Bykowski family needed was some short-term aid, specifically temporary housing and funds to feed and clothe themselves while they awaited the good news from the "Professor." It always helped, or at least couldn't hurt, to refer to Stefan as the "Professor."

Their Plan B was well received by the volunteer at the help desk. It would lighten this volunteer's load considerably, relieving her of the search for a qualified sponsor. Temporary housing would be secured, survival funds would be disbursed as needed. The Polish relief organization was not well funded, but it could, and would, provide short term aid for its fellow Polish refugees. Within a day Jan's letter went out, housing was found, and a few basic provisions were purchased to stock up their modest apartment. And, as was the recurring pattern here in their new homeland, they waited, and they waited.

Chapter 24 - Broadway Lights - Maybe

"Give my regards to Broadway
Remember me to Herald Square
Tell all the gang on Forty-second Street
That I will soon be there."

George M. Cohan

With good spirits and high hopes, the family boarded a cab and set out to its newest home. No, they weren't close, no way close, to the fabled lights of Broadway. And they weren't treated to some glitzy tourist tour. But this was everyone's first real introduction to America and to its Big Apple. It was also a striking visual contrast to everyone's images from Camp Fallingbostel and Hannover. That German image, still vivid, was one of squat nondescript cinder block buildings and factories, then equally nondescript barracks, all gray and colorless and with little, if any, glass. Those German streets were mostly dirt and the German sky remained perpetually gray and smog filled.

The streets of New York were paved, not dirt filled. But it wasn't a totally pleasant, comfortable concrete drive since those New York city streets provided an endless supply of potholes waiting to ambush any unsuspecting tire. The sky, or more specifically the skyline, did offer them an endless variety of skyscrapers. All of them tall, some seemingly reaching to the heavens, all of them enclosed in glass or gleaming steel, and all shining brilliantly. All of this was visual overload for not only the children but for Jan and Polya as well.

The slow drive, with windows wide open, also assaulted the family with a cacophony of noises. There were shouts, blaring horns, roaring truck engines and a deafening mix of voices speaking, or trying to speak, in countless international dialects. The melting pot of their old DP camp didn't begin to compare to this linguistic Tower of Babel on the streets of New York. The endless mix of dialects was matched by the indescribable ocean of people. Out their window they saw every possible ethnicity, every color, every clothing style. There were the elegant three-piece suits commingling with the drab nondescript garb of ordinary blue-collar workers. There were the striking pastel colors of a silk skirt in stark contrast to the dull gray of a cleaning woman's apron. And, as an endless stream of people pushed and shoved its way northward, an equally endless stream fought its way southward.

The slow drive proceeded up Third Avenue though the driver did include a ten-block side trip up Fifth Avenue and one short spin around Times Square. Apparently, this had been prearranged as an extra small gift from the Polish relief agency. It was a thoughtful gesture, offering a brief but eye-popping glimpse of the city's social and economic diversity. The glittering, magical windows of FAO Schwarz would have left the two children speechless but, sadly, the store was not on their escorted route. Nonetheless, there were dozens of imposing and, at times, garish bank facades and corporate logos to view. There were scattered billboards and neon signs promoting a current Broadway production or a new motion picture. The King and I, set in the exotic far east, competed with the rowdy western cowboys and cowgirls from Paint Your Wagon. The African Queen competed with Alice in Wonderland on the big screen.

No, New York City was not representative of America, and Jan and Polya probably knew that. But those bustling streets provided a glimpse of what America had to offer. On that uptown drive, brief as it was, the family was able to see, hear, probably even smell, endless possibilities and opportunities for these two newly transplanted opportunists, plus children, from Borisov. Sadly, the glitter and magic disappeared from view as they proceeded deeper into the far more drab, but still paved, streets of the upper east side. The cab ride finally delivered them to their new, if temporary, home. The skyline now was filled with eight to ten story carbon copy brownstone apartments. No gleaming glass greeted them. There were no imposing skyscrapers, no polished steel facades, no glitzy neon signs. The only glitz they saw was the occasional storefront sign of a neighborhood grocer or deli.

This was all the sightseeing any of them enjoyed for the next six weeks. Their eye opening one time and free cab ride also almost did not happen because of the family's "Gallatin" chest. There they were at streetside trying to hail a cab with the help of the Polish relief volunteer. A cab finally stopped, everyone stepped forward, all ready to load up. But, there, directly behind the family, and strategically hidden from a cab driver's eyes, was the one piece of so-called luggage the family owned: the huge, heavy, handmade chest. Precious, yes, to all of them. But, it couldn't begin to fit in the cab's backseat. And, it couldn't easily fit in the large trunk. The cabbie, grumpy and short-tempered, was ready to leave everyone, including the monster chest, at the curb. Polya again turned on the charm, and with butchered words and gestures, assured the grump that her big, husky husband could easily fit the chest in the trunk. And, he would do so by himself, no help needed. The grump grumbled some more, probably tossed out a few obscenities. But he did allow Jan to wrestle the chest into the trunk. It did fit, at least part way, since the trunk lid could only close halfway. But, luckily the grump had some heavy twine, the trunk was secured, and off they went on their not so grand tour of New York.

Their lodging was on a residential street with tightly packed row houses and apartments. Central Park was to their west and north. It was unlikely they would be taking leisurely walks around that fabled green enclave in the heart of Manhattan. Harlem was to the north as well. The neighborhood was an ethnic and demographic melting pot of first- and second-generation Europeans, all with heavy accents. Blacks and Puerto Ricans added to the multicultural mix. There was also a sizable local population of native New Yorkers, complete with their own distinctive and at times indecipherable accents. The working population was predominantly blue collar. The Bykowski's blended in well. A variety of part-time and day jobs were available which Jan, now occasionally called "John," happily explored. This was not some great American dream the family was living. But, it was a decent start.

The specific address was on the sixth floor of an eight-story old, very old, brownstone apartment. It wasn't filthy or rat infested. But, it certainly was showing its age as well as the lack of maintenance: broken screens, unpainted shutters, cracked and missing bricks. As might be expected, there was no elevator. Consequently, the daily treks, sometimes several treks, were far more than just a leisurely daily workout for anyone. For very young, short legs the six floors provided a daily marathon challenge. And, as they first moved in, unlucky Jan had the additional grueling task of dragging their Gallatin treasure chest up those six flights of stairs. To their credit, the kids and Polya gleefully offered to help push the chest up those six flights. They weren't very helpful pushers, but they were consistent and enthusiastic cheerleaders as their father wrestled with the family's single precious piece of luggage.

The apartment was a one bedroom so-called "studio" with a decent sized living area and a modest but functional kitchenette. The agency apologized for only one bedroom, But that's all that was currently on its inventory. So it was one bedroom plus two cots for the children in their common area. Thankfully, the apartment did have a separate bathroom, though one bathroom for four occupants required considerable cooperation, as well as patience, from everyone. There also was a common hall bathroom on every other floor. But, with six apartments per floor the demands on those hall bathrooms were constant. And, not everyone was as friendly or patient.

Communication was a persistent challenge. Those few survival words and phrases taught by Bob the Bruiser helped a little, but only a little. They weren't housed in some Polish enclave or some Russian-speaking enclave. This was just a working class, melting pot neighborhood with people getting by through grunts, hand gestures, facial expressions, the occasional butchered English. Polya came to the rescue. With her good looks and innocent smile, Polya was able to somehow communicate the family's too frequent complaints about an apartment problem. The apartment superintendent, a sixty something native New Yorker, was always glad to help. And, in their second week in their apartment the "super," Theodore Roosevelt Stanton, surprised the Bykowski family with a marvelous present. Super Teddy, as he enjoyed being called, held a small but working television set, complete with rabbit ears. He had this spare, for whatever reason, and wanted to give it to the family. No strings attached, no payment expected. But, he insisted, in the most serious tone of voice, the family must watch the TV, no matter whatever was showing, as often as possible. TV would be the family's language tutor. Jan and Polya were overwhelmed by this kind man and his extremely kind gesture. But, Jan, with a mix of pride and humility, told Super Teddy they couldn't possibly accept this very generous, probably very expensive gift. Jan had a sizable emergency fund, but this wasn't what he considered an emergency purchase. The Super paused, then countered with a selling price of twenty-five dollars and Jan's commitment to help with building maintenance as needed. The deal was struck with the prompt payment of the twenty-five dollars, a hearty handshake and very hearty hugs from every one of the Bykowski's.

The small television, quickly renamed an American "TV" by everyone, became the family's all important combination classroom and teacher. There was no bona fide actual school classroom anyone could attend. There was no government funded "English as a foreign language" for these "Polish" immigrants in which they could participate. Had they identified themselves as Russian/Byelorussian immigrants there still wouldn't be any "English as a foreign language" program available. No private tutors, no nothing. Nothing except NBC, ABC, and CBS.

The family settled into a regular daily routine. Jan joined in as he could if he wasn't out hustling a day job to earn a few extra grocery dollars. Everyone easily learned and mimicked "It's Howdy Doody Time" and scrambled in front of the tiny screen for their morning "lessons." Pauline became the lead resident translator. She saw a TV object, maybe a fork or a stove or an apple, and connected that object with its English pronunciation. She provided the Russian translation for that object, then commanded everyone to repeat the English word three times. Everyone's English vocabulary grew under her patient tutelage. Pauline never mastered conversational English, and she struggled throughout her life to converse capably and comfortably. But she performed capably here in New York and built the family's basic English skills. The family's growing vocabulary included introducing her children, as well as John, to basic greetings. "Please" and "Thank you" were pronounced countless times each day. And she stressed the importance of using those please and thank you's often. They would not be ignorant, ill-mannered immigrants. To her dismay she also taught the children "why" which they readily incorporated all too frequently into their daily English. Whether in English or Russian or Spanish, or any other language, "why" remains an integral, all too annoying, part of any young child's vocabulary.

There was one other unexpected contributor to the family's TV language education. That contributor, serving as the TV teacher's aide, was Super Teddy. He frequently, actually quite regularly, showed up at the Bykowski door. With a polite knock and without waiting for a "hello" or a "come in, " he opened the door and poked his head inside. At the entryway, fully armed with a hammer in one hand, a pipe wrench in the other hand, and always with a smile, he asked, "Is everything in working order? Is there anything I can help you with?" And still with a big smile he casually noted, "Oh, I see you're about ready to watch 'The Lone Ranger.' I have other jobs to attend to. But, I could stay for a few minutes. Only a few. If you don't mind." Of course, no one minded. This was all pretense, and everyone smiled and understood. He was not there at the apartment as an on-call handyman. He was there to join in on the next episode of "The Lone Ranger." He was always welcome. But as he watched, Super Teddy also assumed the role of an additional, very animated interpreter, asking for a Russian word to match an English word or phrase our masked hero was reciting. Super Teddy was going to language class as well. Frequently he precisely but slowly repeated an entire sentence or two that the Ranger or Tonto spoke and encouraged everyone to repeat along with him. They might not fully understand what was spoken on the screen. Nonetheless, with repetition and the Super's patience everyone spoke more and understood more everyday English. And, on cue everyone enthusiastically shouted out in perfect English "Hi ho Silver, away!"

The family struggled to understand the rapid-fire ramblings, as well as the butchered English, of Lucy and Desi. Nonetheless, everyone enjoyed their zany slapstick predicaments. On balance "I Love Lucy" did add some to everyone's growing English proficiency. So did the eclectic assortment of contestants and entertainers on

Arthur Godfrey's Talent Scouts and the Ed Sullivan Show. One other family favorite, especially for the children, was "Kukla, Fran and Ollie." It was simple, silly, but entertaining and educational. Little Tamara was particularly captivated by the ensemble cast of puppet characters. But she was never able to move past her confusion, maybe a little uneasiness, about that strange Kukla. Watching the program with her mother Tamara repeatedly asked, "Mommy, what's a Kukla?" Pauline had no helpful answer. Those intense, if unorthodox, language "lessons" served the entire family very well, both on the streets of New York City and later in the children's elementary school classroom.

There was very little sightseeing and very little to do during this apartment layover in New York. A dirty, barebones park was a few blocks away, but it didn't look either that inviting or safe. Jan did locate a small grocery store six blocks away, and there was a Jewish deli just a few blocks down their street. As an extra treat Super Teddy's daughter visited him once a week from her more fashionable upper East side townhouse. She wasn't a cook or a baker. But, she knew where there were upscale bakeries selling elegant treats. On her visits, and due to the kind words from the Super, the daughter dropped off a generous basket of cookies and pastries to the Bykowski apartment. That must be the reason all of us developed such a sweet tooth, and lots of cavities, so early in life. For a little variety Jan sometimes invited the children to join him on the grocery run, despite the challenge of the six story marathon trek back up the stairs. No one objected.

Once, but only once, Jan and the two children went on the subway. Pauline, very smartly, chose to stay in the apartment. The game plan was to just take a short ride on the closest north/south subway line, maybe get off briefly to view the Empire State Building and return. The travelers learned, and not so quickly, that it was a considerably long ride down to that building. They did succeed simply by repeating "Empire State Building" and following directions since everyone knew where that landmark was. But, getting back was a nightmare. Jan hadn't paid enough attention to names at subway stops. And, he couldn't read well enough for the signs to be of any help. Somehow, and he wasn't at all sure how, he managed to return them to their apartment. No more subways, no more tourism.

Their first two weeks of city life were somewhat enjoyable. But, that initial joy turned into increasing anxiety. By Jan's calculation Stefan's welcoming response should have been received by now. Jan had even prepared a second letter, ready to send if needed after fifteen days. Just one day after he sent that second letter, the relief volunteer dropped by. She was polite and patient enough. But, she expressed some concern about the lack of progress on resettlement. All Jan and Polya were able to offer was their not very convincing assurance that Stefan would deliver, and any day now. This same discussion took place two weeks later, The volunteer was still polite but more business-like this time. If there was no news, no invitation, in the next two weeks the agency would locate a sponsor. There were available candidates, there were some settlement centers in the Bronx and a job would be found. The Bykowski's would become native New Yorkers. Five days after this latest semi-polite deadline was announced the volunteer reappeared. In her hand was a letter addressed to Jan, posted to the relief agency, and sent by Stefan Mirovich.

Chapter 25 - An Invitation, At Last

"Every gift from a friend is a wish for your happiness."

Richard Bach

Now that a letter had arrived, ever so late, both Jan and Polya feared what the letter would contain. Rejection! Maybe only a vague recollection of their "good old days." "Good luck, but I can't help." Jan hesitated to open the letter. He just stared at it, unable to muster up the courage to do anything. But, Polya prodded him gently. Then slowly, very slowly, he opened it. To add to the tension of the moment, the volunteer remained at their doorway, saying nothing. The letter was very short. But it was oh so sweet. Stefan apologized for the slow response, stating he first needed to deal with some "personal matters." Nothing more was offered except a short, very emphatic "Yes! Yes! Please come." A train schedule was enclosed as was more than enough money - real American dollars - to buy four tickets. He ended by emphasizing, "Yes, you absolutely should come, must come, and do so as soon as possible. See you soon!"

Jan, the one who could best read that old, familiar Cyryllic script, stood there in silence for an eternity. That's what it felt like to the children and to the volunteer in the doorway. And, then he exploded with a thunderous shout, unintentionally tossed the train schedule into the air, and nearly crushed Polya with a loving embrace. The volunteer understood immediately and received a bear hug from Jan, an equally bone crushing hug. But she did not complain. The children understood as well. As their parents had promised them, they all were going to visit their beloved Uncle Stefan.

Jan and Polya spent the next two days packing up what few possessions they had. It meant another grueling trek down those six flights with the huge chest. But, down was friendlier than up. And, their invaluable television "tutor" was hardly that heavy. Jan even allowed the children to hop on the chest during those last eighteen stairs to the lobby. Super Teddy was also waiting in that lobby, offering a firm handshake and hugs. Polya received the most tender and longest hug from the kind superintendent, who also urged her to keep working on that butchered English. As a small, final good-bye he presented the children with a box of those decadent, cavity-creating pastries, compliments of the super's daughter.

The volunteer helped Jan to book the train westward to Davenport. She also surprised them with one more cab ride, and gratefully this time with a semi-grumpy and more cooperative cab driver. And off they went to Grand Central Station. The Grand Hall on Ellis Island was indeed grand. However, Grand Central Station, with its stunning architecture and its cavernous main lobby, was even more impressive and grand. The countless thousands of bodies hustling, running, shoving and shouting were overwhelming and frightening. Gratefully, the volunteer alsok provided Jan with very detailed directions on where to go, what to look for, and how to successfully board their train. The family navigated through the chaos, turned the wrong way only twice, and eventually they found their assigned train. All four cheerfully scurried to the assigned passenger car. The children smiled and waved at the waiting porter, not knowing that the porter's outstretched hand wasn't intended to be a courteous handshake but a hoped-for tip. The little children struggled up the steep stairs, then scurried once again down the aisle to their assigned seats. Excited, but understandably nervous about this new chapter in their odyssey, they bid goodbye to their temporary New York City home, and, forty days after arriving at Ellis Island, the Bykowski's were westward bound to heartland America.

Chapter 26 - And Home, At Last

"Mid pleasures and palaces though we may roam,
Be it ever so humble, there's no place like home."

John Howard Payne

The two-day train trip was uneventful. The family stayed on board the entire route, except for their one transfer to another rail line. Both Jan and Polya were visibly nervous and fearful during the entire trip though no one bothered them, no one asked any questions. They couldn't rid themselves of a nagging fear that they might be denied rebounding if they hopped off. Or they might accidentally be late to reboard when the train paused at some stop along the way. All that fear and anxiety was irrational. But, their entire journey still felt surreal. Surreal until they pulled into the terminal in Davenport, and there on the platform was the Professor.

"Welcome! Welcome! My dear, dear Polish friends. I hope the long train ride was worthwhile," Stefan shouted out to the weary travelers as they stepped off the train. He gave that welcome greeting in crisp, clear English, with no hint of an accent. And he shouted out the "Polish" part of that greeting with extra volume and emphasis, maybe to ensure any bystanders would hear "Polish" loud and clear. As soon as the children stepped onto the platform they bolted from their parents and collided into Stefan. All they shouted over and over was "Dyadya Stefan, Dyadya Stefan." He prudently braced for the collision and then swept both scrawny, but otherwise healthy, children into his arms.

The fluent English greeting was surprising but again possibly intended for a wider train station audience and not just for the

Bykowski's. Stefan was also smartly dressed in tailored slacks, a sports coat and tie. It was not an ostentatious appearance but certainly it conveyed the impression of prosperity and sophistication. Our professor was maybe a few pounds heavier since Fallingbostel, but still very fit and healthy. And, adding to their surprise, Stefan was deeply tanned. It was an enviable tan one might expect from a long tropical vacation, but definitely not from the day-to-day grind in an industrial midwestern town.

Before Jan and Polya could bombard him with questions Stefan raised his hand, ever so politely, to silence them as he turned his attention to the children still in his arms. He gently lowered them to the platform and then turned around to grab the large bag he had brought to this reunion. From that bag, like some playful magician, he pulled out two neatly folded American flags and presented them to his adopted nephews. "Take good care of these flags. Treat them with respect," he whispered to the youngsters. All the children could do was smile and start again with their "Dyadya Stefan" cheer. They did also shout out, in decent English, "Thank you for the beautiful flags." Stefan replied, in his perfect English style, "You are very welcome." And he added, "My, my, you both have been very good students in front of that little television Mr. Super Teddy gave you. The Lone Ranger must have been a good teacher. Maybe Howdy Doody helped a little also? Hey, I have to tell you I also sure don't know what that strange Kukla character is. We'll have to watch together and maybe we will figure him out. Or maybe it's a her? Oh, and Super Teddy sends his love. So does your favorite British soldier, Bob the Bruiser." Jan and Polya could only listen and smile and be amazed by the depth of Stefan's knowledge.

Stefan returned to his large bag and pulled out two very official looking Army officer's caps. The brims were clean and polished, the gold braid was equally clean and shiny. The caps, though very impressive looking, were too large. And as the children tried them on the caps fell down over their eyes and ears, stopping at their respective noses. But the children, now little soldiers, didn't care. They marched around and bumped into one another, laughing all the time and shouting out, "Thank you! Thank you!"

While the kids marched around, Stefan turned his attention to Jan and Polya. He explained in a much quieter voice, and in Russian this time, "I have some friends at this army depot who were very happy to donate their service caps as a welcoming gift. I also suspect you have many, many questions. There will be plenty of time for us to talk later after we get you settled. And, I'll answer all your questions, or try to. I promise." They certainly had countless questions: the impeccable English, fancy and expensive clothes, that out of place tan, military friends. And where did he work? Where had he been since Fallingbostel? How did he know about Super Teddy and the television and TV shows? Ongoing British connections with Captain Fisher? As Jan and Polya heard time and again in the coming months there was invariably something Stefan had to do, someplace he had to go. Never enough time to answer questions for the moment. But, as he always promised, they would "talk later."

"Let's go to your new home," Stefan shouted out, putting any probing questions on hold. Jan and Polya prudently held back on questions, frustrating as it was to them. Instead, they focused their attention on their few possessions and their gargantuan trunk. But as they were busy exchanging greetings and hugs and watching the childrens' heartwarming marches, two porters had loaded their possessions, chest included, into Stefan's rental truck. As the three started walking to the truck the children decided to hitch a ride. With army caps still covering their eyes and ears, they plopped their tiny bottoms on Dyadya Stefan's shoes. Stefan cheerfully obliged, offering his best Bris Karloff impersonation of a stiff legged, lumbering Frankenstein, with arms extended straight out and groaning and growling at his attackers. None of these refugees knew anything about Boris Karloff or Frankenstein or Mary Shelley. Nor did they care. Everyone was innocently laughing, or groaning, and enjoying this first day in their new hometown.

While "Frankenstein" lumbered toward the truck Polya noticed a limp in Stefan, specifically from his right leg. She shouted for the children to slide off Stefan's shoes, fearing they might aggravate an obvious injury. But he politely, though firmly, insisted they continue the ride. "It's an old minor injury, and it's completely healed. There's no pain, only a permanent stiffness at the knee. Just a little accident in Chicago, on my first trip here. And foolishly the leg didn't receive the timely attention I should have given it." And, on cue, Stefan again preempted any further discussion or questions with what would become his signature response. "There will be plenty of time to talk later." They never did.

Another flood of tears and hearty hugs followed. It was a sunny, mild day, and Stefan had wisely rented that truck to collect his new family. The monster chest fit in easily. The children were allowed the luxury of sitting in the truck bed, on their precious chest, as Stefan provided a leisurely tour of the city, Then it was off to Stefan's home. It was a modest two-bedroom rental, complete with a modest, but clean and safe, backyard. The Bykowski residence was to be the entire finished basement, complete with two small bedrooms and a bathroom. It was a grand palace for the family,

Everyone settled in comfortably. The kids started school, even though late in the fall semester. Stefan arranged a job interview with J.I. Case, and Jan began work on the factory floor the next week. The family stayed in that basement "palace" for only six months. The following spring Stefan relocated the entire family, except for Stefan, to a modest but pleasant rental in a Norman Rockwell neighborhood of neat little homes, working class families, adventuresome alleys to roam, small gardens, cute postage stamp front porches with front porch swings. Though a rental, this was the realization of the Bykowskis' American dream. We were crowded but comfortable in this rental home, in this charming portrait of Americana, for six years.

During those six years my parents were befriended by a Russian family, Vassily and Anna Sluzinsky, who lived just four doors down the street. From that nucleus of four Eastern Europeans the social circle expanded to include Poles, Ukrainians, Lithuanians, even a half-crazy Cossack and his equally half-crazy wife. This became the extended family of immigrants that stayed together and played together on those rowdy Saturday nights.

We two siblings found friends, though I hit the jackpot with Nick, the only son of the Sluzinsky's. He was wild, fun-loving, reckless and perpetually in trouble with his parents. Nick became my tour guide through the single lane alleys with their fruit trees, small gardens and small garages that begged to be explored. He also introduced me to the small, immaculate Catholic convent only three blocks away. The grounds were beautifully maintained as were the convent's dozens of trees and its massive vegetable garden. The entire property was protected by a tall wrought iron fence with just one ornate entry gate that was always closed and rarely used. Though the fence was tall, it was easily, very easily, climbable. And for us two boys that fence and all the treasures on the other side were simply too irresistible. Year after year and season after season, Nick and I climbed the fence, shamelessly but happily picked the various fruits, pulled the countless vegetables from the ground or off the vines. We were semi-smart to indulge in this petty theft at dusk or after dark. But, every so often a meddlesome nun stepped out to survey the grounds and spotted us either up in a tree or kneeling among the vegetable rows. She shouted, we screamed. Then we darted to the fence, scrambled over the top and disappeared down a nearly dark alley, usually spilling half our stolen treasure on the sidewalk. When my little brother turned old enough and agile enough to climb that fence, we introduced him to that petty thievery as well. This could have been another Norman Rockwell moment: two young foolish boys scrambling over a fence, one little brother and our scattered produce safely positioned on the other side, and an angry nun in hot pursuit. We never were caught.

That's how American life began, simply but with such great possibilities, for "John" and "Pauline." At Stefan's urging, they adopted these slightly more Americanized names. John and Pauline were no longer refugees, immigrants, aliens or even escapees. Theirs had been a powerful, if at times troubled, partnership. But, with the combination of John's never-ending opportunism and Pauline's charm and street smarts here they were: Americans, very proud and grateful Americans.

Epilogue

We four refugees, now John and Pauline and their two children, became true, legal Americans just six years later as our parents recited the Pledge of Allegiance and each one received a Certificate of Naturalization. A third child, George, was born in 1952 in America and was automatically a U.S. citizen. We proudly stepped over the threshold into our first real home, not just a rental, a year after the citizenship ceremony. We three children enjoyed successful careers, in business, in the legal profession, and as a beloved wife/mother/grandmother. Though Stefan gave the train funds freely, our father insisted on paying back that invaluable "loan" and did so two years later. Eighteen months after they shared that first rental home Stefan startled everyone one day by announcing he was moving to Cheyenne, Wyoming the next week. He offered no further explanation. Nor did he ever offer any explanation as to what had caused him to delay sending that invitation in 1951. This just added to the lifelong mystery and contradictions about Stefan Mirovich. It was also fitting and not so surprising that our ever ambitious, now thoroughly American John switched careers, leaving the assembly line for a carpentry apprenticeship. Maybe that decision was influenced by the sight and memories of that backbreaking Gallatin chest. Whatever the reason, he retired thirty plus years later as a well-respected finish carpenter. In the interim he also built and realized a handsome profit selling three homes. Our slightly less American Pauline, though still the dutiful wife, enjoyed some measure of independence as a much sought-after senior cook at various restaurants. And, it was always a tough call as to which was the family's favorite: ambrosia pie or meat and kraut filled piroshkies. Throughout those seventy plus decades together, good decades overall, it literally was "til death do us part."

Acknowledgements

It has been a decades-long desire to collect, organize and eventually document the fragmented oral history of my parents in a biographical novel. Suzanne, my dear wife of fifty plus years, has repeatedly and lovingly urged me to do so, saying so often, "Don't talk about it. Write it." This is that very overdue end product. It might be labeled historical fiction. But, the core story line is very honest and accurate, built upon that oral history which, over the years, was reluctantly shared at times, cheerfully shared at times, tearfully shared at times. Because that history is so sparse, as are the few preserved documents, I've undertaken the enjoyable challenge of transforming that bare bones history into a more detailed, lively, and entertaining, half-century odyssey. I've inserted my best guesses and speculation. I've added more characters, more historical details, and more "color" and dialogue, as my two children, Rob and Lyndsey, have urged.

My dear, fun-loving "little" brother, George, and my protective big sister, Tamara, though she is now departed, have been invaluable in extracting bits and pieces of oral history over the years through visits, luncheons, sometimes just simple family room chats. My five grandchildren have been charming supporters, asking thoughtful questions, even volunteering historical research to help advance and enliven their great grandparents' life story.

I am also greatly indebted to Greg Fisher, my dear friend, former work colleague, and an avid historian. He has enthusiastically undertaken countless research projects, discovered important documents, and shared his vast knowledge about Europe before, during, and after World War II. His tireless efforts have enabled me to infuse my parents' half-century odyssey with invaluable historical authenticity.

Most importantly, thank you, my departed father and mother. What a wonderful gift you have given to my sister, my brother and me. Through your struggles and your tenacity you triumphed and realized that sought after American dream. And, through your effort you have allowed us to enjoy that American dream as well.